Our Adv

The
CHALLENGER

A Novella by

Jesse Zimmerman

(originally appearing on schlock.co.uk)

Illustrations by

Jasper Davis

TABLE OF CONTENTS

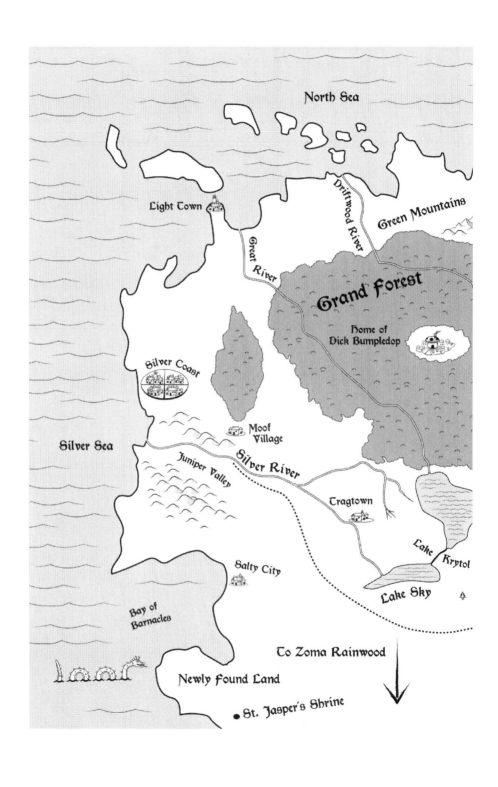

North Sea

Light Town

Driftwood River

Green Mountains

Great River

Grand Forest

Home of
Dick Bumpledop

Silver Coast

Moof
Village

Silver Sea

Silver River

Juniper Valley

Tragtown

Lake Krytol

Lake Sky

Salty City

Bay of
Barnacles

To Zoma Rainwood

Newly Found Land

• St. Jasper's Shrine

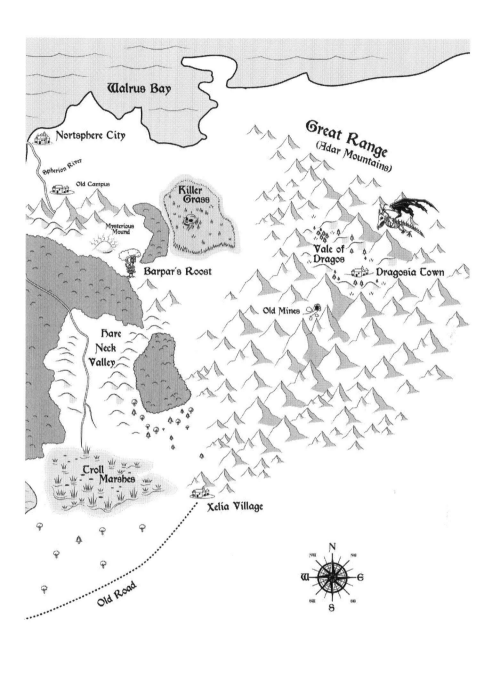

Gamer's Gates
or
The Challenger in Hare-Neck Valley

We turn about and Dick Bumpledop begins singing from the stoop of his fungus cottage. I strain my ear, barely making out the words: *'hopping along our way, danger is not for today!'* and *'When the trail splits in half, to take the left would be a gaffe!'*, his usual semi-nonsensical rhymes.

The morning is late. We're tired despite our medium-length rest. My sister, Fauna, is clearly impatient as she stands in the cool mist of the woodland path at the front of the giant mushroom with a door and windows where we'd just spent the night.

"Okay, well, so long!" she says loudly to our host who stands singing at the little entrance-way. Fauna then looks at the Challenger and me, mouthing for us to start walking…fast.

In truth he has been really good to us, this fellow, yesterday having rescued us from a muddy marsh. We appreciated his help, though I'm sure we would've found a way out eventually, especially with our ranger friend, the Challenger with us. The beds Bumpledop lent us in his mushroom home were comfortable, the loaves he gave us scrumptious, yet the three of us are relieved to be going from him now.

"I thought he'd never shut up," the Challenger mutters when we get onto the forest trail. These are thick woods that we'd been crossing for nearly three days. The thirty-something ranger is decked in dark colors, with some light chain-mail covering his torso, a forest green cloak fit atop his broad shoulders, his dark brown breeches held up by a birch-bark belt. At his waist he wears a leather belt, a scabbard with a sword hangs from it.

"He hasn't," I say, hearing distant singing.

"Just keep moving," instructs my grumpier-than-usual sister. I would've expected her to be in a better mood after being hosted so well out here in the rugged wilderness, but the constant merrymaking of Dick Bumpledop was too much even for her.

"So you don't like it when people are nice to you and give you food and a place to sleep?" I ask my two party members, my tongue firmly in my cheek.

Fauna glares from beside me. I wonder if she's readying words or fists. "Flora!" she snaps. "I know you wanted to leave almost as soon as you entered that fungus flat!"

"Yes, but I'm not known as the *nice* sister!" I tease.

Usually it's her teasing me, so I enjoy this bit of gloating.

I say to the Challenger. "She's the outgoing one, always since we were little!"

"You *are* little," the ranger remarks, shaking his head.

"Littler," I say. "Always talking to everyone, wanting to join in on activities while I watched from afar!"

3

In truth I usually had my nose in some tome or other I got from Mother's library. I can read of things far away and not get a mark of dirt on me, but not my sister, not her. She needs to touch and feel things, even bad things.

"He *did* rescue us," says the Challenger, running a hand through his dirty-blonde hair, twirling an especially long strand over his forehead. "Not that we were in danger. I would've thought of some way out of the mud."

"Sure!" Fauna agrees jestingly, pulling the straps on the big knapsack on her back. "But it was good that he got to us when he did. I was exhausted."

"Me too," grumbles the Challenger, stepping ahead of us. "Babysitting is hard work!"

"Oh, this is babysitting to you?" Fauna asks with a high laugh that is likely heard throughout the woods.

"Feels like it," The Challenger remarks with a half-smile as the trail splits in two. He pauses before us and we arrive at his sides. Sister looks at me and tells me I'll be carrying the knapsack next.

"You should be thankful you're on this quest with us," is all she says to our ranger companion. "When our names get written in the history books alongside the great heroes of the past, you will be grateful to be so remembered!"

"When I get the rest of my coin I will be grateful," he says, alternating his gaze between the two trails, sniffing the air.

"The quest still hasn't really started, has it?" I say more than ask her.

"Oh, yes it has, Flora! This *is* our quest…to find a quest!" she proclaims, placing both hands on her sides, stamping a foot, turning to the Challenger. "So, which way?"

"It's your quest. You tell me," the rugged ranger responds. He turns about, shutting his one eye for a second and I can't tell if he is blinking or winking. He wears a brown patch over the space where his former eye once was. Across his chest rests a longbow, a quiver of a dozen or so arrows strapped to his back. Both he and my sis are trained marks-folk. Not me though, I only have a dagger from Mother to use as a weapon.

We are indeed on a quest to find a quest. What quest? We don't know yet, so long as we do *a* quest and have *an* adventure worth telling. We twins, after our birthday when we came of age, decided to set out. Actually, Fauna decided to set out and I followed at some urging. She said I could write about it when we get back.

So now we're here at this fork in the woodland path.

"Ah, doesn't matter. Try left," says Fauna, charging on ahead, the big bag on her back bouncing. This trail is thinner, the trees on the sides so close together they resemble wooden fences, the ground littered with short shrubs, tangling vines, and woodland flowers. Despite the pleasant appearance, I have a feeling we should be going right instead, yet I follow my sister.

We kick up pollen and floating seeds as we jog. Flocks of butterflies vacate the miniature ecosystems at our feet. Above us the canopy is thick and green, sunlight streaming down in narrow streaks. I feel calm as I inhale the smoky wooded scent these northern forests are known for. I see the Challenger has unsheathed his sword and is cutting some of the vines and twigs in front of our path. I also notice Fauna's long red cap bouncing up and down as she navigates the thicket.

"Maybe we should turn back?" I call up to them, glancing about the trees, spotting very tall ones to my left side. I wonder if I could go up and get a better look. I am about to suggest it when I hear my sister shriek.

"What is it?" asks The Challenger, pausing in his side-to-side slashing.

"Ow!" Fauna shouts and I hear her unsheathing her sword. "Yeah, just pricked my shoulder. Stupid sharp twig!"

We all proceed through the brush. I feel some prickly stuff on my face as I push through the thick mess, feeling encumbered, but I press forward, breaking apart the remaining bits of thorns and twigs in my way. Amid the sounds of cracking I hear something in the distance. I strain my ears, detecting the noise from behind us, but I can't yet tell what it is. The ranger, a small way before me, suddenly turns around, his eye wide, his face forming into a deep scowl. Fauna stops as well and I see her spin about, an anxious look overtaking her fine features. Her green eyes seem to jolt in place.

Then I begin to make out the sound:

Hey there, my newest friends,
Alone and caught in woodland glens,
Who fares upon that forest path?
Who dips in sparkling river bath?

The ranger groans. And then he shouts: "Move!"

Fauna is already tearing through, snapping branch and root as she runs, while the Challenger thumps his feet wildly, no longer bothering to slice his way through. I wince, coming up behind them, and then I force myself to smile as I turn around as see our host again.

From far away he looks big, but as he approaches his height seems to shift, getting shorter and shorter until he is just a bit under my height, his tall pointed straw hat stretching up another foot from his head. He wears big boots and earthy trousers (likely due to caked mug) under a big green overcoat. There's a bright yellow scarf wrapped about his neck, his big salt-and-pepper beard waving as he hops jollily towards us.

"Hello again Mister Bumpledop," I greet. He is about ten or so paces away, his usual big grin on his round face.

"Hey friends!" Dick Bumpledop calls to us, removing his hat, revealing a full head of silvery hair. "It looks like you there are stuck again!"

"We aren't stuck," insists Fauna. I look over and see she is leaning sideways over a long, low-hanging branch, a wall of vines stretched out before her.

"We're just cutting through!" adds The Challenger.

"Oh! These woods can be treacherous!" our former host says in his booming yet friendly voice. He raises both of his hands, waving his fingers and calls out: "Life force of the wood-land! Be calm, for these are friends of the Olds! You tuck your vines and branches away, spirits! Let them pass in peace!"

I hear a series of churning-like sounds and I turn to the way we had been going and I see the woods shift. It's subtle at first, branches slightly parting and tall grasses flowing apart from the trail, but soon the very trunks of the trees lean over, loud creaks and woody grumbles emanating as they move. Now there is a clear path through the woods where two could walk through side by side. The Challenger places his sword in his sheath. Fauna does the same with her blade. I look back to Dick Bumpledop who is grinning even wider than before.

I sigh before asking if there is anything we can do to thank him. When he tells me he has some folktales to share with us I can almost hear the silent groans. Soon Fauna and I find a log to seat ourselves on, while the ranger stands with his back leaning against a spruce. My sister throws the big knapsack onto my lap, making me say 'oof!' as we wait for our host to begin.

Dick Bumpledop speaks from topic to topic, oftentimes venturing off-topic and starting all new stories along the way, sometimes returning to the original yarns. He tells the tales with feeling, moving his hands wildly at some points, and if we hadn't listened to hours and hours of his stories the night before we would likely be entertained, but I can see the glaze setting in on the faces of my companions. He tells us of the time he tossed out rubbish into a nearby creek and the Lord of the Otters had him brought back to their den where Dick sang to them until they let him go. He tells another story about how he helped a lost hedge-hog, interjecting with a few songs about the movement of water and the growing of leaves. I listen, taking it all in.

Eventually, after the sun has made it to the midpoint in the sky, Dick Bumpledop takes a pause from his storytelling, standing up from the little rock he had planted himself on, stretching his arms and legs, yawning. "Ah, I must be off, friends!"

We all straighten ourselves out as I hear a badly hidden sigh of relief come out of my sister. "Yes!" she says, waving a hand. "We too must get going!"

I agree, lugging the straps of the big knapsack with all our goods onto my back. I don't know how Fauna carries it so care-lessly, probably because she's stronger than me. She always made fun of me for it when we were little. I wear a big pair of specta-cles too. Fauna would say that people called me an owl and when-ever I asked "Who?" she would laugh furiously.

"Move along, friends!" Dick Bumpledop announces, jumping and tapping his feet together before breaking into an-other song. We three exchange glances. Fauna begins stepping to-wards the trail. Bumpledop is busy singing, his eyes closed as he dances, waving his arms and shaking his round waist around while we back slowly, issuing thank-you's between his verses. I am the only one taking in his whimsical lyrics, just in case there is anything I need to know:

> *"Now, you flee deep into the woods,*
> *With your sack all full of goods,*
> *Three friends through old lands do you travel,*
> *Where your adventure must thus unravel!"*

I smile at the last line, looking over to Fauna. Songs are already being sung about her.

"Oh and I almost forgot! Owl sister?" Dick Bumpledop suddenly shouts as he stops dancing.

Fauna laughs, almost hysterically.

"Here!" he calls and produces something from one of his pockets, tossing it to me. I almost fumble the little object he has thrown, a small wooden thing. It doesn't take me long to figure out that it's a flute due to its small mouthpiece and three tiny holes on its thin body.

"Uh, thanks!" I say. "I guess I can learn how to play."

"Blow thrice if you run into trouble!" explains Dick Bumpledop. I thank him and turn around, listening half-heartily to his last words, something about a valley with three mountain peaks where he cannot help us, and I catch a few lines about other folks in the realm, one of which is a giant owl, but I don't know if he's poking fun. He also mentions a friend named Barpar, an ancient one who made the owl larger once by tossing it, or something. We move rapidly through the woods, turning off from the thin trail, the echoes of Dick Bumpledop fading into the afternoon.

"Well, wasn't that nice of him?" I say to Fauna after a short while of us walking in silence.

She shrugs. "Like others before us, we wander the land looking to do good, even if other good beings are irritating sometimes."

"Speak for yourselves," says the Challenger. "I consider myself neutral and chaotic."

"You said that before," I tell him as the three of us make it to a large clearing. "What does that mean?"

The ranger turns around and blinks his good eye. "Oh, you know."

I am confused. "No, I don't," I say, feeling an ache in my back.

We two sisters seat ourselves on some patches of short grass and, with a heave, I slump the big bag off and let it land between us. Fauna slinks to my side and quickly untangles the strings that keep it shut.

"Ah nuts," she says, breathing on me, clear disappointment on her face as she pulls back. "We're near out of food!"

"Really?" I ask, peering inside the flap, feeling a little hungry. I put a hand to the soft blue tunic over my belly.

"We have some nuts leftover, which is why I said that when I opened it," she answers, giving a weak smile. She reaches in and pulls out a handful.

"Let me get something from the forest," the Challenger offers, vanishing behind the walls of foliage before we can reply. He returns soon with a dead bird in his hands, some kind of woodland fowl. Fauna stands up and gathers some wood for a fire while I look over our inventory.

In all we have quite a few items for our adventure, most of it provided by Mother, though some other stuff we got along the way too. We have, aside from nuts, yards of thin but firm rope, some healing leaves, a small bag full of flame-wood (extra dry wood that catches fire after three rubs), a leather bag with a total of ten powder bombs with metallic shells (small bombs I can fit in my hand though the blast they produce is five times as big – courtesy of the Alchemy Department, friends and colleagues of Mother), an extra quiver of strong arrows made of a semi-magical wood/metal alloy, and three skin flasks for drinking. We also have extra socks, blue for me, red for Fauna. We have too a small but effective telescope that I've had since I was littler. I place the little wooden flute inside, figuring we won't be calling Dick Bumpledop.

Fauna makes a shallow pit, fills it with dry leaves, and asks me for a piece of flame-wood. Once she sparks them and the fire begins flickering the Challenger places lunch in and the smell of crispy meat floats into the air.

After eating we all take a stretch around the dying fire. I feel new energy flowing through my body as I look about my companions and the sunny clearing.

"Don't stub your toe," Fauna warns, making a goofy expression as she leans backward against a rock. "Or else Dick Bumpledop will be here!"

"Time to move on," I say. "He's a tiny distraction in this apparently epic quest you're obsessed with having."

"Where to next, girls?" the Challenger asks us, poking his long blade into the embers at our feet. "Shall we stay eastward?"

Fauna nods, turning and pointing with an outstretched hand.

"That's west," I say.

She turns, points the other way. A single brown rabbit, or maybe a hare, hops gaily along the path in the direction from whence we just came. Soon we see two more hares running alongside the trail, and then another, and then a pair of skunks, their tails up in defiance as they move. A few chirpy birds rush overhead, flapping their wings, all going in the same direction as the four legged critters.

"Looks like everything is fleeing where we are going?" remarks the Challenger.

We continue along the trail, the forest thinning as we make our way in the shadows of light canopy. I enjoy the silence as my sister treks a fair ways ahead of us and I am left with the Challenger. I ask him if he knows this realm. He explains to me that he has been traveling this country for the past four years, having gone almost everywhere either on a lonesome sojourn or in the pay of others.

"Four years? No place to call your home?" I ask him, imagining what it must be like to be rootless. We'd met him a few days ago in a tavern on the outskirts of our realms.

He shakes his head, looking down the pathway at his feet, appearing lost in thoughts. I ask him why he has been wandering the realms. He turns his head up a little to meet my gaze. I can see something flicker in his eye, a look of pain, of loss.

I don't ask him again. Soon he chuckles a bit, accidentally kicking a toad that had just leaped in front of his foot as he stepped. "Whenever you meet someone with a mysterious past, chances are something tragic happened to them and that's why they're where they are."

I give a curt nod, looking over at my sister skipping along the trail, a series of low-hanging willows blocking the space before her. She stops and we catch up to her.

"What could be beyond these leafy drapes?" Fauna asks us.

"Hopefully something to fight," says the ranger at my side, pulling out his sword again, pressing its point against the bottom of overhanging foliage, lifting it to reveal that the forest ends abruptly. Beyond is an open space, a great field, perhaps a valley judging by the distant hills I can barely see further away. Near our feet runs a tiny gushing stream, so narrow we each easily leap over it, bringing ourselves into bright sunlight, the brightest we had seen in days.

Fauna stammers, spinning her body about while she continues to skip along the grassy trail. As I follow my sister, I take in the green fields, the ground under us sloping gradually downward until it reaches a low point in what appears to be the middle of this huge open space. There, at the base of the descending ground, sits a great hill, near perfectly round. Fauna gasps. "Look!"

I gaze where she gestures. Far in the distance, beyond the hill at the base of the sloping ground, stands a tall peak covered in trees all the way to the top, this mountain carpeted by forest. Fauna begins running for the round grassy hill. I call for her to wait, but the Challenger laughs. "Let's go check it out!" he shouts, waving his blade above his head before charging after her.

I groan from the weight of the bag on my back, but manage to follow. Propelled by the downward slope, I keep behind our ranger friend as Fauna reaches halfway to the hill. Here the ground evens out, running flat until it reaches the foot of the hill. I see a small clan of rabbits running past us, heading towards the neck of the woods we have just come through.

I mutter to myself: "I would call this Hare-Neck Valley."

"Look!" my sister calls as she stops and I reach her side. She points to the entrance-way of a tunnel at the bottom of the hill, just to the right of where we stand. "And look there!" Fauna points leftward to another identical archway.

"Flame-wood!" my sister orders. I am about to fling my heavy bag in front of me when the Challenger suggests we climb the hill instead of going into it, just to get a better look at the area. We two agree, but I insist he carry the bag up.

The hill is somewhat steep, but we climb with relative ease, our feet finding little nooks and indents as we make our way to the top. At the summit it is flat, this big circular space about thirty paces around. In the center of the summit is a short well made of stone. Gasping at the odd sight, I peak over the rim, seeing weird bright blue mushrooms growing all about the sides of it, running downward to what looks like a dimly lit chamber below. I can only see some big rocks down there, flickers from unseen light sources dancing upon their surfaces.

"Look at that," says Fauna, busily taking in the immense sight around us.

"Wow," the Challenger adds, dropping our bag.

The sight is indeed amazing. First, I look to the far mountain I saw earlier, somewhat closer now, the ground rising steadily towards it like it does on the other side of the hill. It stands alone, mere woodland hills running alongside of it, a few streams crossing the land here and there. I continue my gaze northward (where things look similar) when I set my eyes upon another treed mountain.

"Weird," I comment, pointing to it. "That mountain looks just like the other."

Fauna nods. I then turn about halfway and see another mountain, this one not far from the way we came, to the southeast. Like the other two it rises suddenly, a series of hills between each of the three mountains, forests covering all of them.

"Uh oh," I say as I realize something.

Before any of my companions can ask me what I'm on about the Challenger cries out, raising his sword, pointing to the first mountain across the great way. Both of our heads turn to where he's pointing.

"What is that?" Fauna asks in a sharp puff.

Near the peak we see what looks like some kind of floating ball or bubble. It's green and, as it gets closer, I realize it's big, twice the size of a person, yet perfectly round. It approaches us, drifting twenty or so feet above, and then slows down as it nears the single round hill. A face emerges on its surface. It's simple; two black eyes, a single dot for a nose, as well as a line for a mouth. It appears to be looking forward, seemingly not noticing us as it moves overhead.

"Are you ready?" a booming voice emits from the weird thing.

"Ready for what?" Fauna shouts.

"I sure am!" another voice roars from behind us, startling my sister and I while the Challenger flings out his bow and plucks an arrow, lining it up, pointing it upward at the new big blue face that has appeared across from the green one.

"Alright then!" says a third face, a red one that has emerged to the southwest, its voice also loud, though somewhat softer spoken. "Lobster-Man is ready!"

"So is Frog-Bro!" declares the green face.

"And Slug-Lord!" cries the blue one before declaring: "Let the games begin!"

"Games?" Fauna yells at all three of them, pulling out her sword, raising it toward them. "What games?"

Without a further word the Challenger shoots an arrow into the blue face, which harmlessly flies through and continues soaring into the valley. Fauna shouts at him, reminding him that our company is supposed to be a force for good, but the Challenger explains again that he is neutral and chaotic.

The blue face lowers its eyes slightly, seeming to notice us, asking: "Who are these?"

The other two faces sink a little in the air.

"I don't know about this," says the red one, its beady eyes blinking.

"Ah, look!" says the green face. "One in green, one in blue, one in red! They must be non-playable characters!"

"Someone gifted them without telling us?" asks the red one, the closest thing to a look of confusion on its simple face.

"No matter," says the blue one.

The big green thing, Frog-Bro, laughs dryly and says: "I get the man! You guys are toast!"

"Let's start already!" snaps the red face. The others dip slightly and they all vanish at once, all saying: "Good luck, have fun."

Fauna asks me: "What was that all about?"

I shrug, looking to the Challenger.

"No clue," he asks. "Maybe we should get going? We don't want to get caught up in something."

A deafening trumpeting noise erupts from one of the mountains then. We all duck and I feel powerful vibrations in the ground. Another blast follows from the mountain across the way, and then a third blare echoes across the valley. I know now why the animals were all fleeing this valley when we came in.

I cry out to my sister: "What have you gotten us into?"

"Me?" she shouts back, crossing her red-sleeved arms.

Before I can say anything more we hear distant rumbling. I look to the mountains, one after the other, and on each I see what appears to be huge swathes of darkness tearing down the mountainsides from the peaks. At this distance I can see the trees on the mountains crumble and snap before these great clusters that are flowing downward toward the valley.

I grab the knapsack, fetching the handheld telescope while Fauna reaches in at my side and grabs the extra quiver of arrows, strapping it on her back before grabbing something else as well. Hands sweating, I bring the eyepiece of the scope up to one eye, closing my other, pointing it to one of the mountains.

"Oh no," I say.

"What is it?" Fauna demands.

I want to describe it, but the words get caught in my throat. "There are...charging down the mountainside...whole armies of...things!"

Even with my scope I cannot quite make out what they are. At the front, and making up a bit more than half of the total mass is a sea of black, brown, and grey furry things. They move so fast I just see shifting fur, red eyes, fangs, and spears! Everything in their wake is getting crushed; everywhere they move as they descend emerge clouds of dust, dirt, and pieces of flinging trees they crash through. They must be small creatures, the bulk of them, I figure, but I also see larger things among them—what appear to be large lumber with arms and legs! They stamp downward among the masses of furred things, these walking logs wielding lumberjack axes in their branchy hands. Flying above them, moving in the same direction, are what appear to be wooden barrels with great white wings spreading from their sides, flapping madly. Among the crowd I see too what look like enormous rolling eyeballs and I spot what look like gigantic stone men marching among the other monsters.

Hearing my sister yell, I spin around, seeing her angry face magnified for a moment before focusing on the next mountain over. Here I see the same, an army of furry things, walking logs, flying barrels, rolling eyeballs, stone giants, and the many other weird monstrosities. I notice that these ones are shaded red, or have red among them—the eyeballs have red pupils, the winged barrels red stripes, and so on. I zoom back to the first hill, noticing that the same applies but with green, and then I take in the third mountain and see that the same things are coming down the valley but with blue tinges and stripes.

"Three teams," I mutter.

The scope is violently yanked from me. Fauna looks through it, spinning around at the three mountains like I did. "Crap! Crap! Crap!"

The Challenger next looks through with his one eye and grumbles.

My sister reveals the flute in her hands, having grabbed it from the bag, and she cries out: "Help us, Dick Bumpledop!"

Dread sweeps over me while butterflies explode within my belly. Fauna puts her lips to the whistle as I fall over, landing on my butt. There's no sound emitting from the flute. She blows two more times, her face already pinkish. I start giggling.

"What's so funny?" Sister shrieks, placing the flute at her belt, grabbing her bow.

"B-B-Bumpledop!" I stammer from the grass.

"He told us to blow this flute thrice!" she shouts back. "Even if it's a silent flute! It must be magic! He'll come help us!"

I stand, retrieving the little scope from the Challenger. "Fauna, Dick Bumpledop can't help us. He said so in one of his songs. I didn't catch all the words, but I remember him saying that if we come to a valley with three peaks that he can't help us."

Fauna's tan face nearly turns paper white. "We should flee," she simply says and points her bow toward the East.

"Back from whence we came then!" our ranger companion declares, pointing his sword westward.

I peer through the scope to where he's pointing and I see it, the little gushing stream and now distant curtain of foliage, but now there is a great metallic wall beyond them. It must have risen from the ground, for I see that the bottom of the fence ascends directly into the earth. I turn about in a full circle, noticing that this immense wall wraps around the whole valley, stretching between each of the three mountains.

Handing it to my freaked out sis next, I tell her what I just saw. She looks through the scope and swears worse than before.

"Well," says the Challenger. "You wanted a quest!"

My sister's face goes wild. "Is being stuck in the middle of a battlefield between magical automatons and summoned monstrosities a *quest*?"

The ranger shrugs. He takes the telescope and searches the scenery. "Our best bet is hiding until it's over."

"They look like three teams judging by their colors," I say. "That's why they think we're on their teams."

"We're on no one's team!" Fauna shouts angrily. "We don't belong to big ugly faces!"

"That's right!" yells the ranger. "We're afraid of nothing! Now, let's go hide."

The Challenger scoops up the knapsack and the three of us nearly fall down the sloping sides onto the ground below, heading for the closest tunnel entrance at the hill's base, plunging into blackness for a few frantic steps until we emerge down a rock corridor into a dimly lit chamber, the one I'd seen from above through the well. This place is big, as big as the mound from the outside, which was to be expected. There are lit torches on the walls, too high from the cave floor to reach, six in all. The ground is flat and hard, a bluish hue, and there are rocks, really big ones, with flat tops not unlike the mound itself that each stand about an average elf's height, easily surmountable. In the middle of the room is a single big rocky raised platform. A bright light shines from above through the hole in the roof, the well. We cautiously approach the center rock, taking in the strange atmosphere.

Soon the ground shakes and we hear heavy crashing and footfalls. Flakes of dust and tiny bits of stone fall from the walls. A great battle is being waged outside.

"Maybe we can wait it out," Fauna cries over the erupting noises.

I am about to agree with her when I hear something that freezes me in place, something more chilling than the commotion outside—the sounds of hundreds of tiny feet scurrying, getting louder, combined with the sounds of flicking tails and chirps and squeaks. We three exchange anxious glances before shoving ourselves over the edge of the central rock platform. Whatever's coming is going to be all over the floor soon.

Upon the level summit there is enough space for six adventurers, just enough for us to move about. The sounds have multiplied, echoing down all three of the tunnels that lead outside. In the light of the torches I see a dark mass moving in the tunnel we'd come through—it looks like one long flat creature at first, but then, in the torchlight I see many creatures. These must be the furred masses I saw, the smallest units, all bundled together. They seemingly move as one, all scurrying inside, curving their forms about the big rocks. These are tiny things on two feet, each a third my height. They're frail-looking, with skinny arms and legs covered in brown or black or grey fur, and they're wearing little robes or minuscule chain-mail armor. In their paws they carry different weaponry, wooden spears, little axes, and daggers held like swords, some with small wooden shields. The heads of the critters are ugly, looking too large for their bodies, with whiskered snouts, pointed ears, beady black eyes, and sharp fangs that show when they screech unintelligible gibberish.

I turn, sighting another swarm of them on the other side, and then a third huge cluster sneaking in from the third tunnel. Now I realize they have different colours on their clothing, signifying whether they serve red, green, or blue.

"Kobolds!" the Challenger yells from beside me.

There must be a hundred on each team. As the groups meet around us they all squeal a piercing battle-cry before they charge. In the middle, all around our big platform, green pushes into blue and blue into red and green while red brushes against green, much of the red cluster moving sideways to take on the front of green's vanguard forces (from what I can tell). Knife, spear, and ax all thrust while black blood spews everywhere, the front-line fighters covered in it, while little furry bodies fall over and are promptly stepped upon by the next line of forces.

"Kobolds?!" I stammer, noticing my sister is covering her ears, the screechy noises overwhelming the room. I'm feeling sick as the little monsters slay one another.

"Yes, kobolds!" our hired friend repeats as the chamber completely fills with the diminutive fighters, not a single bit of floor visible beneath and around us.

"Wait! I read that kobolds were little reptilian things? Like, tiny dragon-kin that stands on two legs?" I ask, my dagger drawn in place of the scope.

The Challenger shakes his head, giving me a strange look. "What are you reading? Kobolds are little furry rat beings, but they're super weak. Watch!"

The ranger grabs a large pebble from the floor of the platform, points out one particular kobold near the far wall, a grey one that's hunched over and carrying a long dagger, a lit candle set upon its head. The Challenger throws the tiny stone at its face. It shrieks and falls over, tongue lolling out at its side before another clump of kobolds step over the body.

"So they die easily!" yells Fauna. "But if I get stabbed enough times with those weapons I'll still die!"

"Yes!" I agree, looking to her. "Let's wait until their numbers are thinned?"

Fauna gazes around the room, looking impatient before she points to the ceiling. All three of our eyes look up with hers to see the roof is covered with light blue mushrooms.

"Trippy," I hear her say, but this is no time for experimentation.

"I bet arrows stick to those," I say, scratching my chin. We return our attention to the fighting kobolds. The reds seem to be winning for a moment, pushing back on both the blues and greens, but after some time, when green and blue temporarily cease fighting each other the reds are pushed back on two sides, eventually leading to the annihilation of the remaining reds, the last of them, a round brown kobold in red, screeching as blue and green spears thrust into both of its sides.

Now there are two bunches, maybe a few dozen of each, more blues than greens. The blues move swiftly upon the greens and in short time the entire floor is littered with dead kobolds with about thirty or so blue-clad ones standing. The victorious kobolds begin cheering, some hoisting their weapons above them in celebration before they all gather near the middle of the room.

A voice speaks: "I won the underground fight! Yes! Slug-Lord number one!"

The big blue face appears smiling above us.

"You again!" Fauna shouts.

The face turns about. "Oh, you still here?"

He looks at me. I grip my dagger tightly.

"You! Fight them! I command it!" the face yells, causing the walls to shake a bit.

"No!" I declare, too enraged to be afraid.

"We aren't fighters in your game!" Fauna cries, backing me up.

"Yeah!" the Challenger echoes.

"Look, bud," I say, trying to calm down, to explain ourselves to whatever we're speaking with. "We got lost and wound up here by mistake! So, can you just let us out through this valley and we'll be on our way?"

The blue face goes wild, its dots for eyes growing three times in size. "What?" it roars. "You mean to say you're *actual* girls?"

"Uh," I say. "Yeah, sisters actually. We need to leave!"

"No! This is *our* space!" shouts the head.

"What's wrong with him?" the Challenger asks the two of us.

"No!" it cries again. "I have kobolds left! And other things! You will die here!"

The blue face vanishes.

"What a wiener," mutters Fauna, holding her bow. The blue-clad kobolds begin scampering towards us.

"Good thing for this big rock!" says the Challenger right before the kobolds start pairing up and standing on one another's heads in order to make it to our level. The ranger curses, rushing forward to kick the face of the nearest kobold. The kobold flies off the shoulders of the other, screeching in terror.

A furry head emerges in front of me. I slam my knee into the rat-face, causing it to fall. Fauna loads an arrow and points it at the next kobold that appears, causing the kobold to scream and turn tail out the tunnel it came from. The Challenger jumps down onto the flat ground, facing the remaining ten of them. The group of furred adversaries move forward in a makeshift phalanx, shoving their spears and knives at him, but the ranger swings his sword once, managing to hit every one of them with ease.

We all smile at each other, feeling relieved, and I wonder if all the monsters are as weak, but I doubt it. I'm considering staying down here until the competition, or whatever it is, ends. This is when we hear it, the returning sounds of frantic scurrying. Fauna looks sickened.

The Challenger loads an arrow and points his bow upward, having placed his sword back at his belts. "Pass me the rope!" he calls to Fauna. My sister throws him the whole thing, the long and thin rope Mother had gifted us. Our companion takes a fairly long bit, cutting it from the rest with the side of an arrow tip. Next he ties the rope tight to the middle part of his arrow and then reloads it on the bow, shooting it upward at the mushrooms on the ceiling.

"Genius!" I cry.

"You gave me the idea," he says, tugging on the firmly attached rope. The Challenger then climbs onto the next nearest rock platform, one of the smaller ones that looks like stools, and he says: "Now, when they get here, take your bombs, your firewood, everything you have!"

I nod over to him and then crouch and begin rummaging through the knapsack as the sounds of tiny footfalls become louder and louder. I glance and see three enormous swarms, kobolds all blue. They are funneling through the entrances, more than enough to kill us if they get close enough.

The Challenger swings, using the rope attached to the ceiling, back to us at the big middle platform, his feet taking out the first line of kobolds that make it near the center of the chamber. He immediately swings back as more kobolds stream through the same entrance. His boots must be heavy, I think as I see a pair of kobolds splat against the wall. Another had managed to grab hold of the Challenger for a moment, shooting upward with him before losing grip and falling upon a raised spear.

Here I am in the middle of the central platform, having taken from the knapsack a bunch of the small bombs and two pieces of flame-wood, now briskly shoving the rest of the rope inside the bag again and closing it up. My sister is shooting arrows the whole while, picking off kobolds as they close around our platform. After I kick another ratty face from the lip of our rock, I hastily smash my two pieces of wood together, causing both to ignite at once!

In one hand I hold the two flaming pieces, winching at the heat on my fingers, in the other hand I take one of the little bombs and light its fuse with the burning wood – I toss it towards the middle of the far side of the room, away from where the Challenger is swinging. The bomb explodes after five seconds, tossing up flames and little bits of kobold. Fauna grabs a bomb at my feet, raising it's fuse upward at the fire at my hand. She chucks the bomb over her shoulder, letting it fall towards the tunnel entrance furthest from us. It blows up in the midst of the streaming kobolds, creating a huge blackened hole where the archway had loomed.

She grabs two more bombs, lighting them, handing one to me. The Challenger sweeps by again, grabbing a bomb from the small pile beneath me, next flinging himself towards one of the torches, lighting and tossing the bomb in one move, taking out more kobolds under his feet kicking feet.

I sweatily turn my head to the bomb pile, seeing that it no longer exists.

The burning fire make it's way down the pieces of wood in my hand quickly and I feel even more intense heat on my fingers as I throw one at the nearest group of kobolds. It's flames take out three of them.

The Challenger once more appears at my side, praising me for my idea. He lets go of the rope, pulling something from his tunic pocket, a copper flask. He takes a big swig while tilting his head, and then he rips off part of his sleeve, shoving it into the open flask before lighting the fabric on fire with the last of the burning wood in my palm.

"You had that the whole time?" I ask him, tossing the wood that dissolves into ashes before reaching the ground.

"How do you think I got through Dick Bumpledop's stories?" he asks and winks (I think). He throws the burning flask, hitting a large cluster of the tiny beasts before the platform, embroiling them in flames instantly, the fire spreading madly as the kobolds shriek and run. Their numbers have thinned, but more quickly flow into the chamber, as if all our fighting had just been in vain. I feel fear again as I see something coming in from behind them, a big blue blob thing squeezing through the tunnel like an octopus fitting through a hole smaller than itself.

"We should get out of here!" I shout as I notice a second blob coming in through another entrance, edging its way forward, tendrils flailing about the wall of the cave. In panic we leave the bag behind, but I quickly take out the remaining small bombs (four of them) and two pieces of the flame-wood, stuffing them into my deep pockets. Fauna quickly grabs a few items as well, including my scope.

"Nice quest," I tell her dryly. The Challenger begins climbing the rope attached to the mushrooms along the edges of the well, making it up to the cave roof quickly. Fauna grabs the rope next, beginning to climb. I kick a wandering kobold off of the platform.

Sister makes it to the top and I can see the ranger's hands pulling her upward. He has climbed up and out of the well. I go next, feeling the firm rope. I make it halfway when something tugs on my leg. I cry out, looking down to see a blob. Its tendril pulls hard and I barely keep my grip on the rope. Without thinking, I release one of my hands from the rope and use it to grab a piece of flame-wood in my pant pocket, quickly rubbing it three times downward against the other piece inside, pulling them both out as they erupt in flames. The blob tugs harder still, causing me to lose one of the wood pieces. It falls onto the ground below, hitting some kobolds.

"Pull me up!" I scream to my sister. In the wild moment I see her red cap above for a moment. My hand that still grips the rope is hurting, having already been singed earlier.

I try to wag my foot. An enormous mouth appears underneath me, the blob is reaching upward, thinning it's body, trying to swallow me. I feel my hand against the rope sweating before feeling the sensation of ascending movement; my companions are pulling me up!

I place the fiery piece of flame-wood in my mouth, biting down on the unflaming end to steady it as I pull out a single bomb from my other pocket. The rope raises again, bringing me nearly to the ceiling, the sunlight from above pouring onto my face now. The blob beneath shifts shape, making itself taller still, its mouth wider and bigger, and I look down and see an immense hole leading to its dark insides. I bring the little bomb up in my hand, bring its wick against the burning flame that sears my cheek and, letting go of both the wood and the bomb, I watch as the pair of items fall into the gaping maw below.

"Up!" I cry.

The slimy abomination bursts apart, balls of fire flying outward in every direction, slaying kobolds in its wake. I emerge into sunlight, my tunic getting caught on the sticky mushroom clusters for a moment. Outside I fall over once they manage to squeeze me through, gasping, falling into the arms of my sister, my feet meeting the grass.

"Flora, are you okay?" Sister asks tenderly, something I haven't heard from her in ages. I look up and smile, getting to my feet, relieved that the blob no longer has my foot.

Once more we are atop the summit of the green mound. The valley is alive with combating creatures. I see kobolds and blobs fighting between the feet of great tall beings made of stone. I spot among the commotion what appear to be horseless wagons that are full to the brim with the weird armed logs.

"Rubbish lot," mutters Sister.

The Challenger tears across the space as a walking log with green stripes fends off a dozen red-clad kobolds at the far edge of the summit. The ranger has a piece of flame-wood with him that he'd just lit up and, as soon as the fighting log smacks the last of the kobolds off the mound the Challenger leaps and sets it ablaze, causing it to drop its ax and flee, a smoky tail following it onto the battlefield beneath.

"This has to end!" Fauna shouts as we two take in the sight of a giant eyeball being chucked far over our heads by one of the giant stone brutes. I gaze as the round thing zips through the sky, seeing right beyond a multitude of flying things.

"Winged barrels?" I groan as I place my dagger across my cap's brim for additional shade. Some of these fly randomly, others in formations, all bobbing forward like geese, dropping flaming debris upon enemy units below as they sway.

"Got any ideas?" the ranger says, having just returned to our side. His bow is raised, and he careens it in a semi-circle at our rear. My sister too has hers, an arrow notched as well.

"The rope again?" I ask, pointing to the Challenger's loaded arrow, it's rope attachment having been removed already.

"You mean, maybe if we are attached we can try to steer it away from the battlefield?" the ranger asks me.

"How about riding up to one of those?" Fauna suggests, pointing to one of the distant three mountains. As she finishes saying this a chevron of six winged barrels shoot forth in the nearby sky, whizzing by a little over from where we stand. They rise slightly in the air, hurrying when they approach one of the walking statues, this one of reddish tinge, that stands tall over the battlefield. The great golem thingy waves a thick arm, hitting two of the incoming barrels, causing them to plummet while the remaining barrels ram themselves directly into the stone-walker's torso, their bursts all converging into one massive fireball. The statue's upper body cracks apart over its lower body, both of it's arms waving feebly as it crumbles into two big pieces and a mass of smaller ones.

"So we're not riding those," the Challenger mutters, turning from us, placing a hand over his forehead to scan the field further. "Those," he says, pointing in the distance, which direction I know not, halfway to one of the mountains. All our eyes follow his finger, noticing he is referring to the wagons that zip through the battleground. Fauna pulls somethings from her pocket, I don't have time to see what.

The battle, from where we stand, looks like a three way tie so far. Colours shift and change before us. Sometimes the reds have certain fields and hills, but are quickly supplanted by swarms of greens, while the blues display a strategy of backing off temporarily and then striking the victor of a scuffle in coordinated clusters, overwhelming the enemy bit by bit. There are parts of the valley where it looks like a three way contest, armies fighting melee, pushing back and forth against one another. Near the base of our hill we see one of the wagons zoom by, its ax-wielding logs with red stripes hacking at the greenish kobolds at their sides. A big green blob emerges before them from the throngs of fighters, leaping before the wagon, the log driver unable to stop in time. The wagon jolts, sending half of the logs flinging off the sides.

"Opportunity!" states Fauna and the Challenger nods eagerly. All three of us tear down the side of the mound toward the stopped wagon. It's not far, and we only need to evade around some kobolds to get there. When we reach it we all jump in the back, the remaining three logs not facing us, too busy stabbing at the blob beneath them. A tentacle-like appendage reaches up, snatching the log driver, pulling it off the wagon.

Fauna lights two of the flame-wood pieces then, waving it at the other two logs from behind. The woody warriors turn about quickly, letting out terrified screeches from unseen orifices before they vacate the wagon. My sister moves to the front swiftly, finding a set of wooden levers. She pulls one backwards, sending the cart back from the near blob's gaping maw just as a larger red blob appears to grab the green one, swallowing it whole. I nearly fall over when Fauna pushes a second lever and our wooden wagon shoots forward, running over the red blob, hitting a group of kobolds, smacking their furry bodies.

She veers rightward. I fall to the side, nearly banging my head against the rim, watching the wheels crush a small eyeball monster, sending goo splattering.

"Yuck!" I yell, getting up and stepping over the Challenger, who is now laying on the floor of the wagon, his legs tugged beneath him.

"Which mountain?" Fauna calls back to me.

"Whichever!"

"Hang on!" she yells, sending the cart zooming through the battle. Things shriek and splash underneath us. I peer forward aside Sister, ducking in time to dodge a low-flying barrel bomber.

Fauna runs the wagon through a long space between opposite lines of combatants. She yells at me to stay down, so I kneel aside the Challenger, grateful for her warning when arrows begin flying overhead, causing Fauna to hunch down at the front.

We come upon a pair of fighting statues, the biggest we've seen yet, the one on the left green, red on the right. Fauna nearly drives into the left one's shin, turning quickly to pass through its legs. The red stone fighter suddenly slams its shoulder against the one we're under. I turn to my right to see a huge foot rushing toward us. Fauna, through miracle or quick hands reverses the wagon hard, backing us off at full pace to see the two colossal rock-men falling and crushing a company of kobolds beneath, dust and earth flying up along with weapons. My sister puts the levers in forward motion and steers us away.

"I don't know how I know this, I've never even reigned a pony!" laughs Fauna.

"Maybe you just know," says the Challenger. "We all have our proficiency sets."

I get up as my sister slows along an open strip of grassland, finding a pathway that runs to the nearest mountain between two approaching columns of strange creatures. They are blue slimy things, seemingly shaped like men, though faceless, long spears clutched in their hands. They're nearing us, walking stoic-like, for we tread between them and the rest of the battle. Above them I see the blue face. It's floating above them, a big grin on its face.

The Challenger appears at my side, looking sick from the rapid motion. He stands with his blade drawn, urging Fauna to make for the mountain between the files of fighters. My sister takes no time in speeding the wagon through the legions of slime-men.

"What?" a familiar but pestiferous voice calls from above. "Still alive?"

"Let us leave in peace!" I shout up to the face as we veer toward the ground below it.

"Lobster-Man!" the face cries out instead. "Frog-Boy! We have intruders! Stop fighting!"

The Challenger roars at my sister to go as fast as she can. She zips past the blue slime-men to where the ground is gradually sloping upward toward the mountainside. The wagon surprisingly remains steady as it climbs, the wind splashing us all hard in the faces. I turn about, watching the mountain base expand beneath me, the valley and the mound now small in the distance behind.

The armies have stopped fighting, I notice. I see specs of red, green, and blue, some near, some far, wherever they are, all stopping in place. The blue slime-men, partway between us and the mass of the rest of the units, seem to be turning about.

"Look!" the ranger says, bringing my attention to what's ahead of us. We are turning upward toward a great alcove near the top of the mountain. It's an open space, nearly as wide as the mountain's peak, the roof a good twenty or so feet above. Our wagon arrives at the curve into this alcove, bouncing a bit as it returns to flat ground. Fauna stops the wagon. The sight before us causes all three of us to gasp. This huge place runs back to a far wall shrouded in shadow. From the left to right, located about fifteen paces inward, there are immense iron cages, empty now, likely where the kobolds and other creatures had been released from. We step out of the wagon, our boots meeting bits of blue goo. And then I see him, the one I assume to be Slug-Lord.

He is hunched over, ten feet away from the edge of this massive indentation in the mountainside, this bulky figure clad in a bright blue robe that covers most of his body, facing the battlefield, leaning over a small pond encircled with stones. Waving his hands over it, I gather that he controls his army through this pond, this device that is likely magical.

31

My sister and the Challenger move forward slowly, sheathing their blades, opting to pull out their bows and prepare arrows. I follow, dagger in hand, unsure of our game-plan here. I notice, down towards the opposite side of the edge of the alcove, there sits a small shiny blue ship, and I realize that this must be a flying ship, which makes sense since there is no large body of water nearby.

"Slug-Lord!" Fauna calls mockingly.

He looks up and scowls at us. On his head he wears a brown short brimmed hat. He tilts this as he sees us, and now I notice, as he leans upward, that his name suits his appearance, for he actually has the body of a slug. I see no legs, only a big blue body that ends in a flat tail at the end of his robes. His face looks not unlike the round blue one we saw in the battlefield, just with thick tufts of coarse brownish-black hair running down his gullet underneath his chin all the way down towards his lower neck.

"Ooh," he says in a voice that sounds like he speaks more through his nose. "How dare you come here to my sanctuary! This is *my* space!"

"Let us leave here!" my sister barks. We move in on him, now only a few feet in front of him and the little gaming pond.

"Yes!" I shout, gazing into the pond from where I stand. I can see, beneath the rippling waters, a mini-map of the valley.

"No, milady!" he yells, placing one of his short, stubby arms over the pond, waving his fingers over it. "You will die here, all three of you NPCs!"

"We don't want to be here!" I protest, trying to see if he can be reasoned with. "We stumbled in by mistake!"

He shakes his thick head, looking as if he is trying to straighten himself before us.

I decide to try again, making my tone more sympathetic: "Look, what is this all about? What are these games?"

32

"This is the championship game!" he states, curling his lips a little at the mention. "We have been playing for years, so long I cannot remember! We've been cursed by witches, though we are warlocks ourselves, warlocks who have been spurned too long!"

"Okay," my sister says.

"The point is," declares Slug-Lord, with more than a bit of spitting. "We have this place, this one valley where we can play our games and win our championships without interference!"

"Fine!" shouted Fauna, stamping her foot hard on the ground, bringing her bow up to point at our captor. "Then show us the way out!"

Slug-Lord only shakes his head at the suggestion, waving his short hands at us.

"The ship!" shouts the Challenger. "We're taking your flying ship, alright? We don't have time for your whining!"

Slug-Lord chuckles further, his laugh as annoying as expected. "My flying ship only works when I'm on it, you idiotic fool!"

The Challenger approaches the slug, raising his bow and bring the arrow inches from the side of his face.

"You're coming with us!" Fauna then orders.

"Lobster-Man! Frog-Boy!" Slug-Lord shouts, leaning over the small pond. "The intruding females and their man-servant have invaded my space! Bring all your units here to slay them!"

"Move!" barks the ranger, but the slug-man stays in his place.

"You won't get out of here alive!"

"Then neither will you," says the Challenger, pulling further on his bowstring.

"I think not! Look behind you!" Slug-Lord giggles, pointing to the battlefield behind us.

We all turn to see them, the blue slime-men, a whole line of them standing at the edge of the alcove we just came up on, spears ready, all aimed at us. They step forward as another line of blue fighters emerges behind them.

"Crappy," says the Challenger before turning his whole body and propelling an arrow at the first line. It hits one of them, but flies through its body, streaking out the other side. Fauna shoots some arrows at the other ones with the same results.

They both reveal their swords, charging at the blue slime soldiers. I am unsurprised when their blades harmlessly cut through them, their bodies completely undisrupted. I reach into my pocket, remembering that I have no more bombs or flame-woods pieces. I had fumbled the last few bombs on the wagon. Panic overtakes me, and I can see Fauna is fearful as she and the ranger begin backing away from the impending rows of slimy spear-men.

Anger then takes me. I leap behind him the slug, placing my short blade at his hairy neck. "Call them off!" I whisper harshly in his tiny ear.

One of the slimed ones seems to see me, turning a faceless head before its free arm shoots forth like a tentacle, slapping my fingers, causing me to cry out and drop my dagger. Slug-Lord laughs. Both my sister and the Challenger are now near me, the slime-men, some of them green and red, now overwhelming us, a whole cluster of them blocking our way as more arrive behind them.

The slug guy slinks away from my grip, leaving a blue trail behind him.

"This isn't looking good!" Fauna cries.

"Our quest to find a quest looks like it's going to be cut short," agrees the Challenger. "Girls, my friends even for a short time, it's been nice questing with you!"

"And you too, Challenger!" Fauna says and I see a renegade tear moving down her soft cheek. She turns to me. "I'm sorry I brought us into this!"

I place an arm around her. "We're sisters!" I tell her, trying to sound brave though my voice is shaking along with the rest of me. "Where you go, I go! We'll make a brave end worthy of all the great heroes!"

"Let's fight until we die!" declares the Challenger before dashing into the midst of the slime-men. He spins about, his blade whirling like a top, but instead of taking all their slimy heads off, the blade merely cuts through and does nothing...as expected.

Fauna charges. I follow. There is no escape. This is it.

"I love you!" I yell, assuming they are my last words as the slime-men form a shrinking circle around us, their spears pointed inward, inching closer and closer.

"Ditto!" my sister shouts sweetly.

We grab one another. I press my forehead against her face. I can feel the strong arms of the Challenger around both of us, and then I feel the end tip of a pair of spears at my back.

A forceful wind beats down upon us from above, stirring me from my shock.

I pry my eyes open and gaze up to see a great shape, a shadow before the sunlight. The winds keep hitting me, and I notice that this huge thing above me has wings, two big ones! A pair of giant claws appear above. Whatever it is, it grabs hold of some of the spears, three in each talon, and then crunches them up before us. The slime soldiers all jump back at once as the wind from the wings beats stronger, causing some of them to fly apart.

A piercing screech follows.

Fauna points to a hole in the circle of slime-men. We all run through it, turning around in time to see a colossal owl about the size of the biggest bull or bigger land atop half of them, crushing them beneath its feathery mass. The remaining slime-men begin striking their spears at the giant owl, causing it to back up, shrieking at them, its huge eyes looking maddened, and its tufts of fathers upon its head raised like a menacing hunter-beast. This is when I notice a figure riding atop the giant bird's back. It looks like a man, larger than most, with broad shoulders covered with coarse brown hair. He is shirtless and his chest and back look like thick carpet.

"Ahoy there! Be you friends of Dick Bumpledop?" calls a thunderous voice from atop the bird.

"We love Bumpledop!" exclaims the Challenger.

Streams of relief flow through me. Fauna laughs hysterically. "An owl!" she shouts.

The hairy friend begins throwing something from a sac strapped upon his shoulder, little pebbles, yet as he throws them they grow larger, multiplying in size so fast that by the time they hit the nearest row of slime-men they are big rocks! The slime-men on the level ground are dispatched quickly, streaking down the side of the mountain as the visitor continues to throw fast growing stones at them.

"No!" shouts Slug-Lord as he rushes toward his magical ship behind us. "Not Barpar!"

"Yes Barpar!" says the new friend in his powerful voice before he turns his attention back to us. "Dick Bumpledop cannot enter this valley, yet he heard your flute calls and here I am! Any friend of Dick is a friend o'mine! Now, come, get upon Screech and let us make haste!"

We dash to the owl named Screech, mounting its immense back that thankfully fits us all, clasping our hands onto its feathers.

"We love Dick Bumpledop!" repeats the Challenger merrily to our furry rescuer.

"He's my boy!" Barpar replies, smiling with big perfectly white teeth.

As the owl flaps and ascends from the alcove's edge, we hastily introduce ourselves. Barpar tells us he is another old one who has lived in the realms for ages. He explains to us that it's best to avoid these type of lonely game-playing warlocks, something we have already learned.

I look down at the battlefield below as it shrinks from view. The mound sits in the middle, while the open fields between the mountains are still filled with the three armies. And then I see that we are being pursued. Slug-Lord has boarded his flying ship and has risen from the alcove and the slime-men have suddenly all sprouted wings. They all follow Slug-Lord's ascent while flying barrels rise to join them. From the other mountains I now see other shapes moving, red and green flying ships at the lead. The other game-players are chasing us! We are far above them, yet they are all moving fast, and it looks like they will take us in quick time.

"Barpar! Any magic you have would be helpful right now!" I shout over the high winds of this extreme height and the frantic flapping of giant wings to our sides. The Challenger is seated behind us, towards the owl's tail-feathers, while my sister and I are seated beside one another comfortably upon the big bird's shoulder blades. Barpar has his hairy legs flung over near the owl's nape.

He shouts to us over the winds: "Everything I throw becomes bigger! And the longer it flies the bigger it becomes! That's how old Screech here got so big. I gave her a great toss one day! Isn't that right, old owl?" The big bird screeches.

"Ah!" I reply, finding his explanation strange but interesting. "Fauna, what items do you have left from the bag?"

She suddenly winks, grinning, reaching into her jacket pocket. "Two pieces of flame-wood and one mini-powder bomb."

"Ah," I say. She hands me the bomb while proceeding to take out the two wood pieces next.

"They're going to catch us if we don't think of something fast!" the Challenger says to us. "Look, the owl cannot beat its wings fast enough to outrun those ships!"

As Barpar steers Screech steeply through some clouds, going higher and higher while we all hang onto her feathers tightly, I tap him on the shoulder. He turns his furred head and I ask him if he can toss the thing I hand to him. Fauna tells him to wait as he takes the tiny bomb and keeps his other powerful hand on the owl's nape.

She then hands the Challenger a piece of flame-wood, and then, with her free hand, she reaches into her jacket to take out the second bit of wood. Each of them gripping one hand upon the feathery hide, they manage to rub the two pieces enough to produce a spark, a miracle in these high winds.

"Careful!" calls the ranger, tossing his fiery piece, taking hold of the owl's feathers with both of his hands. "Don't singe Screech here!"

"Okay, throw now!" my sister shouts after she lights the fuse of the bomb in Barpar's hand She too tosses her piece and holds tightly onto Screech with both hands. I understand what her plan is immediately, taken aback by my sister's quick thinking.

"The fuse *should* stay lit," I say to her. "Flame-wood fire is one of the strongest of all fires!"

Barpar smiles warmly and chucks the bomb downward beneath us. As the bomb falls it enlarges, to us almost looking as if it is staying the same size and not falling at all, although we know it is. It passes by the blue boat, the closest one to us, and Slug-Lord gazes as it becomes nearly the size of his ship. He peers over the side as it continues to fall and grow. It passes next by the flying blue slime-men and then the green and red ships with their winged legions chasing after us. I see Slug-Lord turn his head towards us and scream when the bomb finally lands on the fields below.

"Hang on!" I yell. Screech flies faster and higher than ever, while my sister, the ranger, and I peer down at the dots below that make up the armies. This is when the blinding white flash overtakes my vision completely, a sound of thunderous eruption following.

When the flash is gone I see a titanic ball of fire!

It spreads, red and orange, from the point of impact to the sides of all three mountains, huge cracks appearing in the surfaces of the mountainsides. Flames engulf the entire open space, covering everything, and then a black cloud emerges, mushroom-shaped, rising outward and upward. I see it overwhelm the flying creatures, and then the red and green flying ships further below. The blue ship speeds up, but doesn't escape the fire and the cloud. I can hear Slug-Lord's high-pitched screams as the explosion overtakes the entire ship.

As Barpar brings us higher and the air becomes thin my eardrums pound. Screech swerves sideways, and then hovers for a short time. Below the smoke and fire clears, blown away by prevailing winds.

"Chaotic," mumbles the Challenger as the sight unfolds beneath us.

The ground is black, the grass scorched. The mountains have had much of their masses blown apart, huge rocks and pieces crumbling down the sides towards the valley. There is no sign of any of the players, their ships, or their fighters.

"Well, didn't see that coming!" laughs Barpar. "I guess they won't be bothering anyone anymore and creeping!"

A huge grin emerges on the Challenger face, the widest smile I've yet seen him make. "Well, my friends, you've *had* a quest!"

"Yes, we have!" Fauna agrees, nodding eagerly, revealing a smile rivaling his own.

"Oh!" cries Barpar, bringing Screech slowly downward where immense forests sprawl beneath us. "I am sure you'll have many quests yet! But first, let me give you some hospitality! They say that no one tells greater, longer stories and songs than Dick Bumpledop! All save I! I own a great brewery in the lands just eastward of here. I shall have you all over for beer and good scrumptious food and I shall tell you all manner of tales!"

The three of us give one another concerned looks. We owe him. He saved us.

"There's beer this time," says the Challenger.

As the great owl takes us down we all share a lengthy laugh. We have one quest down, but the adventure carries on!

THE END

Lobster's Revenge

This morning we bade farewell to Barpar and Screech, the giant owl who rescued us from the perilous valley of the hair-necked ones. This mighty bird roosted upon a branch high above the tree that Barpar calls home, the majestic creature having flown down to us from above the foliage when we emerged from Barpar's front door. For three days we stayed at the tree-home of our rescuer Barpar, twice as long as we had lodged with Dick Bumpledop. The big furred man's stories were entertaining, or at least seemed so with his brew of thick malty beer. Our three member party endured our latest host's songs and tales while we passed along some of Barpar's herbs from the forest.

Our party now proceeds our trek through the woodlands of the great northeast, my sis running on ahead of us as usual – a wide ancient road between heavily treed ridges is our first path-way of the day. Here the tall grasses and woodland weeds have reclaimed most of the aged road, leaving only islands of half-broken bricks that look alike pebbles in the midst of an overflowing river. I opt to tread on the grasses. Fauna hops along the crumbly bricks, leaping from one to the other, same as she would pass over the metaphorical river that I mentioned above. The Challenger stays with me, the 30-something ranger clearly exhausted, his visible eye having been half closed all morning.

It's around midday when we take a rest, seating ourselves along the mossy side of the cracked road, the ground diving downward into a thicket under our laid out legs. Fauna, my twin, energized as always, refuses to sit, standing near the midpoint of the road, glaring out at the way ahead. After downing half a flask of something watery, the Challenger turns to me.

"I'm hungry," he says, bringing the knapsack Barpar had gifted us off of his back. Our furry rescuer had given us this backpack and filled it with loaves of seedy baked brown bread with cinnamon, salted strips of sirloin, a bushel of giant apples, and a jar of deep orange honey. Barpar had even stitched his name into the gift, just so we'd remember him.

The ranger licks his lips as he takes out a piece of steak and dips it in the honey jar. I grab a big dark apple, needing my full hand to clasp it, opening my jaw to take a big bite—when it flies out from my hands, an arrow shaft emerging in sight as it plunges through the apple, sending it whizzing through the air and sticking against a thick willow trunk that rises from the ditch.

"Fauna!" I shriek, turning to see Sister with a big grin under her bright red cap, her bow in her hands.

"I'm sorry, sis, just that apple looked so perfect for me!"

"What, red on the outside but full of worms?" I snap back, not even sure what I mean.

The Challenger chuckles, dabs my knuckles with his fist from beside me. Fauna steps over to the edge of the ditch, leaping to the bottom to reach the tree.

"It's because of your reckless attitude why we ended up in that so-called Hare-Neck Valley and almost got killed!" I snap as she retrieves the apple from the tree and bites, taking a tiny piece with her small mouth. In truth I know she is a near perfect shot.

"No worms!" she laughs.

The three of us eat silently, save the Challenger's slurping as he gobbles the honeyed steak. When lunch is over my sister puts on the new backpack and we continue our journey, moving eastward to where the trees suddenly stop and we enter an immense golden field. Here the air is exceptionally warm with no breeze to balance things out. As we make our way along a thin trail I notice that the tall grasses on our sides are mostly dried out. Our sojourn under the canopies had concealed us from the hot sun thus far, but within moments I feel a layer of nasty sweat running down my forehead, my skin feeling warm as I wipe away the moisture with the back of my hand. I call to Fauna to pass me a flask of water.

"Wait until we take a break, Flora!" she calls back, her hand on her sword's hilt, the blade in the scabbard that she keeps at her belt.

The Challenger groans and mumbles something. He looks overheated in his jerkin armour, his two belts, and his long green-ish-brownish cloak. His blade is also kept in a long sheath at his side, slung upon his leather belt. He and my sister both have bows and quivers of arrows on their backs. I'm relieved, at the least, to not have so many things to carry. All I have is my trusty dagger in my pocket. We lost a bunch of items back in Hare-Neck Valley, including the little scope that Mother gifted me.

"Ahh," I say loudly, thinking about home. "I could use a day on the coast, or inside Mother's library!"

This immense library is always cool. There are tunnels that are designed to suck in the air from outside and send it spiraling down long pipes that lead to the chambers, the breeze cooled by tunnels of water that it flows through on the way. Right now I imagine myself reading an old book, leaning back, drinking from a cup of icy water as I enjoy the calming silence in one of the giant rooms or corridors, a perfect way to spend a hot day.

A long hour passes while we make our way through the tall grass. The landscape stays the same. There are mountains and hills in the distance to the north and northeast, a half a day's trek perhaps, and beyond the field eastward I can see woodlands again.

"Trees!" the Challenger shouts as he too notices them.

"Shade!" I cry in agreement.

"You guys really hate the heat, aye?" Fauna asks, waiting for us to catch up to her, hands on her hips, a typical adventurous grin on her face.

A dragonfly buzzes past her. She swaps at it but misses, the long-bodied bug speeding past her. Sis charges after it, pulling out her bow as she runs, loading an arrow. The Challenger and I share a shrug and take off after her. We run ahead a short distance, coming to a creek (not a metaphorical one) with a shore of dry mud. We peer into dark green water, its surface covered in thick peat.

"I bet it's deeper than it looks," says the Challenger, pointing his hand at the width of the river, which looks two times too wide to leap across.

"Wait a sec," says Fauna, pulling back her bowstring. "I think I got it."

Just as she is about to lose the arrow at the dragonfly that now rests upon a particularly tall cattail, a long pinkish thing, a tongue, flings up from beneath the water and snatches it. We see a pair of olive green lips emerge from the creek.

"Ew," says Fauna as a frog that must be as large as a medium-sized dog raises its head above the water, chewing before belching louder than any person I've ever heard.

45

The Challenger laughs at my side and says: "Alright then, how to cross?"

Scanning the far side of the dank creek, I begin to say something when my sister backtracks a few steps before charging and then leaping from the edge of the creek, her feet landing nimbly upon the big frog's head before jumping again and flipping in the air, landing perfectly upon the far shore.

"She's such a show-off," mutters the Challenger. "I can do that, probably."

The frog in the middle of the creek raises its bulbous head, opens its lips, and lets loose its mighty tongue, aiming directly at Fauna's back. The tongue latches onto the knapsack with all our food. She cries out, falling back, landing on her butt on the dry mud of the far shore. The ranger at my side grabs his bow in haste, lining up an arrow just as the knapsack flings off of my sister's back, splashing green-brown water as it lands atop the frog's face, and then both sink into the gloopy water.

The Challenger lowers his bow, having not bothered to shoot the arrow.

"Ah!" Fauna shouts, cursing. "That's our food! We need to find it! Kill that toad!"

"I think it's a frog," I say and the Challenger nods.

A series of big bubbles rises to the surface of the spot where the knapsack sank. Another loud belch rings out. And then something splashes and shoots out of the water, landing beside Fauna. It's the knapsack.

Fauna sighs really loud in relief, grabbing the now slimy bag, forcing it open. "Hey! The toad ate all the food!"

The Challenger reloads the arrow. Fauna grabs her bow off of her torso and does the same. They both let loose about five arrows each before I yell at them. "Stop it! You're wasting them!"

"Kill the toad!" my sister cries angrily.

"Slice its belly!" my ranger friend agrees.

"Get our food!"

"Do you really want to eat the food after it's been inside that thing?" I ask them.

They both stop. My sister continues swearing. I look away, sighting a wooden bridge down the creek, cursing a bit myself as I realize if we'd just looked around when we came to the water we'd still have our food.

We cross the bridge soon after, meeting Fauna at the other side before continuing into the woods.

"What are we going to do?" Fauna asks as we get into the shade of the first trees, finding a thin trail to tread upon.

"I'm hungry already," moans the Challenger, rubbing his abs under his jerkin.

"You can catch us something as you always do," I tell him. "Great Challenger of the Wilderlands they call you right?"

He nods, gazing about, taking off down a smaller trail, telling us to go ahead only to meet us further down without any food. He tells us he saw a mother deer and a fawn, but thought they were too cute, as well as a few skunks that he was too hesitant to eat lest we bite into its stinky parts. The skilled hunter promises to get us something later. We continue on our way, our quest to have another quest proceeding, the forest pathway widening, forking at some points as we keep to the North and East. I look about the trees and bushes for apples, pears, or berries, finding nothing but leaves and buds. At one point, as the three of us are walking side by side, we hear a deep, low grumbling noise. Thinking a ferocious beast is near, we all prepare our weapons, only to realize it was the Challenger's belly.

I'm beginning to feel hungry too. Soon we come to a high point, the forest floor having run uphill most of the afternoon. Here there are only a few short trees, this place relatively clear, almost a clearing, and we can see the treetops ahead and below us where the pathway plunges downward again. A short way away we see a single pillar of smoke rising from between canopies, a sweet roasting smell accompanying it.

"A camp!" Fauna shouts, pointing.

"And they're cooking something nice!" the Challenger adds, licking his lips. "Although I wouldn't count on them sharing."

"No?" I ask. "Why not?"

He chuckles a bit, rubbing his belly. "You don't know wandering folks so much as I do. Some have great hospitality, sure, but others would slay you for asking."

"We'll see," says Fauna.

"I say we take a small bit of the food," says the ranger, shaking his head. "Why risk a fight?"

"We can't do that!" I say.

"Yeah!" agrees my sister. "I already told you we're a force for good."

"And I told you I'm—"

"Yes, yes, neutral and chaotic!" both us sisters say at once, to which the Challenger nods.

We descend the path cautiously, our soft boots making barely any noise, the succulent smell getting more intense as we get closer. Fauna points out a pair of prints in the earthen trail, pointed toes looking more like a beast than a man, but clearly the work of two feet rather than four.

The Challenger says "Kobolds," under his breath and retrieves his sword from his scabbard.

I groan.

"Look too big for those little rat-beings," Fauna says.

Eventually, as the scent becomes stronger than ever, we hear voices. They are deep, guttural voices. The three of us slink along the narrowing trail, finding ourselves on a ridge overlooking a camp. The fire burns in a clearing down the way, a thick pair of bushes concealing us as we peer down at a pair of two-legged creatures. They resemble the kobolds we saw back in the valley, furry and rat-like, dressed in red mail armour, though they are nearly the size of a person, and their snouts look longer compared to the smaller kobolds we saw days prior. They hold in their hands long iron-tipped spears, and both of them are facing away from the fire.

"What are they?" I whisper to the Challenger as the three of us huddle in the little space upon the overlooking ridge. He shakes his head, his unpatched eye looking confused. At his hands his blade is ready, while my sister prepares her bow.

There is a big slab of gigantic meat on the fire, part of it blackened and crispy. Behind the flames, where the larger-than-usual kobolds are not looking, runs a trail beyond a wall of massive tree trunks.

"No," I say, wanting to be cautious. "We can get food elsewhere."

The Challenger shakes his head again.

"Let *me* go," says Fauna. "I can grab it. I'm small."

"No," says the Challenger.

"Why, because you're a man? You sound like Slug-Lord," Fauna hisses at him, but it's too late. The Challenger has already parted us, making his way down the ridge towards the trail that leads to the rear of the camp. Fauna grunts, pulling back her bow, ready to cover for him. We see him sneaking through the back trail, his arms sprawled out at his side, each step he takes gingerly, gazing at the two kobold guards. They stand side to side, leaning slightly against their spears which they hold before them upright, still gazing away from him.

"Mmm," one of them mutters, the one on the left, then says: "I'm starving, I am!"

"Ah! Quit yer whining, worm!" returns the other. "Captain says we ain't taking food until 'e and the others are back! Those are our orders!"

49

The first of them grunts. "Starving, I am!" he shouts. "Oh, just a little piece, guv?"

"Shut yer rat mouth!" snaps the second. "Is you still a kobold, or did Master make you a proper alphabold like the rest of us? Stand straight, mate, like Master says, lest you be a sniveling cluck!"

The first one snarls angrily, but says nothing more.

The Challenger steps on a twig that snaps loudly. I see his face grimace as both kobolds (or *alphabolds*) turn about. One thing about the Challenger is that he always has a snarky line ready. The ranger sees that he is spotted and straightens his posture, saying boldly: "Looking for me, boys?"

The two creatures grip their spears firmly and run over to the Challenger side by side. Fauna curses. I try to stay calm, tapping Sister's shoulder, noticing a large buzzing wasp nest hanging from a tree branch above the clearing. My sis raises her bow slightly.

"Eh, who are you?" asks the more aggressive of the two, shoving the tip of his spear an inch from the Challenger's chest.

"No one," says the ranger, putting both hands up while still clutching his sword.

"No one? Aye, that be your name then?" says the first of them, the sniveling one.

"Sure," says the ranger.

"We got No One we does!" says the first, quickly side-stepping to get behind the Challenger.

"Quiet yer bloomin' snout!" says the second. "Eh, we's got a prisoner 'ere! A prisoner for Master! Oh, he'll make us the first alphabolds, he will!"

The first of them then grins, curling his rat lips, his front teeth pointed and yellow. The Challenger shakes his head, waves his sword about for a split moment, and then ducks. The second kobold shoves his spear forward, missing the Challenger's head by a half a foot, the end of his spear plunging into the chest of the first kobold behind the ranger.

"Ah!" the sniveling creature cries out, grabbing the spear shaft. "I thought we was friends, I did!"

Fauna shoots, dislodging the nest from its branch, causing it to dangle for a moment.

"Get here, you twit!" the surviving kobold guard shouts as his companion falls over. The Challenger leaps backwards, dodging the proceeding spear thrusts.

"Ow!" shrieks the kobold as the wasp nest lands on his head. "Ouch! They're stinging me!"

The Challenger sees his chance and he takes it, striking his blade hard against the foe, bringing him down. He cheers. I pat Fauna's shoulder and we both laugh.

And then the clearing our friend stands in erupts with furred bodies, all clad in the red armour as the first two were. I count quickly, gasping as I tally nearly a dozen of them. The Challenger's eye goes wild. He looks ready to begin slashing, and I know he can likely still win here, but a great net is flung from one of the big kobolds, trapping him instantly. The many furry bodies move in, tie up the net, take his sword, and then clamber on through the woods, grabbing the meat off the fire as they move, all vanishing as quickly as they came down the trail.

My sister and I exchange fearful looks. She mouths the words: "What do we do?"

The Challenger is alive but taken by the enemy.

I don't know how long my sister and I gazed at one another, warming in the glow of sunlight. We remain on that wooded ridge overlooking the clearing, the two fallen kobolds still in place, untouched by their own party that had captured our ranger friend. I would never have imagined such a thing happening; the Challenger is a great fighter. I would have expected him to chop off all their hands – good old Challenger! – instead he was captured by these strangely tall and bulky kobolds, taken before our eyes.

Eventually we slip down to the clearing, finding a hidden trail, the one the Challenger had taken in his attempt to sneak up on the two guards. The troupe of kobolds had taken the roasted meat off the fire, of course, leaving nothing but ashes and crisped wood. I stand over the dead campfire, looking at this new trail the kobolds had just gone down, while my sister inspects the two kobolds.

I step on a leathery small bag on the ground, some weird green ooze flowing out from its tied-up mouth. Leaning over, I grab hold of the bag by its single string, peering inside it, seeing nothing but this bright green goo, wondering if it's some kind of kobold food.

"What are these things?" my sister asks as she steps upon the chest of the kobold that she had just dropped a wasp nest upon.

"I don't know," I say honestly. "In all my readings I've never heard of kobolds that stand as tall as people-folk. Mind you, until a few days ago I thought kobolds were lizard-like creatures rather than rat-like things!"

These kobolds are different from the ones we'd encountered in Hare-Neck Valley. While furry and rat-like, these two and the ones that took the Challenger are far larger and stockier than any we've seen. They are dressed in mail armour with a reddish tinge. The kobold underneath Fauna's feet suddenly groans; he is alive (for now). We saw the Challenger slash at him, but as I look closely I see that he merely clinked the mail armour, and the black blood that was on the kobold had splattered on him when he stabbed his mate by mistake. Sister grabs her bow, loading it with an arrow that she hovers over the injured kobold's swollen snout.

The beast grunts as I move to my sister's side, pulling out my dagger in case she needs back-up.

"Speak swiftly!" Fauna shouts down to him, pulling her bowstring further.

"Nice line!" I compliment from her side.

"Thanks," she says, pink appearing on her cheeks. "Now speak, what are you? Who do you work for?"

"Whom," I correct her. She gives me an annoyed glare.

"Ah crikey!" grumbles the creature beneath us, spittle and blood spewing from his mouth as he speaks. "You's too late! Chaos will be defeated!"

"Another weirdo," Sis groans. "Where did they take our friend?"

"Your friend? The thief? 'E is doomed if we have taken him!" the kobold mutters with a laugh. "The Master knows how to deal with such folk!"

"Master? Where is your master?" I ask, waving my dagger over his face.

The kobold guard grunts, spits, and then laughs again. I see him moving one of his arms slowly, reaching for his spear, which had fallen earlier.

"Fauna, watch out!" I yell.

He moves his hand swiftly, grabbing the shaft, about to strike it upward at her. "Hold! Hold!" Sis yells at the wretched creature beneath her, stepping hard with her boot onto the midpoint of the spear, snapping it in half.

"You busted me spear, you has!"

"She'll bust more if you don't listen to what she says!" I warn him, Fauna giving me a small grin, clearly impressed that I've taken over her bad-ass role.

"Bloody girls!" curses our captive, kicking away the wasp nest that had earlier landed on him.

"You'll be bloody if you don't shut up!" I retort.

"That line was just banking off the last one," says Fauna. "Anyway, get up! Up, slowly!"

The tall kobold scrunches his rat-like maw, shaking his head a little as he leans upward, both of his black eyes on the arrow-tip that rests apprehensively a few inches from his furry face. "Should've known we was being watched! Failed we did!"

"Tell us about this master you speak of?" I ask. "Whom do you serve?"

"Labstruman," he declares, a hint of pride in his gravely voice.

Fauna pulls her bowstring back again. "Where can we find this Labstruman?"

His beady eyes narrow in on me, and then he chuckles, his raised upper snout revealing sharp canine-like teeth about a lolling red tongue. "You girls wanting to listen to Labstruman? Ha ha!"

"We want our friend," I say, realizing this big kobold may not be cooperative. "Now lead us there!"

He shakes his furry head. "No! You are not worthy of our Master! You will bring only chaos!"

"We're getting nowhere!" Fauna suddenly snaps, and for a moment I think she's going to pull so hard on the bow it'll snap. "Let's toss this loser and find his master ourselves!"

At this point I am so frustrated I almost agree. I raise my dagger before his ugly face and shriek: "This is your last chance!" I snap, unbelieving how tough I am acting.

The kobold grins, licks his lips, and stares at the small blade I wield. He is bold, strangely brave. I realize that he won't tell us. "Fine," I say. "Then we'll let you go."

"Flora!" Sis shouts from my side. I turn myself about, still carrying the bag of goo. I slyly make a tiny cut in it with the tip of the dagger. A tiny bit of goo slowly trickles out. Reaching behind me, I loosen Barpar's knapsack about my backside, flinging it to the ground, placing the leaking bag of goo inside it. I turn about, tie up Barpar's bag, and throw it the kobold, yelling him to take his slime with him. He straps it to his back.

I nudge back, wink to her. "Go and don't look back or my sister here will shoot you as you run!"

The kobold laughs loudly, his voice coarse and high-pitched at once, a truly hideous sound. And then he charges off, clambering out of the clearing and onto a hitherto unseen forest trail, the same one his mates had taken the Challenger down. My sister loses an arrow that slams into a trunk by his side, clearly visible to the fleeing enemy, and then she loads another.

"Why did you give him our bag? And why did you free him?" she asks me, her face going from pink to bright red.

"Shoot Barpar's bag, just do it," I tell her in reply. She does so, striking its midpoint, the kobold leaping up and down as he tears away from sight.

"Come," I say, waving my hand, taking off after the foe. She immediately understands. As we make our way down the path we see tiny drops of the green goo here and there. At one point, as we turn alongside a woodland creek, we lose the trail, only for me to spot a dab of the goo on the other side of the stream. We vault across and continue on. Thankfully we find an apple tree and satiate our hunger for the time being.

Evening falls when we find ourselves at a treeless mound in a large clearing. This earthen barrow raises nearly four stories above the ground, covered in tall grasses and weeds, some rocks jutting here and there along its rising surface. I tell Fauna that it looks like an ancient burial spot. It is not too different from the mound we saw in Hare-Neck Valley a few days ago, and just like that hilly mound back there, we see an entrance-way, a man-sized portal in it's surface.

"Not this again," my sis mutters, sword in hand, bow on her back, pointing with her free hand to the drops of green goo that lead into the doorway and down some steps into darkness. "We can't go in the front door. Here, I feel a breeze from elsewhere, a gust of hot air."

"You've been around the Challenger for too long," I say, meaning it as a compliment. Fauna walks around the stony doorway, stepping onto the mound's upward sloping surface, sifting between tall wobbly flowers with bright red petals. Further up she finds a rock that is around her size. She kicks it off the hill, revealing a small hole. I run up to join her while she pokes her head in the hole. It is the size of a large dog, just enough for our smallish, thin forms to fit through. I feel what she was referring to, warm air coming through.

As usual, she goes in first, disappearing quickly, the soles of her red boots the last thing I see. She calls back to me, tells me it widens further down. I hesitate for a moment, but remember the Challenger, and I dive in next. At first, I can only wiggle forward, kicking at the earth walls behind me, nudging forward towards my sister's stinky feet, but, like she says, as I move forward I slowly find I can move my arms and shoulders more. Soon we are crawling on our hands and knees through a space, bumping our heads lightly on a rocky roof. Hot air pushes past us, and, as we descend deeper into the earth, we begin to feel heat, and hear voices.

They are grumbling things, likely the kobolds. After some time in the darkness we see a reddish-orange light at this tunnel's end. I see the walls of the space we crawl through flicker beyond Fauna's bobbing head. And then we hear a singular voice. It is dry, a near monotonous tone, the voice echoing off the walls of a nearby chamber.

I listen carefully:

"Ye have all assembled here to harken to me rage,

Cognizant of all obstacles of our incongruous age,
'Tis I who advert your clans from disaster,
Look upon me, your leader, your hard-shelled master,
Who took you from sniveling rats, useless and poor,
Whose fuzzy buttocks hovered inches from the floor,
The antidote to any chaotic insipidity,
'Tis an expeditious acceptance of all hierarchy,
For in power structure we find our meaning,
With logic, reasoning, and fact-leaning,
We strive to keep things as they are,
To cease life from getting too bizarre,
Remain hierarchical at all times,
But now I tire of generating these rhymes,
Now you shall have a lecture, straight and fast,
To teach you of the future and times of past!"

Fauna groans under her breath as we make it to the end of the low-ceiling tunnel, finding ourselves upon a rocky perch in a large chamber. We must be underneath the ground, for this big room is far too large to be contained in the mound alone. It's like a balcony, this place we find ourselves on, and we look down and around a great open space. Beneath us we see them, a great many kobolds—or alphabolds—these large man-sized beasts, all clad in the same red armour. There have to be at least thirty of them, all facing the front of the chamber, away from where we peer over.

They all face a tall earthen wall, the roof made of rock with immense stalactites projecting downward like stone knives, their shadows casting nightmarishly upon the walls, mingling with the shadows of the spears wielded by the two-legged creatures. Beneath this wall sits a great stone chair, a throne of kinds that looks like it could support five of me. Seated upon this is a bulky figure clad in a black cloak, its face unseen under the hood, as well as its arms and hands. All I can see is a pair of thick red feet in big brown boots that rest underneath the cloaked figure.

"So, you've toughened up," the dry voice speaks from behind the draped hood. "Today I am told there is news, but first, let me enunciate a narrative for us to ponderously observe. We all know I grew you, taught you of the intrinsic value of hierarchies, but today I speak of *my* past. I once lived in a place called Silver Coast, a great city."

"Represent," Fauna peeps, but I am too shocked to respond. This being is saying he is from our home-city?

"I was once a lonely thing, great and wise, familiar with all kinds of knowledge of embodiments and patterns. In my youth, as I learned at the campus, I found myself a victim of a great injustice. It seemed that those with great minds like myself were destined to be alone, while those at the top had all the opportunities to engage in all kinds of craft. It is an injustice and it continues! Things ought to be changed, made more fair, so all of us lonely things can flourish!"

There are grunts, squeals, and screeches from the standing crowd. Spears rise and fall in waves that start from the back rows and end at the front nearest the cloaked thing that speaks. Fauna and I turn to face one another in perfect sync, and I am sure that I look as perplexed as she. Sis's face is scrunched up like a stress ball.

"Did he not just sing a whole song about *not* challenging hierarchies?" she asks me.

"I thought that was the point, so not sure what he's saying now?"

"Well, don't correct him. Let's not give ourselves away."

"Oh, it's *me* who is going to leap down there recklessly?"

"Got to be ready," she says, turning back to the assembly. While we gaze over the ugly things I wonder if there is a way to convince them that this leader of theirs is a fraud, but as I look over the sniveling, slobbering mass, I start to doubt that they can be convinced. For creatures as dim as them, this leader probably appears very intelligent.

"Look at your spears striking above your heads in perfect order, harmony," the speaker says next, his voice echoing off the walls just as it did when he had been rhyming. "Before we start, have we any news? Patrols?"

A kobold steps forth. I see Fauna at my side sliding her bow off of her nearly flat body. It's the kobold we'd followed here, stains of green all over his furry backside. He takes off the decrepit knapsack, raising it in both of his hairy palms.

"The prisoner has friends, he does!" the kobold squeaks. "This came from them!"

"Ah!" cries the figure on the throne. "A backpack covered in the antidote!"

Fauna nudges me, pointing with her arrow down the way to the side of the first row of kobolds. I see him. It's the Challenger!

The ranger stands before two of the kobolds, his hands bound with rope, his face showing no sign of fear. He blinks with his one eye, looking about the chamber, turning away when I try to give him a tiny wave. He does not see us. Maybe they will question him. Maybe he will lie and convince them to let him go. He always tells us he has a high charisma stat, whatever that means.

A small kobold, half the size of these others, like the ones we've seen before, scatters out from the crowd, running toward the gooey knapsack at the feet of the throne-sitter. The creature grabs it from the larger kobold, bringing it over to the concealed hands of this leader being. This is when I see a dark claw emerge from the cloak, and as quickly as it appears it becomes covered from my vantage point by Barpar's bag.

"Uh-oh," I whisper to Sis.

"What is it?"

"Labstruman," I say, realizing it, whispering harshly: "Lobster-Man!"

And then the thing with the hitherto monotonous voice goes wild, a booming gasp shooting out from beneath the dark hood. "Murderers!" he shouts. "Usurpers!"

The kobolds all reel back, even from our sight appearing confused before they all echo: "Murderers! Usurpers!" making the cave walls shake.

"Be you a friend of Barpar?" cries Lobster-Man, writhing in his throne.

The Challenger speaks: "What's it to you?"

I groan, hearing the tightening of the bowstring aside my left ear.

"Barpar! Murderer! He has slain my best friends! Frog-Boy! Slug-Lord! I barely made it here alive!" the voice shouts, less flat as before. The cloak falls back as the big thing stands up from the throne.

"Ew!" says Fauna, but no one hears save me because the crowd below us is now roaring and clashing their weapons. Lobster-Man is tall, taller than these kobolds by nearly three feet. His legs and arms are spindly, but his middle thick and pink, his claws three times the size of his big head. The face though, it looks not like a lobster's, but of a man's – circular, red, with big round black eyes, a tiny nose and a grinning mouth without teeth. Upon his head, above four small antennae and two dangling, long pink feelers, there is hair, greyish, a brimmed brown hat, similar to the slain Slug-Lord's cap.

"You're Lobster-Man!" the Challenger shouts. The kobolds all murmur angrily, while the two behind the ranger both grab his arms tightly.

60

"Yes! And you're going to pay for burning me in that blast! I'll slap you happily!" retorts the Lobster angrily, raising one of his claws, this one black, the other red like the rest of him.

"You wouldn't let us go!" the prisoner exclaims. "We didn't want to be in your stupid game!"

"Well now you'll die for Slug-Lord and Frog-Boy! For the sake of order over chaos!" Lobster-Man shrieks, his kobolds all rushing forth at once towards the Challenger.

"Chaos wins! And don't think I don't know where you got that green goo from! It's not yours! You didn't create it!" we hear our ranger friend yell as the furry bodies cover our sight of him. Fauna and I stand to our feet at once, my dagger already in my hand, her arrow already fired. It hits a nearby kobold in the back, and he falls and screams, wiggling in pain at the feet of the others, but none of them notice. She readies another.

"What'll we do?" I ask her, hearing the fear in my voice. Part of me wants to run, or rather crawl fast, back from where we came, out of this cursed place! But I know we can't leave him.

"Stop!" cries Lobster-Man, his voice louder than ever. The crowd of kobolds freeze, and I see the Challenger as some step back from him, his face already a little bloodied. The lobster being raises both claws over his head, wailing in apparent rage. "Bring him here! I shall show you how to deal with chaotic soy-folk!"

Laughter follows from the so-called alphabolds. Some near the front step back, while others behind the Challenger nudge him forward, spears at his rear, the man-like rat things cackling as he moves.

"Tell me your name, so I will know whose head I claw off!" the master demands, his grin taking up most of his face as he leans his long, flat shelled-covered neck forward.

"The Challenger!"

61

The crowd is silent. Lobster-man shakes his head and says "I ask for you *real* name, not some name you made up! You cannot force me to say your made-up title!"

"I am the Challenger! Is Lobster-Man even your real name? Repeat my name before me and remember it!"

Fauna draws her bow once more, this time aiming for the lobster. I hope she can get him right in the soft spot, wherever that is.

"I *am* Lobster-Man! I have the alpha spot on the food-chain! I control an army of enhanced kobolds, alphabolds, my servants!" he shouts, turning to his soldiers. "All you alphabolds I have made! My fighting soldiers! Who do you serve?"

"Labstruman!" they all shout back at once, the walls throbbing once more.

I can't take any more of this!

Standing in place upon the high perch, I just shout: "It's *whom* do you serve, not *who* do you serve! How can you preach lessons when you don't even know rudimentary grammar?" my voice leaps over the precipice and flows throughout the chamber, echoing like Lobster-Man's voice had.

There is silence save the sound of their thirty or so bodies shuffling and turning about. They see us.

"Ahh!" cries the big crispy lobster in his plain yet booming voice. "Crazy! I can't control them! Reinforcements!"

"Give me back my bloody sword!" yells the Challenger.

The kobolds, alphabolds, or whatever, are now facing our elevated rocky perch. An army of little eyes and whiskered snouts peer at us. I feel my knees turn to jelly, yet stand my ground, dagger in hand, no idea what to do. Sis swerves her loaded bow, under a dozen arrows in her quiver, not nearly enough. I hear the footfalls of more kobolds approaching the chamber. There must be tunnels in the walls. Below us are the bulk of them, all gathered in a massive cluster that is thickest directly under the lip of the perch we stand on. I now see the Challenger is taking this moment to do something, fiddling with his two hands behind his back. Within seconds he has untied the ropes that had bound his wrist.

"Come on, you weaklings!" Sister shouts, seemingly seeing her chance. "We've slain dozens of kobolds already by throwing pebbles!"

Fauna downs one kobold as they rush forward, and then another, before having to duck a beneath trio of thrown pointed shafts. They're chucking their spears. I, having no projectile weaponry, have slunk backward a little. I kneel beside Fauna as four more spears hit the rockwall above and clatter upon the floor, two spears landing inches from me.

"Idiocy!" she cries with a classic Fauna laugh, ducking beside me. More spears. We have ten now on the floor beside us. Fauna gets up, launches an arrow, and hides once again, shouting: "Stop slaying us!" down at the foes mockingly.

"Should we do something?" I ask her frantically.

"Okay, on one," she starts counting, putting her bow on the floor, grabbing a spear in each of her hands while I do the same. "Two..."

"Three!" I finish and we both stand, chucking our four missiles. We fall in time to avoid getting skewered by a line of spears aimed right at us. We repeat this, the kobolds seemingly not catching onto our method. The luckless creatures scream, some getting hit, one of them goes flying towards the back of the room where the big bipedal lobster roars in frustration, wagging his large claws above his face.

"Chaos!" Lobster-man shouts.

This is when I see the Challenger already punching his way through the kobolds, dodging spear thrusts and ax slices, sending a fast-flying kick into one of the bigger one's faces. He grabs a spear from another then, spins about in a wide circle, smacking all the kobolds surrounding him before the spear snaps apart in his hands on a charging ax's blade. He headbutts the ax-wielder next!

Fauna raises herself, shouting to the ranger, throwing a fresh spear clear across the chamber. He catches it and continues fighting, felling another two before a fresh circle of fiends surrounds him.

"We have to help him!" Sis cries to me, pulling out her bow again, shooting a few arrows off. Kobolds are still chucking spears up at us when we decide to jump. The moment feels so hopeless so I just do it without thinking, landing hard on the floor of the chamber. The first kobold I see sneers at me, bringing the sharpened end of his spear toward my face. I manage to roll out of the way, catching sight of my sister leaping onto one of the tall brutes. I get to my feet, dodging a furry foot, and now I can see the Challenger rushing towards us. He fights with his new spear, leaving a trail of sapless kobolds in his wake, a good ten standing ones making chase after him.

He yells: "Run!" as he speeds past us. My sister takes off after the ranger and I follow, both of my legs sore from the jump and landing.

The path is clear before us at this far wall across from the throne underneath our former perch spot. We see a set of big wooden doors, twice the width and height of a normal door. Fauna reaches it first, her and the ranger pushing one door each. Once they are open we see a small chamber that sits just beyond the great archway. We three run inside, having no choice as the kobolds are mere feet from us. Fauna and the ranger slam the doors behind them. The Challenger uses the spear in his hands to bolt the door.

We all take a series of short relieved breaths. Here inside there are four tall metal torches around the same length that we then take and bolt across the door as well, leaving only one torch to keep the room lit. The big doors quake as we hear the creatures pushing their weight against it. And then we hear the sound of axes hacking.

This chamber, as stated above, is small, no bigger than my room at home (which is quite big for a bedroom). To our left and right, about ten paces on both sides, are grey rock walls, the ceiling lower in here, about seven feet high. There are no doors or windows or passageways or anything we can escape through. At the far wall from us, another ten paces away in this square-shaped room sits an immense black cauldron, as big and wide as an aristocrat's bathtub, bubbling to the brim with green ooze.

"This must be the antidote the lobster spoke of!" I cry.

"Oh, how observational of you," says my sister.

"This is it," agrees the Challenger. I hug him, so glad he is okay. At first, he doesn't hug back, but then he puts his arms about my shoulders and I see one of the rare times that he smiles.

"Thanks for coming to get me, guys," he says, patting my sister on the back. She nods, but has no time to smile.

"Okay, let's not get ahead of ourselves in celebrating," I say, beaming back at him.

"Not get ahead of ourselves!" a shrill voice calls from within the room, whistling before repeating: *"Let's not get ahead of ourselves!"*

Above and a bit to the right of the steaming cauldron rests a small iron, dome-shaped cage that hangs from a hook on the ceiling. Inside this cage sits a single bird about the size of a chicken, horrid in appearance for it is completely bald, featherless, looking more like a bird on a rotisserie spit than a living one.

And yet it whistles and then it speaks again: *"It's only temporary—only temporary!"*

"What is?" asks Fauna.

Sharp crashing sounds echo against the doors behind us, shaking the whole wall.

"What's only temporary?" I ask.

"The antidote," the ranger says, stepping over to the brim of the cauldron. "*This* is what is only temporary."

The bird flutters both of its fleshy wings at its side, cocking its head sideways and then right-side up again, and then sideways again. *"Let's not get ahead of ourselves!"*

"You said that already!" snaps Fauna, bringing up her bow, pointing the arrow at the birdcage. "And I'm still hungry!"

"You said that already! Still hungry!" the unfeathered bird chirps while I extend my hand to lower my sister's bow.

"We don't have time," I say.

"Time!"

We all gaze at the birdcage. I notice that four letters: **ECHO** are scrawled on the bottom of the birdcage. To my side the Challenger stamps his foot, peering over the side of the goop.

"No time to make more! Have to go back to source to get real stuff!" shrieks the bird.

"None of us ever said that!" snaps Fauna.

"None of us ever said that!"

"Yep," mutters the Challenger, placing both of his hands on the cauldron's brim. "It's as bad as I thought, but at least it's not permanent." I realize that he seems to know something about this ooze.

This whole time the doors behind us have still been shaking, the distinct sound of axes chopping into wood blended with the multitude of bloodcurdling yet anti-climactic war-screams. I spin about, seeing the first plank of wood splinter and a long whiskered snout stick inside the new space. Fauna turns about as well, shoots an arrow at the hole, and we both return our gaze to the talking bird.

"We need more! Need more! This batch is only temporary!"

Fauna moves to the side of the big pot, picking up a small yellow sack off the floor. It reads: **Birdseed. "**Let's see how this works," she says, tearing off the top of it and pouring it into the goo. Echo (so I assume it is named) rattles the cage above, fluttering its meat-stick wings, the bird's head frantically poking through the cage's bars to peer below at the tiny seeds floating on the green surface. I see where Sister's going with this once she loads another arrow and fires it at the little chain that the birdcage is held up with, sending both the cage and the crazed bird into the goop, a massive lime-coloured bubble bursting above the sinking cage. For a moment I wonder why Sis bothered throwing the birdseed in if her plan was to sink the bird, but I figure this out soon enough.

"No time for tests!" declares the Challenger, leaning right over, putting his face into the goo while he shakes his head about. He flings his head back up, his slimed hair flying, sending bits of green everywhere, hitting me in the face.

"Ow! Why'd you do that for?" I yell at him, although I realize that we must do this.

Another wooden plank gets chopped behind us. Fauna replaces her arrow, shaking her head. "They're coming!"

I scoop up a handful of the goo, gagging as I stick my hand in and feel its warmth, bringing a big slimy glob of it towards my mouth. It tastes—as I figured it would—disgusting! It reminds me of this cake that I baked with Mother when I was littler but had accidentally left out in the summer sun. As I force my tongue to lob creamy gunk to my throat, I remind myself of the impending danger.

Fauna lets out a tiny, almost terrified giggle, and then reaches into the bowl of goop, pulling out the birdcage. Inside is a bird so large the bars of the cage have already bent, while its ravenous bill begins to tear apart the front wall of it, the mutated creature quickly diving for its birdseed, gobbling it up along with more of the antidote. Sister takes a mouthful next, in her hand like I did, her face scrunching up again as if she'd just swallowed a giant ball of salt, lemon juice, and earwax.

The Challenger dashes to the crumbling door. An ax's blade swings through, lodging itself in the wood in front of the ranger, who promptly grabs the sharpest part with two fingers, pulling it from its wielder. A kobold's face appears in the hole. The Challenger punches with his free hand, sending the furry face back from whence it came.

"Come on in!" he shouts, now swinging the ax, winking as he gives me a quick nod. "I feel it now! It takes only a moment! Things will seem to slow down when you rush, but it's not time, it's *you*!"

Things already feel unusual. My vision seems clear, like I can sort the things I see before me and focus on one thing at a time with all of my energy, ready to switch to another thing instantly if need be. I see one blow on the door, turning my gaze to its source, and then I see a furry claw reach in and grasp about. I move forward to stand beside the ranger. I breathe deep, feeling calm, and ask Fauna to join us.

"In a moment!" she calls. I hear the cauldron crash upon the floor behind me, feeling no need to look back to confirm that she has tipped over the antidote. I hear it stream into an unseen drain.

My sister emerges to my side, carrying her sword, her left hand clasped about the birdseed bag. She is larger than before, only slightly, but still noticeable, her sleeves having become torn as her biceps bulged up. My arms and legs feel heavier, more powerful. The left door gives way completely, the wood falling off from its hinges, crashing to the ground, the edge of its broken surface landing directly in front of us. The right door bursts apart seconds later, revealing the first four rows of menacing alphabold soldiers, the very first six of them sneering and snapping their snouts as they leap into the room. Fauna moves first, turning her unarmed hand, flinging the contents of the little bag onto the front row of them, none of the them flinching, some laughing as they realize they'd just been assaulted by birdseed.

A giant squawk rings up from behind us, and a speeding pinkish brown object shoots towards the next kobold like a bolt of pinkish brown lightning. Echo the plucked bird jumps from one birdseed covered kobold to the other, pecking faces, eyes, piercing chain-mail, and pulling out chunks of fur, the featherless creature moving so fast to be like a blur of speed to my eyes!

Confident, I charge, making my way to the closest kobold to my right, the left and center flanks already being taken care of by my sister, the ranger, and the frenzied bird. In this state it feels like the kobolds are weak once more, like things have just been reset to the way they were before. I don't even use my dagger on the first of them, just hit the nearest with my fist, sending him flying to the opposite wall. My new strength is immense! I feel bolder than ever when the next kobold shoots his spear at me, for I slice apart the shaft with my small blade, and, with improved speed, kick the falling tip of it toward the middle of the furry critter's body.

"Ouch!" the kobold cries as it bounces off of him, grasping his belly. "That hurts, it does!"

"They're antidoteded!" a raspy voices shouts before Fauna headbutts the source of it, sending him flying against the others behind. The supposed alpha creatures begin fleeing, some dropping their spears, one of which I pick up, as Echo charges after them, shrieking: *Not enough! Need more! Need more!*

The Challenger and Fauna appear as if they have barely broken a sweat. My sister has a big grin, flexing her arms for a moment, raising her sword above her cap. "I love this!" she yells.

"Welcome to my world," our ranger friend groans before raising a blackened ax and pointing it beyond the smashed door.

69

"Aye, let's crush Lobster-Man!" Fauna shouts.

"We mustn't allow him to escape!" the Challenger adds hastily. "If he finds out how to make this goo potion permanent, the world could be in very big trouble!"

I am unsure of what he means, and I wonder if we could capture him, maybe take him back to Silver Coast as a prisoner, but before I can begin a conversation about the ethical issues my two companions are out the doorway. I follow, stepping over a row of dilapidated kobolds. In the big chamber we see a tiny clearing before an entire army of alphabolds. They stand, spears and axes in their hairy paws, faces twisted in hideous scowls. The reinforcements have come. There must be nearly a hundred.

We hear, but do not see Lobster-Man: "Get them, my loyal followers and patrons! Get them!"

They begin chanting in a dark speech, clashing their weaponry, stamping their feet, sifting their tails. Fauna stands at my side, the Challenger at hers. The bird called Echo appears at my feet and says: *"Alright mates, let's do this!"* whilst flexing muscled wings.

"Hm?" I ask, looking down to the naked bird. "Are you repeating something?"

Echo turns to look at me and I think I see a smile at his beak: *"For real now! I speak and understand! I was just playing dumb parrot before because I wasn't sure who you were! I have been playing dumb since these scum captured me!"*

"Ah," I say, surprised.

"Before it wears off, let's strike! We might have a chance!" the bird chirps.

"If I die, then at least I die taking these scums out!" spits my sister.

'Likewise!" agrees the Challenger before bellowing a battle-cry, slashing his new ax madly before him. If the air in front of him could be hurt it would be in terrible agony now. The first row of kobolds lunge and the rest follow, overwhelming my sight. All four of us begin chopping our weapons (or beak) at once, readying to be overcome, all steadfast in our desire to die upon our feet! I manage to tear apart one kobold's spear, kicking the foe from me, sending him into the two behind him, but then four others emerge where they fell, charging at me, slobbering as they swipe. I back up, nearing the rock wall behind me.

Just as I accept this is likely the end it happens.

One tall alphabold strikes his spear. I dodge it, moving to my left, and then duck as he pierces the air above my head. And as I rise again, I see that the humanoid beast is no longer taller than me, but half my size now! A swift slap from my left hand flings him six feet from me.

Now I see it's happening to all of them! One by one the alphabolds shrink back into the diminutive kobolds we are used to.

"The antidote! Their effects must've worn out!" I cry in relief and amazement.

"Thanks, self-appointed narrator!" the Challenger shouts back.

"I still feel it!" says my sister.

"As do I!" laughs the Challenger as the remaining army of kobolds diminishes into three-foot tall rat-beings, their little black eyes bulging as they realize their predicament. I see Lobster-Man standing at the back of the room aside his throne, his blackened claw near his round chin. He looks worried.

Usually the Challenger and my sister would give me a quick instruction on how to strategically proceed but this time— nah! We all just run in, slashing, hacking, pecking, kicking, and slapping.

I see the Challenger bash one tiny kobold as it attempts to flee, sending the critter flying to the ceiling, shrieking as it hits a hanging stalactite. Fauna, I see in that brief second when I charge forth and steal a spear, slashes her sword from left to right, sending dozens to the farthest wall. The cowering mob moves as one mass of fur, this sea of brown and grey bobbing heads revealing more and more of the cave floor as they retreat. Fauna is twirling like a top now, hitting them one by one, sending them flying forward, knocking over the ones in front of them. Closer to me the ranger moves his right arm close to a trio of the running vermin, his ax swung downward and sideways, catching them and another four as he steps up.

In this moment, where I feel more clear-headed than I have ever felt before, I decide to simply jump. It's dream-like when I push my feet off the cave-floor and float upward, halfway to the ceiling, and begin to fall forward, the tip of my right foot stepping onto the head of one kobold, my left foot kicking the back of another. I land in a crouching position, the other little beasts parting in fear as I jolt myself upward again and stretch out both of my arms to my sides. I feel hairy faces crash into them and, looking left and right, I see that I have clothes-lined four in all, their feet flying out from beneath them as they fall onto the floor. Echo leaps upon one of the ones I just knocked out and tiny tufts of fur fly everywhere while the bird mauls it like a floppy pillow.

The screeches bounce off the walls and ceiling, causing the great chamber to shake. In our frenzied state we feel each movement, the grounds beneath us seemingly rising and falling under our feet. I hear a crash. I am turning, seeing Lobster-Man falling over as the kobolds stream over and past him, a great piece of rock falling nearer the wall to my right. It crushes at least five of them. A stalactite plummets down next, falling on two kobolds, pinning them to the ground like flies in a bug museum.

Lobster-Man roars as the last few rat beings run over him, raising his two claws above his head. "Stop running! You're supposed to be at the top of the hierarchy!"

"We're licked, we is!" one of the scampering scum cries out, passing the enraged crustacean.

As the remaining kobolds funnel into a pair of side-by-side tunnels, we hop over to Lobster-Man, stepping between the piles of the furry unlucky foes. The chamber stops shaking when the last of the living kobolds run out of it.

Only Lobster-Man and ourselves remain. Both of his claws fall to his sides. The red creature smiles as he eyes us. "So, this is it, my band of virtuous heroes? You warriors of justice and supposed do-gooding!"

The Challenger spits, bending over to pick something up from one of the fallen kobolds. "I am chaotic!" he then declares, leaning back up, waving a sword, *his* sword!

"You stand in the way of order!" Lobster-Man hisses, pointing an accusing pincer.

"Where did you get the antidote from?" the ranger demands, looking ready to throw the ax with his other hand.

Lobster-Man laughs and I find his dry monotone laughter irritating.

"Answer him!" Fauna barks, stepping towards him, ahead of the rest of us. I want to call to her to stop, and I feel the effects of the goo wearing off now as my normal cautiousness reasserts itself in my mind.

"Oh, you little girl? Why are you wearing that red cap, you want attention?" says the lobster mockingly.

Fauna starts after him first, the Challenger second, Echo third, me last. All our voices dart about the tunnel that Lobster-Man flees down. We hear heavy footfalls, the clinking coins, and hurried gasps just ahead of us, darkness overtaking our vision the further we follow. The antidote does not give us the ability to see in the dark! The tunnel floor goes flat soon, and then starts moving upward. The blackness lifts the further up we go, a disc of sunlight visible now further through this straight passage.

I can hear the others panting now, and I too am feeling tired. It must be some kind of hangover. I raise a hand over my brow, trying to see the circle of light ahead of us. It's the end of the tunnel, the surface! This is when I see a strange object moving towards the center of the path of vision. It's a ship, for I see a single sail, a red sail upon a crimson hull.

"Drat!" curses Sister, unstrapping her bow. "He has one of those flying ships!"

"It's too late! Too late, it is!" squawks Echo, the fleshy bird slowly catching up to us. *"Lobster-Man escapes! You will see him again, I am sure of it!"*

"Might be," says the Challenger, angrily slamming his sword against the rock-wall, taking a big gasp, bending over for a moment.

Beside me Fauna takes off her cap, squeezing the rivers of sweat out of it. "I hope not," she says. "He's just a big red clown. Blows my mind that anyone would ever listen to him!"

"Well, we saw his fan-base," I agree, turning to our new bird friend, technically our second bird friend so far. "Hey, thanks for helping us!"

"Yeah!" says Fauna, putting her cap back on and tipping its brim towards him. "You know, we're on an ongoing quest. Why don't you join us?"

"Yeah, you could be a regular character!" adds the Challenger with an eager nod and a welcoming open hand.

"No! No! I have a family and friends nearby! But now we know where there's some antidote!" Echo answers as he bops his head appreciatively. When we eventually reach the end of the tunnel and emerge into a sunlit meadow he parts from us, thanking us once more. Now the antidote is completely worn off and we are back to our normal selves.

Here there is no sign of Lobster-Man, just this idyllic scene with butterflies and puffy white clouds in a baby blue sky, a world that looks as if the horrors we had just encountered never existed. Sister notices a few small coins on the nearby grasses, one silver, another gold, and she quickly pockets them. I suspect that the running shelled being may have dropped them. Soon we take a short rest further down the way near a calm green creek. The Challenger is strangely silent. I catch him gazing out at the distance as if he is working some things over in his mind. I wonder what he knows about this antidote.

"Our quest continues," Fauna sighs. "But first, I'm starving!"

A big frog emerges from the bank of the creek, looking very much like the one that ate our food. It burps and from our spot we can vaguely smell honey and sirloin. Fauna chuckles, loading an arrow and letting loose.

Soon we got a nice fire going. Normally I wouldn't, but I'm hungry and tired and even a fried amphibian is helpful for getting that awful gooey aftertaste out.

THE END

The Challenger: Origins

When we last left our three heroes they had escaped the reactionary claws of Lobster-Man. In a random tying up of loose ends they ran into the same over-sized frog that had eaten their food, and in turn, ate the frog. Little did they know that it was one of those magic frogs…

My vision is watery, slightly swirly, and the forest in the distance is alike a running oil painting with bubbly sparkles floating. Fauna looks odd, the reds of her cap and outfit twice as bright. In her hands is a fried frog piece, her face gnawing at it, getting juices on her cheeks.

"Fauna-aaaah," I say slowly. "Do you feel?—and how?"

"I feel…like…" she sniffs, looking about apprehensively like a chipmunk. "When did the sky become green?"

"The frog," I say. "Was it one of those magic ones?"

She shakes her head, smiling, showing her bright teeth.

The Challenger—that is, the ranger, our friend of two other adventures, is seated on a tuft of grass. He pulls out a bone from his mouth and nods. "Oh no, I was worried about this! Sorry, I was just so hungry!" he says. "I can't tell you how many of these babies I've eaten! Other stuff too, like cave glow-worms, meditating mantises, and been sprayed by certain skunks that give insight, you know?"

"Never read about those," I say, standing up, managing to adjust my stance on the shifty land. "Whoa…okay, so, don't tell Mother or we won't get supplies for the next time we decide to find a quest!"

"Look," says the Challenger. "There are ways of neutralizing the effects once eaten. There are flower petals that grow nearby. I can get some and we can be on our way."

Fauna shakes her head. "I feel fine enough."

The ranger asks us if we are sure, offering once more to retrieve the petals to undo the strange feeling. My sister shrugs. I pay it no more mind. I feel both panicked and relaxed. Without any words, we all lay on our backs, putting our weapons and things between ourselves. I trust my sister and the ranger more than anyone, so I decide to let myself calm down. Things pass by in the sky before us, distant birds flapping long wings slowly as if they beat against a current in the ocean, some of the birds surfing in the wind, looking cool. A soft gust comes in and we see a flutter of seeds flow over us, white fluffy stems spinning to keep them flying, spinning as they move over us. I imagine myself among them, floating carelessly on the wind.

"You look good like that," says my sister to my side.

"Hm?" I ask, my face warm in the sun.

"Oh yeah," says the Challenger calmly. "We all see what the other person is thinking. If you imagine something and see it, then the other people who also partook in the frog meat will see it. It's kind of a collective group activity, this frog-eating thingy."

I don't want them seeing all my inner thoughts! I block them, thinking of everything I'm trying to block; images of our city, Silver Coast, streak through my mind, memories from when we were growing up, the two of us sisters running through the hallways of our home, through fields in parkland, Fauna always showing off and climbing the biggest trees. There is in a great central square the immense statue of a javelin that we play tag around. I am on the big campus next, the Academy where I learned everything I could! In truth, I cannot wait to return to there and take more courses. In my mind I see the face of all my old classmates, all of them, including that purple-haired girl.

"Was she that one you told me about?" Sister asks me in jest.

"Look up there," says the Challenger as I'm about to make her shut up.

"Wow," says Fauna. "Flora, look, you'll like this."

In the clouds is a great building with walls of marble. This structure is wide and tall, atop it ascends three domed towers. At the building's base opens a gigantic doorway, a long, thin blue carpet rolled out to the courtyard before it.

"That's an Academy," I slowly say, feeling a smile. "We have a great one back home; Mother's Library is part of it. We grew on the edge of that campus, Northwest Quadrant. This one though…where?"

I look to my left and see the ranger holds his stare with his one uncovered eye and then he answers: "Northsphere it is called, back when I dwelt in urban places, before I was the Challenger."

"Oh," says my sister. "This is before you were a woodsy kind of guy. Sorry, that came out wrong. Blame the toad."

"Frog," I correct her. "Ah yes, I've heard of Northsphere before. I think Mother visited before we were born."

There are now tiny figures in the sky, all crowding around the courtyard. Our vision zooms, the Challenger's mind taking us closer to the people in the shadow of the great building. They wear white robes, the ones who have First Honours, while the rest are clad in simpler things, these newer students. I focus my vision on the image that the Challenger has mentally sculpted before us, and I feel a tingly warm feeling inside me as I look out over the book-bearing, robed pupils. I want to be there. Then I see the scene turn to night. From one of the domed towers black smoke rises. Thin flames begin to crackle from the windows, thickening as the pillars of smoke become ballooning clouds of black.

I am about to comment on the change of mood before the Challenger speaks: "That night long ago. I had to have been around your age then."

Night fades backwards into day. In our vision emerges a boy with only the faintest trace of fuzz on his upper lip, his frame thin under a plain robe, his face soft and barely boyish. He carries books in his arms.

"Aw!" Fauna declares loudly. "Is that you?"

He looks so different. As his doppelganger walks I see an awkward gait in his step.

"I was granted a sponsorship by an old sage. He took me out of the orphan temple and straight into the Academy," the ranger narrates from my side. We see the pre-Challenger standing in a room that glows in afternoon light from slanted windows. Here there are small wooden desks all set in a semi-circle. The door at the far side of the room swings open and a man who is seemingly ancient enters, leaning over a curved cane, wobbling over to the front podium.

I am there now.

"Where am I?" I ask loudly, uneasy. No one reacts. I see the early Challenger waving to someone else now, a green-haired girl a few desks over. At the front of the classroom stands some-one new. Here is a big man, older but not nearly as old as the last. This is a barrel chested brute clad in a robe that is black on one shoulder, golden yellow on the other, and then black on one part of his belly, and golden yellow on the other and so-on; a checkered pattern that accentuates his shape. His face is the middle place between red and pink, and he is yelling.

"Who is he?" I hear my sister ask. I see her in the room seated near the front.

"Bumbly," says the Challenger. "He was once our alchemist. A strange man. He feared the students and faculty from other Academies."

"What?" I say, almost laughing. "You mean like Silver Coast?"

"He was paranoid, Old Bumbly," says the Challenger. "He spoke badly about Talen, so that estranged him from most of the educators. He manipulated others though."

"Talen," I say, remembering that name. I see the book in front of me, the Book of Gods, something I read long ago. There is on the page an image of a robed figure, a tall thin being with face unseen, hands bearing a glass beaker and a quilled pen. "Talen, God of Knowledge. I know of Talen. I wish I had better memory to remember more about Him."

"Uphold knowledge, reason, and temper it with wisdom through experience." I hear the Challenger's voice.

"Then why are you neutral and chaotic?" Fauna asks. I see the look on her face, both here in the room and here on the field. She seems concerned for him. It is legit, what she asks, for Talen is known for being lawful and ordered.

"Bumbly showed me that there is no order," he answers and I hear anger in his voice, fixated at the sight before him. "I was the symbol of everything he hated, an orphan who defied the odds. He hates the weak becoming strong. It was his gold, along with the gold of every rich man, he said, that was spent by the Academy through a tax to bring a street child like me into high learning."

81

"Be Objective!" booms the one called Bumbly from the front of the classroom. We are in another chamber now, one with stone tables and no chairs. Fauna stands beside me, both of us over a table, tools and instruments of brass and glass before us. The young man who becomes the Challenger is across from us, the green haired girl, a year older now, with him. Both wear white robes with blue sashes, and I see their hands clasped, hidden from the other pupils.

I get a closer look at our friend in front of us. I see both of his blue eyes and fair cheeks, the same as our Challenger, but he *is* weak, I can see it. His arms are thin, his shoulders nearly not existing. Across from him I see another boy, also thin, shorter, and clad in white with a golden yellow sash. Underneath a mop of straw-like hair I see a deep scowl, his face all bunched up like he just ate a salted lemon.

The room gets cold. The walls collapse, the wooden planks fading like sand. Everything is white for a moment, and then colour begins to emerge. I see the young Challenger again. He stands in white robes, three colourful (blue, red, and yellow) sashes strapped against his chest. Suddenly I see many colours about us, the scents of rich flowers reaching my nose before the image of the lovely gardens emerge. Forms and hues come into being, for an unseen paintbrush creates them. A small crowd materializes and now more people are near. To the Challenger's side she stands, the green haired girl—the green haired young woman. She too wears the tricolour sash.

"She is beautiful," says the disembodied voice of my sister. The woman has emerald eyes that contrast with her fair skin and soft features. I hear the Challenger, *our* Challenger, mutter something. The young couple embrace and the crowd cheers. Everything goes dark, the blackness around us suffocating. I want this to end now. I've seen enough. Bumbly appears and he reads from a scroll, repeating some words, long words:

"Amberiousite, Magilidium, and Tristogralinite!" barks Bumbly, and now at his side I see something, a towering being twice as tall, four times as wide. Its skin is a swampy dark green, face devoid of feature, no eyes, nose, or mouth, only a pair of pointed ears that shoot out at the side of its head. The thick arms nearly reach the floor, long scythe-like claws on each of its hands.

"He made us create that thing," the 30-something Challenger tells us solemnly.

"When alchemists of the last era mixed these elements together, always they resulted in fire and blasts! But never have all three been combined at once! Sages once theorized that it would create greatness!" declares the one called Bumbly.

"Those tomes are out of date! They've been debunked! Can I not convince you not to do this, Professor?" young Challenger says.

"No, Mister! Recall what I say, be objective! Do not give in to your fear!" grumbles the big professor. Something scurries at his side—the pupil, the weird one with straw-like hair and a scrunched face.

"He is called Rand," says the Challenger to our side. "His nickname was The Straw Man. Bumbly was a mentor to him, those of the gold and black patch."

The spindly youth grins at the young Challenger. "Listen to him! He comes from a long line of blood! Best pedigree! You should see how well his dogs are bred!"

"That's enough, Rand!" says Bumbly, turning about to a white stone desk for a moment, grabbing a tall bottle in his big hand. "Here, have something to drink!"

The young Challenger waves his hand in refusal. "No, got an examination tomorrow. She's expecting me."

Rand, half the size of big Bumbly, leaps up and grabs the bottle from his mentor's hand. Bumbly grumbles, and he whispers to his ward. The whisper is faint but we hear it; *"This isn't for you, fool. This is for him, to knock him out."*

The little assistant nods eagerly and leaps towards the rival pupil, throwing the bottom of the bottle up into the young Challenger's forehead. He falls over and Bumbly instructs the giant green thing to pick him up.

We are now in a small room, in a tower from what I can tell, for there is a small window with no glass or curtain, and through this portal I can see the rooftops of the city of Northsphere. Lightning strikes in the distance, because of course it does! The young Challenger is there. He is up against the far wall, wrapped by his wrists in ropes, his ankles in chains attached to the wall behind him. Across from him sits a cauldron of bubbling blue goop filled half to the brim.

"Antidote," I hear his voice beside me. I figure that this must be *the* antidote, the same that Lobster-Man had, though this one is not temporary like his.

The young Challenger awakens, shaking his head, noticing in panic that he is tied to the wall. "Let me go!" he shrieks. I never thought such fear could come from him. I gaze at the shelves that line the room's walls; I see vials and beakers, sealed bottles, dusty books, a few rolled up linens, among other weird things. Torches glow on all four of the walls. Now I see Bumbly, Rand, and the big green thing. The monster carries something in his hands, something the size of a small person in a leather sack. This sack begins moving.

"Now, when you signed—when you signed your papers!" Bumbly shouts, pointing a single finger at the abducted pupil at the wall. "You committed to Talen, committed to finding out truth and we are here to do that! My antidote! It works! It is mixed of the elements!"

"Amberiousite, Magilidium, and Tristogralinite!" shouts Rand at his side.

"Be silent!" roars Bumbly at his overly eager lackey.

"You mock Talen!" young Challenger snaps.

"Now drink of it!" Bumbly calls, taking a long wooden spoon from one of the shelves and dipping it in the blue antidote.

"I refuse!" the young Challenger barks.

"We are committed to finding out the truth no matter the methods!" Bumbly retorts. "Attomoton!"

The green faceless thing opens up the sack it is carrying, pulls the person out of it, and then tosses the sack out the window. I hear Fauna gasping, and then I hear both the young Challenger and the woman in the arms of the green beast scream.

"No," I whisper. It is the Challenger's wife. Her hair flings about as she struggles to get free of the thing called Attomoton. Bumbly approaches the Challenger. She calls his name, but I cannot hear it properly over the commotion. And then I see Bumbly stick the end of the spoon into young Challenger's mouth. He must have done it from fear.

"Now, show me your strength! Break free of your ropes and chains and save her!" he bellows as the Challenger gulps.

"Let her go!" the pupil shouts with a rage. He still looks too weak, struggling in place.

Bumbly shakes his head, "It's not working!"

"Come! Break free!" chirps Rand menacingly at the bigger man's side. Young Challenger struggles hard. Nothing changes.

The monster holds her over the open window. She screams for her husband.

"Okay," says Bumbly, sounding defeated and Rand sighs loudly. "The experiment is over. The antidote doesn't work. Okay, Atto, bring her back in."

The green thing shakes its head and we hear a deep unworldly voice emanate from it: "Master, no. You who made me and educated me in the ways of the individual's will. You told me that we would do all to find the truth, yet you are unwilling to take it all the way."

Bumbly repeats his order for the thing we assumed was mindless to bring the green-haired woman back inside from the perch, but the monster refuses. The pre-Challenger calls to her. She calls back, tells him she loves him as she tries to break free, struggling in place.

Attomoton drops Challenger's wife over the window pane. I hear two screams, one from Fauna, and one from Challenger's wife as she falls from sight. The student does not cry out. He merely snaps the chains at his ankle, rips the ropes apart, and charges, leaping over the cauldron, pushing the green beast as he reaches him. A claw flings up as Attomoton falls over the edge, following the poor woman he had just dropped, managing to scratch out one of Challenger's eyes before falling.

"The antidote," I say to the ranger who is silent. "That is why you are so powerful now."

Lightning illuminates the room. I see rage on the young man's face as he turns to Bumbly, seemingly not daunted by the gaping hole where his eye just was. The older man cries out, yelling apologies to no avail. The young Challenger jumps to him, puts his feet on his shoulders, twists around his neck, and then grabs hold of a wooden beam on the ceiling. For a moment Bumbly is flailing above the floor, and then the Challenger tosses him out the window with his legs. Rand, seeing this, cries out for help. Challenger lands and then tears across the room as the assistant makes for the far doorway, the more youthful version of our friend knocking over everything on the shelves, including the torches on the walls, as he runs, causing the room to ignite on fire almost instantly. He reaches Rand and in one move flips him across the room, the little man landing in the cauldron with a goopy splash.

For a moment I think I hear something among the roaring, the sound of Challenger crying softly. The room burns. Young Challenger grabs one of the linens and leaps from the window into the night, gliding with the linen that acts like a makeshift wing.

Things swirl in fire and smoke. We see images of various landscapes—mountain ranges, rivers, dense woodlands, and the rest of our time here on the grass is just us laying there as the world passes us by. The images eventually fade.

When this happens the Challenger is first to stand. Fauna is next, and then I get up.

"Now you know why I am over-powered," the ranger says softly.

A part of me wants to say something, to tell him I am sorry about what happened, how I wish I knew more about his wife, and to remind him that we are glad to be his friends now, but I say nothing. We walk away, onward East to continue our quest to find yet another quest, another adventure.

As we descend a hill, we do not see that the vision in the sky has come back. I look for a moment and see it, though I do not tell the others what I see. In the room, that small room in the tower where our friend lost his wife and became a great warrior, something happens. The cauldron of blue antidote goop that Rand was thrown into, it stirs even as the room turns to ash.

A wet hand rises, and then an arm, muscular and thick, followed by a mop of straw-like hair.

THE END

The Straw Man Cometh

There is a breeze that sends the grass blades fluttering. We move downward on a rocky green mountain through a pathway that twists through trees. There is a meadow before us. I see it through the thick foliage. It stretches onward to a river. I know this place. I've seen it on maps in the library back home. It's called the Spherion River and it ultimately leads to Northsphere—this city that the Challenger came from, where the vision we saw (two days ago) took place. Our ranger friend has been silent mostly since, volunteering first watch each night.

"He's thinking about her," Fauna tells me today, at a point past noon when we are finished a meal of crushed acorns and apples. The Challenger has gone up ahead of us. We see him periodically as we sisters wind through the gradually descending trail.

"Obvious," I say, feeling a chill.

"Do you think this explains why he's neutral, why he's chaotic?" my sister asks me, not jestingly. "Maybe losing his love made him bitter about order, maybe feeling as if there is no true good worth fighting for?"

"Maybe," I say, about to explain how moral concepts are relative, but I hold back, feeling tired. I didn't get too much sleep up in the last tree. I woke up twice, one time hearing the Challenger mumbling things on the ground, unable to make the words out from my perch.

The stuff in my bag makes clanging and shuffling noises. I stoop over a bit, hitting my raggedy shoes against hardening ground. I bring the two straps of the backpack as forward as I can. We have new bags, us twins, and more stuff in them. Yesterday we found a general store out in the middle of some woods on the other side of these green mountains. It's a weird location, but the store manager, this short stubby man with a big droopy mustache, told us adventurers often come this way. He also had inflated prices, but we had some coin left as well as the extra two coins that Sister picked up in our last adventure. We now have four loaves of bread, a jar of acorn paste, dried fritters, a few feet of hemp rope, three faux-skin flasks, two bottles of rabbit milk, and a booklet on the local plants and beasts so I can brush up on my studies and be able to tell what's what out here –
you see, there are different dangers since we're more northerly than before).

"I've been thinking," Fauna says at my side. "We've gone pretty far, haven't we? I've lost track of the days!"

"Well, remember? We left Silver Coast on the second day because the city's so big, then a few days after we stayed at Moof Village, and then we met the Challenger at the tavern on the edge of the Grand Forest."

"Right!" she says sharply.

"And later we met Dick Bumpledop, had the whole adventure in Hare-Neck Valley, and then stayed with Barpar and

Screech for a while. We then proceeded to have our misadventure with Lobster-Man!"

"Yes, and then we ate the toad!" Fauna adds quickly, waving a downward hand. "It's been a while, and we've had quests. Haven't we had enough?"

I stop walking, feeling tension in my back and arms for a moment. "I don't believe this," I say to her after groaning. She pauses a few steps ahead of me, turned from me partway.

"What?" she asks, her mouth hanging.

"Your whole idea was coming out here! You want to go home? *You?*"

Her face flushes a lighter red than her clothes. She shakes her head with clear vehemence. "No! I'm not saying that! I was just seeing what you felt!"

I groan again. Obviously I know she's saving face like she always does and she knows I know. "Also, it was a frog we ate, not a toad!" I add hastily.

"Well then never mind!" Fauna snaps like a turtle, turning from me, bringing up her red cloak over the back of her head, laughing a little. "Fine! Going to go make water! Go catch up to Ranger Boy!"

She zips off the path, her feet crunching over leaves, bag bouncing, the sounds becoming fainter as I see dabs of red blip between the trees further away. I continue walking, catching up to the Challenger. Here is a wide stretch of land, all treed with some rows of mossy stones here and there. He's standing still, eye wide, gazing before him, sniffing the air.

"What?"

"I know this place," he says, raising a hand, his longbow clutched firmly in it. "These trees, they're thinner than the others."

He steps forward. I follow. These narrower trees look like they are not old as the rest of the forest. Some of them bend and

91

twist, teenaged and rebellious, not stout and dignified like the old oaks, birches, and ashes further away. In a nearby distance I can hear the rushing of water, and my ranger friend veers his head towards it, simultaneously grabbing an arrow from his quiver, lining it upon his bow. I've only my dagger, so I grab it off my belt under my blue cloak. As we move we begin to see the river, the Spherion, where the thin trees stop and a muddy bank starts.

"We're near your old city," I say cautiously. "Do you want to avoid it?"

He looks to me sharply. "Please. I avoid all cities, but this one…"

I nod back, gazing about the place, trying to search my mind to remember the significance. "And this place? I think I know of the lands outside of here. Killer…Killer Grass?"

"How do you know that?" he asks with his usual plain face. "Let me guess, you read it?"

"Yeah," I say, remembering. "It was in the booklet I just bought. Killer Grass is in the fields south and east of Northsphere. But there was something else, something nearby those fields, the place where the Killer Grass first came from? I think I read that?"

"Old Campus. The Killer Grass is more eastward from here, so we're safe," the Challenger answers. "Where's your sister?"

As if she heard (probably did) Fauna appears behind us, calling out: "Guys! I just saw an old weird statue!"

"Where?" asks the Challenger.

She takes us through some trees, along another pathway, this one more level than the last. As we walk I ask the ranger if he's been here before. He explains that we are approaching first campus of Northsphere Academy. This place, he says, was built back when the land was more savage and monsters and bandits and monstrous bandits roamed the land freely, when the civilized people walled themselves in great cities.

"This one campus just south of Northsphere was safe though, at least for a few years, for they had thick walls and a grand weapon," he says. I suddenly remember reading all about this place back at Silver Coast, back in Mother's library. I recall a very vague memory of reading a list of words and chants that unleash powerful forces, but I don't remember any details.

"When was this place abandoned?" Fauna asks him.

"It depends whom you ask," says the Challenger. "Some say it was the moment that the new campus was constructed in Northsphere. Others say it was when the Killer Grass experiment overwhelmed the nearby fields. All knowledge was lost, even in Northsphere's new academy, the one I went to. They have no information, no written accounts of details concerning the last days of Old Campus."

"I remember reading about it," I tell him then.

"Where?" he asks, his bow still armed. Fauna has a bow, but she opts to take her sword, hacking at some low branches in way of our new trail.

Before I can answer she points her blade and shouts: "There!"

The Challenger runs ahead of us. We catch up and are soon out of the trees, now in a space paved with broken stones. For the first time in a while I hear him laugh. "Yes, this place! Look!"

We're standing in a decrepit outdoor rotunda with six thick stone columns surrounding us in a great circle. Vines and grasses have taken over, greenery wrapping itself around the columns, snaking through the cracked floor. Even some small trees have sprung up around the edges. What the Challenger points to stands in the middle of this place, a bronze-coloured statue that stands three times as tall as him.

"W-w-wow!" my sister stammers, running around the sculpture.

"Talen," I say the name of the God of Knowledge. It's man-like in shape, garbed in a cloak that reaches the base. Two arms extend from the god's side, grasping in one hand a beaker, in the other a quilled pen. His face is shrouded by a hood.

The Challenger and I circle the statue and I see upon Talen's back a pair of folded wings. "Talen flies?" I ask.

"Yes," says the ranger, placing the bow back on his chest, his free hand now on his sword's hilt in the scabbard at his belts. "His symbol is a bird. With knowledge comes great vision, like that of a hawk or eagle."

"Or an owl," I add and Fauna giggles.

"Sure," he continues, looking about. "I remember this place. We came here on a field trip." I see him flash his teeth. "Let me show you something!"

"Better be a tavern!" Fauna calls.

"Drink your rabbit milk," I tell her, following the Challenger, this time through the other side of the rotunda, opposite from whence we'd just come.

This big place is filled with juvenile trees and I still hear the Spherion babbling on, unseen. We approach structures made of red brick, the nearest of them two stories tall, the next nearest five stories, all of them covered in a millennia's growth of vines. There is a path that leads between the encrusted buildings, and there is, not far off, at the end of this trail, a single tower. I count nine floors, using the tall glass windows as my guide. For one moment I feel euphoria, smooth joy, a whiff of nostalgia. I can see beyond this ruin that's been taken back by nature a place that was once a community. Pupils like me must have been here in the hundreds, and that tower at the end...

The others speed up. When I'm sprinting my knapsack smacks against me. Between the buildings I now see trees, taller ones, and shadows about their trunks. We reach the walls of the tower. It's thick, twice as wide as the open rotunda we just left and there is a huge open doorway at its base.

"What's inside?" Fauna asks.

"Library," says the Challenger.

"Library!" I shout, panting from the run. "Yes, yes!"

My sister slaps my shoulder from my side, putting her sword back at her belt.

"Why put your sword away?" I ask, pulling the straps on my knapsack, leaning towards her.

"It's a library," she says. "What's there, mutated book lice?"

"Walking molds maybe," says the ranger, blade in hand. "But look, Flora, you'll love this especially."

"What about me?" asks my sister as we all walk in, stepping into a chamber, no—an atrium!

My gasp shoots all the way up to top of this hollow interior. This immense atrium takes up the whole tower! There are overlooking interior balconies on every floor leading up and immense leafy plants growing from the sides of the banisters. At the pinnacle I see a glass ceiling. Additional light comes from windows, streaming in from sources seen and unseen. This circular floor we stand upon looks to be thirty paces in circumference. There is a staircase at the far point, the only part of the chamber untouched by vegetation. It winds upward, writhing towards the ninth floor, reminding me of a corkscrew.

"Mmm...I come in around this time, done with lectures. I'm ready to read, study, overview the lesson, conduct arguments, make conclusions. I'd want to take a spot on high up, way above in my peaceful niche," I say, nearly cooing.

"An owl's perch," Fauna says. "Look at the vines!"

"They're roots must all be outside," comments the Challenger. "Otherwise, who would water them?"

"That makes sense," I agree. These vines look like ropes. They are hanging from all the balconies, some of them intersecting and turning into hydra-like formations, some bulging and overtaking the wall. There are thinner ones too, all of the vines pouring inward, all reaching for the floor.

"Let's climb!" says Sister and the Challenger grins, looking excited.

"Not me!" I tell them.

"Ah," says the Challenger. "Keep going, the stairs look to be made of stone-wood, the hardiest wood of all woods. Only fire can destroy it."

I wish them luck and begin running to the old stairs. When I take my first steps the staircase neither creaks or sways. The wood is a dark brown. "Stone-wood," I say, vaguely remembering reading about it. I look over to see both of my companions grabbing at the lower vines, Fauna jetting up to the second level, the Challenger following close behind, their two figures bounding upward like spiders climbing webs. I sigh, knowing they'll reach the top first. I decide to take a leisurely stroll (at a fast pace). I see that there are bookshelves, long rows going in every direction to the far exterior walls where tall windows are, the light from them illuminating the spines of every book. I wonder and hope if we can spend some time here. There must be tons of knowledge, things I haven't read back home. Third, fourth, fifth, and sixth floor are more of the same, more books, and I see desks further towards the windows.

"I could spend my life here," I say to myself at floor seven. This is different. Here there are some bookshelves, but there is, instead of open aisles leading to windows and desks, an open archway a few paces from the stairs. At the top of the archway are some carved words in an ancient language, an older version of common language. Fortunately I can make out the letters: **Experimentation** it reads.

I go in. It's a fairly large chamber. There are columns that reach only a quarter of the way to the ceiling and on the top of these columns, at about my height, are glass boxes. I see some kind of green mask in one, in another I see a silver cup. There are a dozen or so of these displays. Farthest from the archway is a glass cube with no roof, only an open space at the top. I see this last. Inside is a patch of dried out grasses, yellow and brown, only a finger height each. They appear dead, all strewn over, lying on top of one another.

"Could this be?" I ask myself. Ever the knowledge-seeker, I reach for my knapsack and pull out a tiny piece of bread. Taking it in my hands, I drop it on top of the grass.

I hear a rustling, and then a high-pitched growl and a series of inhuman shrieks as all the blades begin flinging about, little teeth barely visible on their ends, the frantic grass consuming the bread in seconds. Once the piece is gone the grasses all wave about, the blades nearest the end where I stand all flinging against the glass wall as if they are trying to reach me.

"Killer Grass," I say with a half-smile. I cannot wait to show the Challenger.

I think for a moment about the vision we saw, his story, his tragedy, a few days prior, about Bumbly and his admiring pupil, Rand, and how their actions caused the Challenger to lose his wife. I also remember how the young man who became the Challenger slew Bumbly and tossed the little man nicknamed the Straw Man into the antidote cauldron in his rage.

I move back to the stairs. Floor Eight is next. Here I see a similar chamber and a similar archway, the inscriptions in ancient pre-Common reading: **Delipha**.

"Goddess of the Sea," I whisper, remembering that name. Inside I peer briefly, able to see inscriptions reading: **Delipha's Artifacts**.

Finally I make my way to Floor Nine. As expected both my sister and the Challenger are already there. We gaze down at the first-floor from here, looking down the many levels of the circular balconies that wrap around the tower's interior. On this ninth floor there are some doors, small ones, and one big one towards the center of the space. We make our way to the big door and the Challenger sighs loudly.

He smacks his forehead with his palm, punching the door with his other hand. "It's locked! How could I forget that?"

"What's in there?" Fauna asks, a little winded by her climb, her knapsack still firmly on her back. "Another vision-inducing toad?"

"Frog. No, but it *is* something we've seen before," says the ranger. "It leads to an open roof. There are flying ships."

"Wow!" gasps Fauna. That would be really useful, for us to have one of those ships like Lobster-Man had escaped from us on. Sister asks: "Can we just break the door? I mean, look at how strong you were made because of the antidote."

The Challenger shakes his head, running a hand up the surface of the door. "This is stone-wood, won't break."

"A flying ship could be useful for a tight spot!" I comment. My words were so badly chosen, or so aptly chosen because what happens next is indeed just that. We hear the sound of doors slamming shut from way down at the bottom of the tower. Fauna and I rush to the side rail of the balcony, peering down over the vines. The light that had been coming in through the front door is gone.

"*Orphan!*" we hear a monstrous voice roar from an unseen place below. "*He who is called Challenger! Your time is over!*"

Fauna curses. We see small figures emerge. Some are on the lower balconies, others on the main floor. They scramble about. I can only make out that they are bulky and green-skinned. The Challenger emerges at my side, grabbing his bow.

"Prepare to fight," the ranger hisses. "This is bad."

"What is it?" Fauna asks in panic, also grabbing both her bow and arrows. I grab my dagger again.

"Challenger!" the voice calls mockingly. *"Remember me?"*

Then we see it him. A hulking figure steps into the main chamber below. His shoulders and arms are massive, as is his chest and back, even at this distance I can tell he is twenty times my size. He wears a great yellow cloak, which he quickly flings off of himself, revealing a bulgy head topped with messy blonde strands of hair.

"The Straw Man," mutters the Challenger. I see fear in his good eye. The one called Straw Man is human, though clearly something else. He stands, from my vantage point here on the top floor of the library, maybe three times average height, and at least four times as wide. His arms, barely contained in his furry jerkin, are as wide as I am. One of his allies, a short and squat green thing, lurches out from the shadows. I see two more moving towards the winding stairs that I just climbed. They carry what look like iron clubs. The Straw Man grimaces as he glares up at us, running a thick hand quickly through his long, straw-like hairs.

He flings his head, his hair leaping like a floppy mop, and cries out in his booming voice: "Surrender! You're surrounded!"

The Challenger, who he is addressing, looks to me and Fauna. "Okay girls, this is *my* fight."

"He's Rand," I say. "You threw him in the antidote those years ago."

"And that's why he's huge now," says the ranger, leaning over the rail. He then yells: "Rand! I'm glad you've hit the gymnasium finally! Now, these two young'uns were just looking around! Let them leave and I'll stay behind! Does we have a deal?"

"No!" roars back the Straw Man, crossing his meaty arms over his colossal chest. "I think not, Jim-Jim!"

Fauna looks at the Challenger. He shrugs.

"Those two sisters in red and blue—I know them! I've been watching you lot the past few days! That blue one with the big owl eyes 'specially! She knows things!" roars the Straw Man. My sister would be laughing really hard in any other situation. Both she and the Challenger raise their bows, Fauna aiming downwards between the railings while the Challenger points his over the vine-covered edge, straight down. I am crouching, peering at the balconies on all eight levels below and catching sight of the scurrying green bodies. This is bad.

"What are those things?" I whisper harshly up at the Challenger.

"Let's see," he says, suddenly veering his bow, shooting loose an arrow straight at the third level of the library.

Blonk!! The arrow bounces off of something that zooms through the hallways by the balcony, one of Straw Man's servants. From this distance I see the face, green and round, without eyes, noses, or a mouth, only pointed ears.

"Attos!" the Challenger shouts and I remember the big thing that killed his wife. These must be smaller versions of that.

"Impervious to arrows?" Fauna asks, tilting her bow downward more, and she fires right down at Straw Man.

The arrow hits true, thudding hard into the great man's chest. He opens his mouth in a huge smile before reaching and crushing the arrow in his right hand. Straw Man slams his left fist into the nearest pair of desks, sending them crashing against the far wall of the lobby. Sister shoots a second arrow, this one aimed at his face, but the brute ducks!

"Rope!" the Challenger yells.

Fauna flings her backpack on the floor and the ranger rips open the thing, pulling out our hemp rope. Earlier I mentioned that we had a few feet of rope – it's actually about 130 feet! I dash to the Challenger's side, for the ranger is now tying one end around his torso in a knot. I grab hold of the other end and promptly cut off four feet with my little dagger.

"It's perfect now," I tell him.

He pats my shoulder heartily and I see a small smile on his unshaven face. "You guys run, just get out of here. Leave him to me!"

"You know us better than that, Ranger!" Fauna shouts after flinging down a third and fourth arrow, both of which Straw Man dodges and laughs menacingly at, making the walls of the library shake a bit.

The Challenger says nothing while he ties the other end of the long, long rope to the banister. "Let's hope it holds!" he says and grunts as he leaps off and into the middle of the room, swinging his sword all the way down.

The great ranger, sword in hand, swings as he flies downward perfectly above the Straw Man.

The sword misses.

I hear Fauna gasp and load another arrow. The Challenger bounces up one third of the way, readying himself for another strike.

The banister column the rope is tied to cracks in half! Down goes our ranger friend with less momentum than anticipated, still managing a strike as he falls. The Straw Man moves and the blade hits the outer side of his great left leg, spilling a thin trail of blood. The big man, making no further reaction, leans over him, for our friend smashed hard against the floor.

The Challenger scrambles, but the Straw Man grabs hold of him, pulling him with one massive hand clenched around both of his legs. Terrified, I look at my sister and see she's made the same face. At once we tear down the hall towards the stairs.

"I'll shoot him from different levels!" Fauna yells after me.

I make it to the stairs first and start descending. On the eighth floor I see the big open doorway that says **Delipha's Artifacts.** I don't think the goddess of the sea can help us now. Seventh floor! Fauna's rapid footfalls are right above me.

"Flora! Watch out!" she calls as she emerges behind me and rushes to the edge of the balcony rail. "Those green things are coming!"

"I need a better weapon!" I call after her, running into the chamber labeled **Experimentation**. I hear arrows shooting downward again. "Okay, okay!" I tell myself, using the sunlight that comes from the far wall to read the inscriptions on the numerous little columns that contain items, items I overlooked before. On one column I see a horseshoe-shaped metallic thing. I grab it. It's a little heavy, not unlike a horseshoe. There are tiny black letters on the interior curve: **Mighty Magnet**. I know a bit about magnetic properties, but I can't figure out how to work the thing. Quickly, I tuck it in into the back part of my belt underneath my tunic.

I see the Killer Grass in the glass cube tank, the blades lying dormant.

"Flora! Look out!"

Turning about, I see one of the green Atto thingies charging at me! It must have been hiding, this round thing half my height, thrice my width, with bulky arms reaching out toward me. Two arrows (from Sis) fly at it from the side but break upon impact!

I shriek. I then turn, grab the tank of grass and I lift it over my head, twisting my back in an arch, and in perfect timing flop the Killer Grass onto the Atto's big ball-shaped head. The Killer

Grass comes alive at once, screeching and churning, little tiny roars and hisses emitting in the frenzy. I only see green and yellow movement, followed by less and less of the Atto's head. The Killer Grass patch begins enveloping its shoulders next, tearing piece by piece through this metallic creature, sending shards and bolts upon the floor. I see my sister beyond and I run, giving the feeding Killer Grass a wide circular berth.

We two soon reach the balcony of our floor again, both of us peering over the side to check on our friend. Any feelings of relief I had vanish abruptly. The Challenger is limp on the floor and the Straw Man scoops him up, flinging him over his shoulder like a felled deer. Sister loads an arrow, steps onto the rail with one foot, leans—Straw Man looks up at us!

He grins. She fires. He dashes, quick for his size.

And then green Attos surround us, four of them. I raise my hand, unsure of what to do. Sister aims for them next, but we know it's pointless.

"Let us leave!" Fauna shouts in her commanding voice. "Your master said he wants *him*!"

One of the Attos barks at us in the same unworldly voice as the big Atto from our earlier vision, tells us to lower our weapons and come with them. Fauna refuses. The Atto spits something at us, some greenish cloud of dust—and I feel exhausted.

I see my sister fall. I have a brief dream. We're back at home with Mother. Our quest is over and we sit with her at a long table full of steaming cups of tea, the Challenger with us, his green-haired wife too, and others. There is joy, even if just for a split moment!

I wake up groggily, but manage to shake myself, not forgetting the situation.

"Where are we now?" I ask.

"In a birdcage," says Sister beside me, leaning her legs between bars. This is no dream here. We're in a hanging cage with golden bars, the spaces between them too thin even for us small sisters to squeeze through. The cage, big enough to fit a pair of large eagles, hangs over cobbled stones. We are outside once more. I see the library towering over us. The cage hangs from a tree. I see another cage the same size swaying at another tree just a few paces over.

"Challenger!" I call to the occupant of the other cage. The ranger's crouched over, taking up most of the little enclosure. He rubs his head. I see a big gash above his brow.

"They have our stuff," he says, sounding gloomy. I see that he's right; our two knapsacks are on the ground, most of our items and food strewn about. There are four Attos in all, the fifth one having been eaten by the Killer Grass that I dumped on it. Two of them stand by the Straw Man, who in turn stands about ten yards from us. There looks to be an evening sun casting a long shadow of the library aside us. In this lengthy shade, further away, another ten yards in an open square is something else, some machine. The other two Attos are there, seemingly inspecting this big thing. Our weapons too are all gone. I see my dagger and their swords and bows near the feet of the big enemy.

"Woken up have we, ladies?" the one called the Straw Man sneers as he turns to face us and picks up the Challenger's sword from the floor.

"Rand!" calls the Challenger. "I've told you before! Your cow-meat is with me! Let them go! I don't even know these two weirdies!"

Fauna shakes her head slightly, but we both know he's trying to save us.

The Straw Man shakes his head, sending his stalks of lochs flinging. "You know me better!" he booms back. "I want revenge!"

104

"Revenge for what?" asks the Challenger. "You two mates took my wife! What did you expect? And me throwing you in that cauldron made you strong, stronger even than me!"

"It made me ugly!" the Straw Man roars.

"You were already!" Fauna snaps. I want to smack the back of her head.

The Straw Man darts his wide face to us, but he chortles loudly and looks back to our friend. "You know, Jim-Jim. You were always my enemy! Since the first day our esteemed academy took in a dirty, stinking orphan from the streets!"

"Rand!" the ranger yells. "I was lucky to be given an education considering what I came from! I deserved the chance as much as anyone!"

He who is named the Straw Man clenches his jaw, shaking his mighty head again. "No!" he retorts boomingly, waving his big hands before his face for a moment. "*You* do not deserve what belonged to me, that belonged to us, the sons of the Big Shifters! It was *we* who built the campus, *we* who built Northsphere and filled it with riches!"

"Is that what this is about?" my sister interjects, standing up. "You're vexed with our friend because he was given an opportunity when he was poor?"

"Shh, we're not friends," says the Challenger, but it looks like he's given up the ruse.

"Oh! Oh!" shrieks the Straw Man, more than a hint of sadistic glee in his wretched voice. "So, you *do* know him?"

"Rand!" cries the ranger. "If I had finished my studies I would've helped Northsphere's prosperity! I would've helped the Shifters, would've helped in their goal!" He is shaking the birdcage he's in, causing it to sway under the big tree branch.

Our captor crosses his arms, grins wide, and says: "Lies! You were a burden! And you, like all reformers, would have brought more lazy orphans in to compete with the Golden-Born!

105

You, like the reformers, would have raised taxes on us gilded folk! All to support poor boys! Bah!"

"Once more, Rand, you weakly support your argument," the Challenger says, sounding like he has calmed: "I worked hard, far harder than you had to! Enough. This is such a confusing motivation. Now, free the girls."

"I think he's much smarter than he lets on sometimes," Fauna whispers quickly to me, and I immediately know she is speaking of the ranger, not the Straw Man.

Now the villain turns away from us, laughing louder. "You're in no position to make demands. Behold my instrument! Upon Northsphere do I aim my malice!"

I shudder, both at his monologue and the big contraption down the way from us. It has started to hum loudly and then it buzzes like a bee swarm. I see it better – wide like a castle's turret, looks to be made of iron. Out of the box-like part sprouts a tube-shaped object (actually it's a tube) that is three times the length of the rest of it. The bulky base is half the height of a village home and the side that we see from here is full of big cogs the size of pigs, all grinding and turning in a complicated system. I know not how it works, but the cogs clearly are charging it.

"Ah yes! This magical cannon!" roars the Straw Man, pointing to it as he stands halfway between our cages and the great weapon. "Aim for Northsphere, my Attos!" he barks and then turns to us and says: "Northsphere taxed me, taxed my family to pay for lazy street children to infest our institutions! No more!"

"You're going to destroy our city?" the Challenger shrieks, stamping his feet, swinging the cage further.

"As soon as I know the magic word to fire it, yes," says the Straw Man. "But I know not the word, but someone here does."

"I don't know it!" Fauna yells. "Let us go!"

He turns to our cage and begins walking to us, the stones cracking under each of his massive steps. The Straw Man stops a few feet from us, and he raises both of his closed fists, opening his left one slowly. In his palm there is a short piece of grain, its golden shaft shaking in the breeze. In his other hand he holds something small and blue, which he places on the floor of the cage between two bars. The Straw Man whispers something and the blue thing moves fastly at me, slinking onto my arm, up my shoulder, into my ear...this slimy thing…!

The knowledge in my mind is strong. In the split moment I imagine everything, the city of Northsphere waiting to be destroyed, the Challenger's past, this great library nearby us in this Old Campus, the fields of Killer Grass to the South and East, the green mountains that we had trekked over to get here. The current hum of the great cannon overwhelms my hearing while the library's shadow leans into a darkening twilight. The Straw Man takes a single step back from the cage.

Beyond him I can see the cannon's turret faces northward to its target, the city of Northsphere. The machinery inside is on full display, the creator of the dreadful contraption clearly having no conception of walls: I see even more gears, cogs, grinding metal chains, and conveyors. Beyond all the clunking bits there is a bright light. This is the ammunition. I know this from the slug critter that Straw Man has placed in my brain. I remember everything I ever learned and each memory I want to revisit, but not now!

"What *was* that?" Sister finally gasps to me.

"Fauna!" I cry, grabbing her in both my arms. "I remember everything perfectly!"

"What do you mean? Remember what?" she asks confusedly.

"Ah!" barks our adversary as he reaches back from the cage and reveals once more the grain in his other hand. He says: "Would you remember this magical item?"

"Yes," I say, nodding. "That is a Grain of Truth. It is grown in Newly Found Land."

"And what does it do?" he asks as he holds it against the bars of the cage, right in front of me.

"It forces you to speak the truth," I say, realizing now that he wants to know the password to activate the magic cannon, to make it fire. I read these words when I was very small.

"Unless you want to bite your tongue off you will tell me – *what* is the word?" sneers the brute.

I speak the word, finding myself unable to whisper or mutter it, some unseen force makes me speak it loudly. The Grain of Truth has taken hold. The Straw Man steps back from us and begins laughing and slapping the ground, sending bits of grass, pebble, and earth about himself. At my side Fauna looks worried. I can see the Challenger over her shoulder. He is staring at the cannon as the Straw Man roars the word and the bulky weapon becomes even louder, shaking.

The noises growing worse and worse, I reach behind me, grasping something that is wedged under my tunic in my pants. I retrieve the horseshoe-looking item, the Mighty Magnet. I still have it! And I remember everything about it. I read about it once long ago in Mother's library, all around the same time I learned a great many of the magical words of ancient speech. Empowered, I clasp the curve of it, the cold metal, and I wedge its two flat ends through the nearest metal bars, pointing at the cannon.

I shout: *"Lirot Nnyrk!"* and I feel the thing power-up in my hand. It vibrates, pulsates, and I manage to turn it slightly to the right, right at the Atto standing in front of the cannon's open mid-section.

"Push!" I shout, recalling how to give commands to the magnet.

The Atto flails its short limbs. It's moving and I yell again: *"Push!"* and it flies into the open wall of the cannon into the nexus of churning machinery! The Atto gets grounded fast, crunched into a starfish-like shape for a split moment before vanishing further into the inner cogs.

The big Straw Man continues to laugh, seemingly not noticing.

Fauna's eyes go to the bars in front of her and I bring my magnet nearer to me, pointing it at the bars before us. I call: *"Break!"* knowing that the magnet can do such feats. Four bars right near my sister bend outward and then crack apart, creating a gaping hole. She gets out first, I follow.

The Straw Man did not anticipate this! I swerve rightward, taking three long steps, keeping the twin points of my new magnetic weapon pointed northward. There are three Attos now. The cannon, having just crushed the first Atto, begins to shake. Sparks emit from within and the charging turns into a coarse, explosive, churning sound! The bits of the Atto are clogging it.

It's now when the Straw Man has noticed something's wrong. I turn the magnet onto the next Atto, taking hold of it, scooping it up with the invisible force! I grab the next Atto too, bringing both of them under my control as they flail in my two magnetic beams.

"Push!" I shout, sending them at once into the grinds, sparks and metallic bits flying everywhere while the cannon begins to quake further like a seaside village before a tsunami.

In the confusion the Straw Man charges towards the cannon. The last Atto jumps about while the big brute bounds towards the machine! The turret of the cannon is jolting, nuts and washers and parts of the first three Attos shoot all over the courtyard now!

Me and Sister back up, back towards the cage that had just encased us. The long barrel of the cannon falls apart at the place where it joins the rest and then the bulky base topples over, crashing onto the grass and crumbled pavement, the massive weapon still trembling.

Both the Straw Man and the last Atto reach it after it has fallen apart. By now the once magical weapon has stopped shaking and is completely still and silent. I can hear the Challenger gushing out a relieved sigh in the other cage when the brutish Straw Man turns his massive upper body about, scowling at us uncaged sisters. The surviving Atto jumps at its side, seemingly also enraged.

I turn my magnet to the Atto, just wanting that last thing out of the way..

"*Grab*!" I yell and the automaton stops jumping. I have it! I heave the mighty magnet upward and to the right, causing the metal critter to fly up and slam into the side of the Straw Man's head.

He falls over, landing against the deceased cannon.

I spin around to see the Challenger cheering, waving his hands in the cage. Fauna scoops up her sword and bow, and then grabs those of the ranger.

"*Grab door!*" I command the magnet. The cage that contains our friend begins to shake and then swiftly swings open, the lock bursting apart by the force of the magnet. The Challenger jumps out, legs through the small doorway first, and then lands in front of us, his hands reaching to retrieve his weapons from my sister.

He grins and pats my shoulder when he is armed again and he thanks me. There is no time to celebrate – behind him I can see the Straw Man is beginning to stir. Out of nowhere the cannon starts to sputter in place behind the monstrous man, gears flying from its middle, the bright light, the ammunition pulsing once more. It doesn't take a well-read person with a brain slug inside her head to realize that it'll blow up!

"Run!" Fauna shouts, she too able to tell. The Challenger dashes away, we follow.

As I run I remember (because of that magical slug) that the fires of this cannon spread faster than any fire known.

"Where are we running?" Fauna calls to the Challenger who has bounded ahead of us.

"Up!" he cries, pointing his blade to the library. We are turning around the big tower now, back to the front entrance. I agree instantly, for I also know that this fire travels slower vertically.

We all charge around the tower, stampeding towards the doorway. Once we pass under the arch and into the great front chamber we hear the explosion. Every floor shakes. There is the sound of glass bursting on every level when colourful fire appears on the far wall of the rotunda! We pass swiftly to the winding stairs. The Challenger surges upwards first and Fauna hits my side with her free hand, insisting I go as she takes one last look at the doorway. The Challenger's feet thump at every step, his heels nearly flying into my forehead. As we ascend I get a glance over the open space where fires have overtaken more than half of the great room below, streaking through carpeting and devouring bookshelves. I hold the rail to my side, but it becomes hot! The fire is growing upward beneath us!

Sister is behind me now, having gotten to the stairs in time. My mind races with my feet. I can't believe that not long ago I was going through this library in a state of euphoria. It was here where I got this magnet and saw the Killer Grass, that same Killer Grass that grows on the lands south and east of here! I wish things were different, that I could stay here. We keep running up and up and up. It's floor seven when flames are at Fauna's back and she begins to cry out. We can't stop! Must move! The Challenger reaches the next floor and dashes onto level eight. I follow him, as does Fauna who somersaults onto the carpet right as the fires reach our floor.

"Ah no," grumbles the ranger, pointing up to the ninth floor beyond the fresh wall of flames. "If only we can find a way up there! The flying ships on the roof! It's our only chance!"

The fires are spreading fast, the flames flickering with a medley of colours, taking over the carpeting before us, and I see the fires rising further up the stairs, beginning to feast on the floor of the ninth level and that big stone-wood door that leads to the roof.

"Run!" Fauna cries as we stand at the eighth level, smacking my shoulder. There is now a full flame wall between us and the stairs below and above us. The only way we can go is behind us, through the big archway, the one that has inscriptions above that read: **Delipha's Artifacts.**

"Delipha, goddess of the sea!" I exclaim as our trio runs into another large chamber, this one painted dark blue, and I see tanks—aquariums full of water filled with the bones of fish – no custodians, I guess. We spot a little ways in there are many rows of tables and desks. I see a short column beyond them, so I run ahead of the others. There I see an item placed on the hard surface of the short column, a rod. I know what this is. It is near the size of my little dagger, the handle made of smooth pearl, made to fit in one's palm, while the very end of it contains a round blue-green stone. This is Delipha's Rod.

I take the rod before me and call for Delipha (as the slug inside my head gives me the power to recall that this is how to activate it), bidding my two companions to part as I aim the rod with the green-blue stone at the huge flames that are seeping into the chamber. An enormous stream of water jets forth from the stone, getting larger as it travels through the space. My sister and the Challenger jump to the sides as the fires fall before them.

Feeling immense joy, I call: "Thanks to the Sea Goddess!"

The entire eighth floor balcony area is no longer on fire, the carpet soggy and black. Below us the fire still rages, and the ninth floor above us still burns and, as we run up to the stairs, we see that the big stone-wood door has burned down. Twilight sun rays beam in from the doorway. There is fire between us and there, so as we stand on the stair landing I call to Delipha once more and point my newfound item, shooting water upward, dissipating the fires. A small fish flops out from the stream of water, bouncing along the floor. I lower the rod and the water stops. Fauna runs first. I go after her, feeling the heat through my shoes as more fires rise behind us again. Soon the eighth floor will be alight once more. We two sisters reach the ninth floor.

Beyond the doorway we see an open space, the roof, which makes up most of the ninth floor. There are, outside on a flat stone paved surface, two ships made of wood, each with a single mast and double man-sized triangular sail aloft.

"Hey Challenger!" Fauna shouts over her shoulder. "You were right! We're out of here!"

"Come back, Jim-Jim!" the horrible voice of the Straw-Man rises up way down from the base of the library.

I turn about and see that the Challenger is not with us. He leans over the rail on the eighth floor. Fires light up around him and the wall of multi-coloured flames re-emerges between us and the ranger.

With his immense strength and dexterity the Straw Man manages to jump straight up to the eighth floor, his huge body emerging from the flames. Dozens of little fires dance upon his body and clothing, yet he seems unhurt. The Challenger backs into the chamber of Delipha, his sword raised.

"Straw-Boy!" Fauna yells and he turns about to reveal his face is covered in grotesque burns.

I am angry, want him gone. I raise Delipha's rod and shoot. Water spurts through flame and hits him in the eyes. I keep the stream on his face, going downward into his gaping maw next, causing the big man to gurgle uncontrollably.

"Challenger!" I call to the ranger and raise the mighty magnet in my other hand. "Hold onto your sword!" As planned the magnet pulls the end of his blade and the Challenger hangs onto it like a kid grabbing a drifting balloon, his legs dangling as he floats past the temporarily blinded Straw Man and through the fire-wall and onto the ninth floor. I shoot more water at the Straw Man's face and then we quickly splash onto the Challenger, dousing any flickering flames on him. Then we three run, hearing the Straw Man scream behind us. We charge outside. I glance behind and see a little crab is pinching the Straw Man's nose in its claw while he reaches to grab it off.

On the roof we are hit with evening breeze. We pile onto the closer of the two ships. This ship is similar to the size of the last flying ship we saw, able to fit five people, about the size of a large wagon. In moments we are hovering above the tower. Fauna has taken the ship's driving mechanisms, two levers at the front of the ship, one for going up and down, the other for backwards and forwards. I look over the side alongside the Challenger at the burning tower below. We rise higher and I notice there are three cannonballs on the deck of the other ship down there yet none on ours.

"Weird," Fauna says as we rise. "The steering is at the bow."

"Flying ships are weird," I say, remembering reading on them.

I see the Straw Man charge out the door and onto the roof. With the whole building now on fire, thick smoke streaming out all the windows beneath, the Straw Man leaps onto the other flying ship, his huge body taking up most of the deck, and with an enraged face he pursues us!

I hear my sister curse. The ranger instructs her to go as high and fast as she can. "Hold on to something!" he then yells, grabbing the side of the deck's wall. I place Delipha's rod in my belt beside my dagger, keeping the big magnet in my right hand while my left grabs the mast in the deck's middle.

"You'll all pay!" roars the Straw Man. With one hand on one of the levers, he raises the second ship, still a fair distance from us, but close enough where I can see the spittle when he shouts. One of his meaty hands encircles a cannon ball and with one move he powerfully chucks it up at us.

I yell at my sister to swerve, which she does, taking the ship leftward, tilting slightly. The Challenger nearly falls over onto the deck, but quickly rights himself. The big ball misses by a few feet off our bow, falling to the earth.

Straw Man hurls another! This one is coming right at us!

I raise the magnet, gripping the rail with my spare hand, and I cry out: "*Push!*" while nearly losing my balance, the moving ground far beneath us making me dizzy. The ball stops midair and then falls backwards towards the Straw-Man's ship, missing by as close as that last ball had missed us by! I move towards the stern of the ship, grabbing the short wooden rail. The Challenger is a few feet from me. Fauna, I see, is gradually bringing our vessel towards the clouds. Below I see the Old Campus passing from sight and the tops of trees and hills taken over my view.

"Fauna!" I call to her, that slug in my head helping me recall something. "Steer us away from the setting sun and away from Northsphere!"

I feel the vessel turn slightly, rising and curving, and then I see the sun as it slowly descends in purple sky and in the distance I see the city of Northsphere, the tall pearly towers and turrets and the Northern Sea beyond. The second ship follows us, the

Straw Man grumbling as he steers the ship beneath and behind us. He reaches for the last cannonball.

I raise my magnet and command: *"Down, hard!"*

As the big man brings the black ball up in his palm, it suddenly drops out of his fingers and with great force plunks into the wooden deck behind his feet. The blonde aggressor curses loudly, twisting his head, seeing that the ship's haul has a gaping hole. I remember that these flying ships sink if they take on too much air! And so the vessel stops moving and begins to plummet towards the earth!

The Challenger laughs, slapping my shoulder. Fauna slows the ship slightly and turns her head to see what's going on. She smiles. I don't. I scream at her to speed up!

The Straw Man jumps, his powerful legs pushing him off the fast falling ship, bringing his great sprawling body towards us, arms out-stretched! Fauna swears, trying to move, too late. The boat shakes. Two immense hands grasp the stern. The front of the ship tilts upward, my sister managing to grip the levers to keep from falling. I tumble, smacking into the wall of the deck at the back, the two big hands grasping inches from me. The Challenger springs to action, slicing at the hands while the Straw Man pulls himself upward onto the deck. I duck out of the way of the ranger's slashing sword, just in time to see one hand reach for the Challenger, grabbing him by his leg. The Challenger falls, but not before taking his sword in both hands and plunging it at the Straw Man's nearest shoulder.

The foe cries out and falls from our ship, losing his grip, not letting go out the Challenger in his one hand though, taking him with him.

I hastily get back to my feet and rush to the end of the ship, which has re-balanced itself a bit on the air. *"Pull! Grab!"* I nearly spit the words, the mighty magnet in both hands, my two feet pressed against the wall of the stern's deck as I lean the rest of my body over.

Beneath me the Challenger's sword's tip is now attached to the ends of the magnet. The ranger hangs onto the sword, now with both hands. The Straw Man dangles underneath him, legs kicking at empty air, a great field of grass far below. It's so heavy! I feel my arms, shoulders, and back aching in great pain! If I don't let go I fear my arms will break off!

"I can't hold...much…much longer!" I manage to shriek to the Challenger.

"Die orphan!" roars the Straw Man, slobbering as he tries to reach with his other hand, his gigantic form hanging over the side of the stern of the flying ship. The weight brings our ship downward, almost halfway to the ground.

The Challenger yells and he starts kicking the Straw Man's monstrous face. "I have had enough of you and your ridiculous arguments!" he says loudly over the whooshing air, kicking again and again.

The last foot to the face causes the Straw Man to lose his grip. The immense pulling weight gone, I pull my ranger friend upward and he side-flips onto the deck, both of us gazing down at the sight of the Straw Man falling, limbs spinning as he cries out.

He lands maybe one hundred or so feet beneath us with a great crash onto the open field below. I see grasses everywhere in the light of the dusk, a great greenish-yellow field.

The Straw Man from so far away looks wounded, but he immediately gets up, small as he is from this height. I feel a pit grow in my belly. I know what's going to happen. He's going to jump, and he may just have the strength still to reach us.

"Bloody…" the Challenger harshly whispers. Fauna speeds our ship, but it looks like it might not be enough.

The Straw Man places his arms behind his back, crouching, ready to give a great leap towards us and we brace ourselves.

Then I see commotion start moving frantically beneath his feet. I can see it, the whole field begins shifting, at first the grasses closest to him and then the rest of the field. All the grasses flutter in a mad frenzy, looking at first like there are creatures moving quickly within them.

But I know it's not creatures, it's the grass itself!

The Straw Man's big face turns from rage to terror. He screams and waves his arms above his head. His legs are stuck, his feet vanishing into the grasses. He looks beneath him, seeing now that his legs are being devoured.

"Killer Grass!" I yell and I slap the Challenger's back.

The Straw Man falls over, half of him consumed already, still waving his arms, screaming in horror. All around the teethed grasses reach for him, the little blades closest to him biting and tearing his flesh in fury, sending bits of him about the field. His arms fall to his sides only to be grabbed by the Killer Grass next, his fingers, hands, arms and shoulders quickly eaten, the last thing we see from the distance are the long blonde straw-like strands of hair that the Killer Grasses envelope in seconds.

And then he is completely destroyed.

The Challenger and I fall onto the floor of the deck and Fauna puts the ship into high speed, zipping high over the fields of deadly grass-blades, moving eastward towards new lands. This is why I told her to curve away from Northsphere and the sunset, to the South and the East of Northsphere where I knew the fields of Killer Grass lay.

"He's gone," sighs the Challenger, slightly smiling. He looks to me and thanks both of us.

"We're a team!" Fauna shouts back to him. "And now we have this flying ship to continue our adventures!"

The two of us stand up and step across the short deck over to Fauna's side, all of us grinning as the air whooshes in our faces and night finally comes. We had another adventure, another quest, and I have two new items and a strange slug in my head that I probably need to have looked at.

But for now, I'm enjoying my newly recalled knowledge. After all, knowledge is power.

THE END

The Challenger in the Vale of Dragos

If you recall, reader, the three of us had commandeered a flying craft, a magical and mechanical vessel, and we flew it east and south, moving away from the city of Northsphere, the place our friend the Challenger once called home, flying high above the immense fields of Killer Grass that had swallowed our last foe, the dreaded Straw Man. As the night aged we saw in the light of the moon and the stars that the world below us had taken on a mountainous tone.

"These are the Adar Mountains," I tell my companions.

The Challenger nods, scratching the stubble on his chin with the end of his sword. "I've ranged here before, treacherous place," he says, adding: "We only call it the Great Range."

Fauna, my sister, who is driving the wooden wheel at the bow, says to us: "I am going to fall asleep and crash this thing!"

We decide to land and sleep for what's left of the night. We all have scratches and pulled muscles. Sis manages to lower the little ship slowly, finding a large leveled area on the side of

121

one of the mountains near the edge of the range. A sheer drop down a side precipice reveals a dark forested valley below.

"*Pssh-soooo!*" says the Challenger, mimicking the sounds the ship makes as it lands.

We sisters sleep side by side on the small deck of the craft while the Challenger takes the rocky ground beside us. I still have this blue slug in my head, placed by the Straw Man, and with this slimy thing I can recall everything I've ever learned! So, I am un-decided if this is a curse or not. I also have gained in the last ad-venture two helpful items — the Mighty Magnet, with which I can grasp metallic objects with its unseen force, and Delipha's Rod, a magical device that shoots forth seawater. For once I have decent things with which to defend myself. Before this, I had only a dagger, while my sister and the ranger have been consistently well armed during this quest.

I sleep well, so deeply, my dreams flying through rows and rows of bookshelves in soft afternoon sunlight. I wonder, even as I dream, if the slug influences my dream-self as well. When I wake there are drops hitting my face.

"Fauna! Stop!" I yell out my sister's name, thinking she's pouring water on me, or worse.

"Stop what? Making breakfast?" she asks zestfully. I can hear burning and popping and can smell something nice. Sud-denly hungry, I look over and see she is sitting aside a fire with the Challenger close to the wall of rock that rises up from the ledge, the other side across from the cliff. I rub my eyes before I crawl over to join them.

"When you were sleeping your sis went out and got us a mountain fowl," says the Challenger to me. "Smells good? I made a fire with my proficiency skill!"

"Thanks for not telling her I accidentally hit it with the ship," says Sister.

"Oh," I say, realizing I haven't eaten in a day. I get up, making a few stretches, my back to my sister and the ranger and the food. I look out over the far side of the ledge, over the forested valley to the North from where I stand. It is beautiful in the daylight, yet there are clouds, dark ones, forming and moving in from the way we came. Soon we eat the bird together. There isn't much meat, but it fills us up enough. By the time we are done those approaching clouds in the distance have gone grey, some nearly black. Not just rain, but a grand storm is coming. As I volunteer to put out the fire by pointing Delipha's rod some raindrops pound down from above and promptly put it out instead.

"Shall we go then?" Fauna asks with a giggle. We get back into the little boat and my sister attends to the wheel once more, flipping the switch to get the vessel moving. It floats upward, granting the three of us a good look at the rest of the mountain in front of us, and once we hover over a rocky summit we see stretched out before us a whole system of peaks. Some of these enormous mountains rise still higher, and as we move forward at a cautious pace I take in the various formations below and around us.

"These are some of the biggest mountains in this continent!" I tell the others, shouting over a sharp wind that howls through the maze-like mountains. It's fun watching the world pass about you as a wooden floor hums underneath your feet and you feel the dual calming and exciting sensation of movement. I hang on to the rail at the side, looking at the sights as the Challenger stands behind me, the ranger inspecting the view on the other side.

"*Shoooooooobbbbppppp!*" he mimics the sounds of the passing air.

Fauna takes us around a great pair of mountains – or rather just two divergent peaks of one gigantic one – and soon we are traveling through the air between two great stony cliff walls.

There are formations in these walls, I notice, shapes that I can discern, some spiral-like, others like curled shells.

"Wow!" I call in amazement. "Imprints of ancient life from when this continent was mostly underwater. You know, the tops of these peaks were once a series of islands!"

"How do you know all this?" Fauna asks, prompting me to remind her of the brain slug. I had read all these things long ago and now I remember it all word for word, every word on every page, every lesson from every educator, all of it. Cooling shade envelopes the ship and I can hear the rain behind us.

"*We'll* be underwater if we don't hurry!" shouts Fauna, and then she tells me: "So you really should get that slug thing removed, aye?"

"And how would we do that?" says the Challenger. "Maybe stick a rope in her ear and pull it out the other side?"

Fauna chuckles, steering us slightly to the right as a big rock projection comes into view from the left side of the vessel's pointy bow. She raises the ship next, bringing us a little higher and then out of the space between the two massive cliffs. We see shorter mountains below and I can spot river valleys winding about the rising and falling land far beneath.

"Why should I get it removed?" I ask her. "I feel more clear and lucid than ever! You know that feeling when your mind is so sharp? Multiply that by a few hundred. I can remember *everything* I've ever learned!"

"You should have it removed," reasons the Challenger, looking back at me from his side of the ship. "Particularly as it was something implanted in your head without your permission."

The best response to him comes into my mind instantly and I say: "You were given your superhuman strength, speed, and agility without your permission, does that mean that *you* should give it up?"

I realize immediately that I shouldn't have said that.

"I wish none of it happened," he simply says.

"I'm sorry! Sorry!" I call to him across the narrow deck. "But, do you guys understand that the circumstances in which I came to have this gift does not undo the fact that I like having it?"

"A gift?" Fauna says, sounding annoyed. "You consider a slug writhing into your brain a gift?"

"What does your perfect recollection tell you about blue slugs that help you recall all knowledge?" the Challenger then asks.

Before I can reply – as I pause because I don't recall ever reading about this kind of slug – I hear a roar of thunder from behind us. It's distant, but still very loud and...thunderous.

"Maybe we can land somewhere for the storm?" I tell my sister.

"There's Flora, always playing it safe!" she laughs, shaking her head, her red hair under her cap waving in the wind. "We've faced monsters and villains, haven't we? Slug-Lord, Lobster-Man, Frog-Boy, the Straw Man!"

The Challenger laughs too. "I keep thinking our next foe is going to be called Snail Lady or Mucus Guy!" he adds and Sis chuckles heartily.

And then the rains come down hard, almost at once flooding the deck. I feel my socks get drenched (thankful that I have another pair in the pack on my back). Water is falling speedily from the sky and although it falls off of the sides underneath the rails of our little flying vessel, it does so at a slow pace.

"Hang on!" Fauna yells. "Left side, guys!"

We do as she tells us, dashing to her left and hang on tight to the rail. All our items are in the packs on me and my sister's back and the weapons are at belts or strapped up, so everything important is secured. I know my sis and I know what she's going to do. She turns the wheel sharply to her right, sending the ship partly sideways, the water splashing over the side of the rail into the deep valleys below. I wrap my arms around the rail, locking them in place, my feet sliding over the turned deck, and then Fauna turns it back to normal. Within seconds the water is filling the deck again.

Lightning flashes and before the thunder can sound she yells to us: "Maybe we *should* land!"

"If you took my advice we would already be finding a safe place!" I snap at her.

"Not helpful! Okay then," she says, lowering the ship a little. "Guys, look for a place and—"

Thunder erupts in the air. Because of this we don't hear the scraping of the ship's hull against something hard and sharp. When the thunder fades out we hear the very end of the discomforting screeching sound and we look behind us and see a particularly tall and pointy mountain peak that has bits of wood falling from it's sides.

"Did that just?" I ask, standing straight.

The Challenger shrieks over the rain: "Yes!"

Fauna steers the wheel, and the ship moves only slightly.

"Get us down!" I yell, grabbing the rail harder.

The Challenger runs to the front of the ship, leaning over the converging rail at the bow. "There! I see something! Land, open land! A green plateau!"

Not letting go of the rail, I slide my way over to him. Up ahead I see only darkness, but when another lightning bolt flashes I can see exactly what he described – there is a big grassy space, huge really, a vale of sorts, all surrounded by walls of mountain peaks that appear to be conjoined together like turrets on the walls of a castle. On the exterior sides of the mountain walls, as we rapidly approach, I see sheer drops down the mountain sides, with land far, far below. The interior is some kind of raised oasis among the sharp and rocky rising and falling landscape.

"Ugh!" Fauna shrieks. "I barely have control! Hang on!"

The ship partly turned sideways as it falls, then glides a bit, and then shoots down towards the open place, my sister presumably doing what she can to aim us there. All goes dark and then everything lights up once again, and in that moment I can see something on the exterior side of the mountain wall we are coming towards—something is there on the outside of the green vale, right above a very sharp descent down below. Upon the mountain wall I make out a form of some kind and with the slug in my brain I manage to figure out exactly what it is, or what it seems to be.

It's a massive skeleton, its bones white like the snowy mountainside, and it is in the shape of a long necked beast with immense jaws, with a pair of horns sprouting backwards from its pointed skull. It also has four powerful leg bones that strike down from an immense rib-cage. Stretched out behind the main bony body is a pair of great skeletal outstretched wings.

"A dragon?" I ask myself, but the sight is gone, replaced by the higher up peaks of the mountain wall, and then the green grass below. We have passed over the walls of the vale.

The little ship swoops sharply, the green rushing up to us, and we half land, half crash. Losing my grip, I fly through the air as the ground meets us, my body skidding away. I don't know if this is thunder or the sound of wood splintering that I hear.

I am on my back from my side, looking up at all the rain falling straight down from a sky that is totally black. I feel pain all over, but I know that I will be okay as my mind analyzes the wounds. I know the feel, the symptoms; I remember everything I ever read about the body. I am going to be okay. I can only hope the others are the same, but that little blue slug makes it so I know immediately that their chances are not as good, not probable that they survived if they were on the ship when it crashed.

Before I know it I am being dragged by unseen hands. *"Please,"* I plead in my mind. *"Please, for once, do not be something malevolent!"*

Here on this green plateau, our story plateaus as well... I wake a little sore, but more confused. I'm resting on a cozy pillow in a small bed that looks like it was made for someone my size. A furry blanket is covering my toes up to my chin. I'm content and warm, my feet particularly toasty, and I'm fairly sure that my hosts are not captors, or lest they make a comfortable prison. Calming sunlight streams in from a window behind the bed. There's only a small desk and chair across from me and a big closed door.

I lean up and wipe both eyes.

"Fauna!" I cry when my sister comes into focus, feeling a rush of joy. Her arm wrapped in a cloth sling, she stands at the foot of the bed, the sun lighting up her red outfit and cap. She begins slowly laughing. I expect the Challenger to barge in the door next and for the three of us to have a big happy scene, but he doesn't and I ask where he is.

"Are your limbs working?" she asks me.

My legs ache a bit, but I am okay to walk. Sister tells me, as I get up, that she jumped from the bow of the ship as it crashed, landing on her right arm, but was quickly found and brought here.

"Is it broken?" I ask.

"The ship? Yes. If you meant my arm, no, only a little hurt," she says with a smile.

"Where are we?" I ask as we leave the snug sunny room and enter a long hallway with brownish-reddish walls. There are doors every few paces on both sides, small torches hung and burning between them. We head to a bigger door at the end of the hallway.

"Well, I've slept most of the time, just like you," she tells me. "I was told I was out for two days."

"Really?" I gasp, realizing that there are some things that my blue brain slug cannot determine; time and space become warped when one is wounded and asleep. I also realize I am not wearing my spectacles. "Are the people here friendly?"

"They tended to us, didn't they?" Fauna says as she pushes the large door to reveal a chamber three times the size of the room we were just in. Warm air hits me as we enter. It feels like a summer marsh. There is glistening fog everywhere, but I can make out the four walls, the furthest of which has a few small windows. The daylight makes little rainbows in the steam.

I hear a man's voice humming some random melody. Before us is a big porcelain tub set in the middle of the room. Our ranger friend is taking a steaming hot bath in bubbly water. He splashes as he turns around and I can make out a smile on his face.

He shouts happily: "I was wondering when you'd wake up!"

"And how are you?" I ask, feeling immediate relief.

The Challenger stands, sending water over the sides of the tub, and I can barely see him in the colourful steam and with my bad eyes, but I can make out that his body is about as hairy as his face. Fauna finds a towel hanging off the wall near the doorway and throws it to him. He jumps, largely concealed by the vapour, splashing, landing perfectly on the marble floor like a cat, snatching the towel midair. He wraps it about his waist and I see red and brown marks over his muscled torso, and I ask him if he is hurt.

"Nothing the good healers couldn't handle," he says, winking, still wearing his eye-patch. "For once we end up somewhere friendly!"

"Healers?" I ask.

"Healers!" a defiant voice interjects from behind and I turn, seeing a slender figure in white stepping over from the left wall, a woman. I can see that she stands slightly taller than me and her hair is a deep green shade of which I can only see a little of under the white shawl that is wrapped about her head. I can't make out her face aside that her eyes are big and also green.

"Hello," I say, her presence both calming and intimidating.

"Greetings to you, Miss Flora," says she in a softer tone. She approaches, smelling flowery, and presents to me a pair of spectacles, wide-rimmed, blue framed, and circular like my old ones. I take them and put them on my nose. I can see her now. She is maybe in her early or mid thirties (an older young person) with smallish features. She too wears spectacles, big ones like me.

"New lenses," she tells me.

I look her over and can see better than ever. "Thank you!"

She smiles, showing dimples and I feel warmth on my face. She then pulls out a tiny feather quill and a small scroll that she rests on her palm for support. "Do you feel any pains in your head or inside your body?"

"No," I tell her truthfully. "Maybe a bit tired. Fauna came and got me." I look at my white gown and my face turns warm. "I guess you took my clothes."

"The clothes were dirty, ripped. We cleaned them, us girls, sewed them. And we have all your items," she says and smiles again as she looks over at my sister and the Challenger. "You guys have quite the interesting stash! I am guessing that you're adventurers?"

"How did you guess?" asks the Challenger with a chuckle, wiping his wet hair with his dripping hand.

She laughs before she turns to me once more: "I imagine you have questions?"

I nod eagerly. "Many!" I say and ask: "What is *this* place?"

"You've never heard of it? Few outsiders have, I imagine. We once called ourselves New Northsphere because most of our people were from there."

"Oh yeah," Fauna says and looks at me. "We literally just saved Old Northsphere."

"Yeah, I'm from there originally," adds the Challenger, coming over to stand next to us sisters.

"Oh? And for a while we were even known as South Northsphere," says Emera next.

"Oh, confusing," says Fauna.

"Our ancestors thought so. Over the generations many others have been brought here from elsewhere too, so we nowadays call our home the Vale of Dragos," our new host explains.

"Dragos?" I ask, my brain slug turning up no reference.

"We've been here for at least two hundred years. Let me take you on a balcony tour and then I can answer more questions," says the green-haired healer. She tells us to meet her in the hallway soon and tells us her name is Emera as she leaves.

"She seems nice," I tell the others once the big door is shut behind her.

The Challenger nods. Fauna tells me that she has a daughter she saw earlier, a little version of Emera who is really cute. My ranger friend turns to me and mouths something, something that I can't quite make out. A pair of attendants, a smiley boy and a girl who looks younger than me and Sis, arrive with my clothes and a tray with three glasses of a juice that is undecided between lemon and orange, but very refreshing. We soon get our items back as well, our weapons and my two magical items, and I go back to my lent room to change. The clean fabrics are nice and bouncy and pressed and smelling meadowy!

Fauna and I then fetch the now clothed Challenger and Emera returns and takes us down the other way of the corridor and then up a set of winding stairs that remind me of the library we were in on our last adventure. We arrive up in a big room, an atrium with a high ceiling, a golden dome with four bronze-hued beams that run out from the circular edges and conjoin in the middle into a cross (or an X depending on what angle). I can hear Fauna gasp but I am looking at Emera, who has moved on up ahead toward one of the walls where there is a big door.

"We see a lot of atriums in our adventures," remarks the Challenger.

I follow our green-haired host out the door to a balcony that wraps around this tall building we are in. Fauna and the Challenger soon arrive at our sides and it is here that Emera tells us it's the Healing House, and she seems to anticipate the next thing I want to ask her.

"There is our library," she says, pointing an arm, moving to the stone rail. I see across the way an even taller tower, about six stories, a pearl-white spire that is set among the roofs of smaller structures. It is far taller than any of the other things I see, most of which from here are just roofs of various colours. She then moves her pointing hand to the next largest building in view, a big pastel green one that is as wide as the library is tall and she tells us this is their great hall.

I lean my upper body over the rail slightly. Spreading out from the base of the Healing House, straight down, I see a brick road and a line of what appear to be markets, typical box-like shops, some with tents over counters at their fronts. Beyond is another street and then a complex of homes, some two, others three storeys tall. I also see great spaces, open plazas among the clustered structures, and I see too what look like wagons, tiny from here, that move through the streets and squares, strangely with no horses at the lead. There are people too, many people, and they swarm the streets. As far as I look are more lanes and buildings, and it all expands on until I see fields and more unpaved spaces with homes further apart from one another. Farther on, between where the buildings end and the far mountain range begins, is great farmland, meadows, and some clumps of woodlands with winding rivers.

"You don't even need a town gate," remarks the Challenger to our host. "You know, for when barbarians and kobolds might try to raid?"

"Doesn't happen here," Emera says with a shrug and a shake of her head, her face bunching up a bit. She then leads the three of us all the way around the stone balcony. It is thin, this balcony, but has enough space for us to walk aside one another. There are beautiful flowers in pots every five feet or so, some with flying insects buzzing about them. Here on this far side of the balcony we see that we are closer to the great wall of rock that rises from this edge of the city. At its base I see wooden shacks and lines of track. I look at my sister and the ranger, seeing all three of their eyes grow wide in amazement.

"Mines," Emera tells us. "There are rocks under these mountains, as far as we can dig. The miners," she says, motioning her head and sighing. "They go only so far."

"Oh, is that true?" asks Fauna and she looks at me. I know what she will ask next. "Can we go through the mines, under the mountains and leave when we're fully healed?"

"Yeah, I probably just need a few more hit points and I'll be good to get ranging again," says the Challenger and winks with his one eye again.

Emera, our host and healer who has been thus far so warm and friendly, suddenly looks sad. She bites her lower lip and speaks: "I am really sorry, but no one leaves the Vale of Dragos."

"What?" I say and gaze at her, trying to recall something, anything I might know about this place, how to leave, or if I saw something as we fell that could be a way out. I find nothing.

"Oh, we don't work well as captives," Fauna groans.

Emera shakes her head. "No, it's not that. It's just—no one *can* leave. We are trapped until Dragos returns and brings us out. Until that day, I'm afraid you're New Northspherians, or Dragosians, or whatever. Sorry. But it's not a bad place to live. And we are told that Dragos will come back soon."

"Dragos?" I ask. Even without the help of the brain slug I can tell where this is going. "Tell me about Dragos…is this a big dragon with horns and wings?"

Emera smiles again and nods and the image of the gigantic draconian skeleton I saw on the other side of the mountains as we crashed suddenly emerges in my mind.

"Ooooohhhhh."

The bones, those enormous skeletal wings, each bumpy vertebra running from its neck to its tail—I see this in my head. That slug in there is helping me remember it perfectly. I wonder in that moment if I should tell her what I saw. I think back to when I was a child, how Mother always told us sisters the importance of speaking the truth, even if the consequences were not good – truth itself, she would say, was a good thing.

We four are soon back in the atrium, looking up at what my sister and the Challenger had been staring at before. There is a dome, white framed, with four quadrants divided by bronze crossbeams. In each quadrant is a quarter of a cheesewheel-shaped canvass. I see the one that Emera is now pointing to. Yep, it's a dragon.

"Dragos," my sis echoes from my side. The dragon depicted in the quadrant is of blue-green scale, of a majestic shape and stature, and He floats above a flooded land, a town I deduce from the little pointy tops of homes that poke out from the rushing waters.

"He brought us from Delipha's Deluge, when the lowland part of Northsphere was flooded."

"Now the city is only on the highland part," remarks the Challenger. I deduce that this flood, which I have a memory of reading about in part, took place long before the Challenger was born.

"Is it? I'm glad to hear that the city still lives then. It was bigger once, back when the lowlands flooded. That's what I was taught when I was Emeratu's age."

"Emeratu?" I ask.

"Her daughter," says Fauna and Emera smiles warmly.

"These paintings could have saved us a lot of exposition," remarks the Challenger and he points his ranger arm to the next panel over. Dragos is smaller here, centered in the middle, for the image is of sky and clouds with mountains at the base. I see a strike of lightening behind the tail of the dragon, and in the next panel I see green. This is the vale, and Dragos looks tiny above the mountains, and there are the figures of people, many folks crowding within field and town.

"And what is that?" I ask Emera as I step past my sister to look up at the fourth part of the dome. I see a scene of white and in the middle what looks like a brown wheel with a square-shaped gem of some kind in its midpoint, a green-blue thing.

"Ah, the foundation of our society," says she to me. "While we wait here in the Vale we have the gems of Dragos. That is what the miners mine. All moving things are powered by them, for we have no horses here."

"That explains why I thought I saw wagons moving by themselves," I say. In the sunlight Emera's face lights up and I feel calm despite the situation.

"You have gems that power things?" Fauna asks her. My sister looks at me, raising an eyebrow. I begin to catch on to what she is thinking.

"Why not create something to get out of the Vale?" I ask.

135

"Well, we are not to leave until Dragos is come," she simply says.

"You've got a real Captain Walker sort of situation here," says the Challenger.

We hear commotion from beyond the room, from the city underneath the balcony outside. People have gathered, I can tell, and the sharp sound of a horn rings strongly. Emera leads us back to the stairs. We have with us our items in new packs on our backs, me and Sister, even snugger than the ones we had earlier. I check as we go down some steps, making sure that Delipha's Rod and the Mighty Magnet are in my bag. They are.

"It's funny," Emera says as we make it to the floor beneath. "There have been talks of making machines with legs to climb over the mountain walls, but the Gem Priests won't allow it."

"Gem Priests?" Fauna asks her, walking with her in front of myself and the Challenger.

I hear a voice in my head, a deep yet soft voice. *"Yes, Gem Priests won't allow much of anything."*

"Did anyone else hear that?" I ask once we step down a new flight of stairs.

"Hear what?" Fauna asks.

"What were you saying, Emera?" I ask, unsure if she had spoken, though the voice I heard sounded quite different, older. We reach the ground floor, a large chamber with two marble pillars. A great double door of turquoise hue stands before us at the end. The floor is heavily carpeted in a dull grey.

"The Gem Priests are instructors," Emera says and laughs a little. "And they forbid anything to move except a wheel. Wheels can't go up mountainsides, can they?"

"Depends on the wheel and the mountainside," says the Challenger and grins. "But generally, no, wheels cannot go up mountains. A skilled ranger, like myself though, just with my two feet, that's another story."

"Many have tried, all failed," says Emera, leading us across the grey carpeting to the big doors to outside.

"Many were not me," is all he says in response.

"There are ways, both above and under, but both are deadly," the same voice rings again in my head. As I rub my face with both hands, feeling sweat dripping down my forehead, Fauna and the Challenger both grab the two big doors and open them, drenching us in bright light.

"That thing in your head," I hear next. *"That slug. It is a gift to a point. Apart from preserving all your memories, it will eventually give you the power to speak with others with your mind as I am doing now. I can send messages to you."*

I shake my head. The gleaming light overwhelms my sight at first, but after a few seconds I see figures emerge, silhouettes at first, but they begin to become focused. The first I notice are two tall ones, really tall things with thick heads and long necks. As they come more into sight I see that they are automatons, machines, of some kind, with wide square-shaped bottoms, each with two large wheels on their sides. They have arms, and they hold what look like great pole-arms with ax-like double blades of green-blue colour. Their tall bodies and necks and heads are one colour each, one is a dark green, the other a dark blue, and they both share the same menacing face with painted teeth upon clenched jaws and big wild yellow eyes that make them appear as if they have taken some plant that gives immense energy or something.

Dragons, they look like dragon-men, yet they stand three times as tall as an average man and are on wheels! The dragon-guard things stand among the people, a blue one to the left, green on the right. One man who stands among the others. He wears an ornate green towering hat upon his head. The tall cap rises from his forehead as one but then splits into two wing-like shapes facing out from one another. In his left hand he bears a blue staff with the head of—you guessed it—a dragon with twin horns that flow backwards from the head.

I see my sister to my left wave a hand at the crowd, while the Challenger crosses his arms. Emera slinks away a little, as if she sees this as 'our moment'. They are murmuring, these townsfolk. I see green and blue hair, as well as some that are in between. There are among them folks in brown, short ones mostly, both men and women, many with what looks like dirt on their faces and round helmets upon their heads. I notice one of them, a small woman who holds a long shovel in her hands and I deduce that these must be miners.

The man with the staff and tall winged hat speaks: "People of Dragosia!" he exclaims in a resonant voice, waving his staff, his long blue robes twirling about his tall figure slightly in the breeze. A short man clad in green tights by his side suddenly blasts the trumpet he bears, a bit too close to the ear of the tall hatted man who grimaces and shuts his eyes at the sound.

"He is Gemok," says Emera to us from behind.

"High Gem Priest," I hear the unseen woman's voice in my head. I look around. We face west and the sun beams on us and I have to raise a hand to scan the faces of the crowd, most of whom are smiling, and I feel glad that they seem welcoming. I notice one face, a thin face of a woman with white and purple strands of hair that fall a bit past her shoulders. The pieces of hair look ragged, matching the rest of her frail appearance. She wears a grey gown and I can see her arms are so skinny at her sides. Our eyes meet and she smiles slightly. She looks truly old, nearly ancient. I know immediately this is her.

"I am Qilla. I am a librarian," she says in my mind.

"We have new peers, new villagers! Tell us your names! I am Gemok, High Priest of Dragosia!" says the tall man and he ap-

138

proaches us and the short green-clad retainer steps forward with him and gives a small curtsy before blowing the trumpet again in Gemok's ear.

The High Priest whups the little man with the bottom of his staff and he falls over, dropping the trumpet.

"Greetings and welcome to your new home!" Gemok then greets us.

"There are ones like Gemok, the Belows we call them," I hear Qilla's voice. *"And there are those like me, the Aboves. Most of the folk here are of my thinking, yet so many of his ilk have power. Meet me at the library and I shall tell you more."*

I realize that I am being placed in the middle of a power struggle of some kind. I do not want this. I only wish to find a way to leave. My sister speaks: "Greetings, I am Fauna!"

"I am Flora, Daughter of Flora!" I then announce to the crowd and the High Priest and we hear our names echo among the assembled.

"And who is this stranger?" asks Gemok, tipping his staff slightly toward our ranger friend.

"The Challenger," he says simply.

"Only problem is," continues Fauna. "Is we are not from here and were on our way home from an adventure!"

"There is no way from the Vale of Dragos!" declares Gemok, telling us what we had been told. The crowd begins agreeing loudly, many of them nodding and chattering among themselves. "Until the day Dragos returns to bring us back into the world, I am sorry to say, you are one of us here in the Vale!"

"See?" says Emera from behind us meekly. "Sorry."

"Only thing is," I begin, hesitating, but I look over to my sister and the ranger before continuing: "Well, thing is, Dragos is long dead! I saw the dragon's bones on the other side of the mountain!"

There is a collective gasp that begins with Gemok, spreads to his little retainer, and then surges through the crowd. And then a few screams rise up from the mass and I can see the two Dragon-faced things, those tall sentinels with the painted faces. The two of them had raised their pole-arms the moment the words left my mouth. Gemok gawks at us, his lofty hat fluttering as his neck cranks backwards. I see mothers covering the ears of children. Sister had always told me to know when to hold my tongue, especially outside of our home. I raise my hands and am about to try to be heard again.

"Lies!" yells the High Priest as the retainer blows his trumpet again. Gemok smacks him down with his staff, sending the small man against the cobbled walkway.

"Hey!" yells the Challenger. "If you're the High Priest you should be more relaxed, especially with all the green you're wearing! If my friend says she saw the bones of a dragon on the other side of the mountain before we crashed here, then I believe her because she's got the highest Intelligence Stats ever!"

"Silence!" declares Gemok, trying to raise his voice over the crowd and he bends his spindly form over his fallen retainer and grabs the trumpet from him and blows the mouthpiece, the booming noise overtaking the crowd's cries.

"What do we do?" asks Fauna to my side. I see the Challenger reach for his sword from his hilt at his waist. One of the miners, a big yet squat man with a sleeveless tunic that reveals bulging muscles, has stepped towards him, spade in hand.

"Challenger!" I call and raise then lower my hand. He looks over with his uncovered eye, and takes a step back. The muscular miner steps forward with two friends at his sides. I don't want us to fight our hosts; they're not monsters, not villains, but folks who healed us and have been hospitable.

"You are unseen, all three of you," Qilla's voice sounds in my head. *"Follow my lead!"*

140

I see her past a thinning wing of the crowd, her long purple and white and silver hairs flap a little in the breeze.

"I think we are invisible!" I tell Fauna, though it seems we can still see one another.

The Challenger steps towards the big miner, who seems to not see him, and waves his hands in front of the man's face before the ranger extends two fingers from his gloved hand and pokes the man in the eyes. He shrieks and covers them and the Challenger laughs and quickly side-steps him and the other two.

"Come!" I tell them in a harsh whisper and I see some of the nearby faces glance around like they heard me, which they probably did.

"Where did they go?" Gemok cries. People rush forth to where we just stood.

I see Emera there, hanging back near the door and I call to Qilla, asking her to help our healer friend. The three of us scramble to our left and we slink through a path between standing bodies towards the older woman.

"Make her unseen!" says the Challenger, seemingly understanding.

Gemok points his staff at the healer and says to her: "Tell us, who are these people that you healed?"

"I—I don't know!" Emera stammers.

"Come this way!" I cry to her as I hear more gasps, a big one from the High Priest. She too must be invisible to them now! Emera rushes to us and the four of us follow Qilla, who's speedier than expected, leading us through the shifting forms of folks and then through cobbled streets, passing by more than a few horseless wagons. I get a look at one as it passes, just barely missing Emera by a tiny bit as she moves. A man is in the front, the carriage filled with bags. I see one of these bags towards the top is slightly open, and I see something bright and green-blue inside.

141

"We're nearly there," says Qilla in my mind. We run by a row of brick homes, and then a single long structure with numerous doors in its front, and then we take a turn into an alley, my sister and me at the rear behind the Challenger and Emera now. As we come to another alley a figure darts out between us, a tall man I notice before me and Fauna crash into him. He falls at our feet and we jump over him. I see his face, pink skinned with a pair of shaded spectacles on his face above a big nose. He wears a black round cap, which falls off. He seems stunned as I see him stand once more when we turn a corner.

"That was the Constable!" Emera cries to me.

"Sorry Constable!" Fauna yells back at him.

We arrive at a small courtyard area that has two tall oak-looking trees set on opposite sides. Before us looms the tall library we saw earlier from afar.

"We end up in a lot of libraries too," notes the Challenger as he takes Emera's hand, for she had been trailing a little behind him.

"What happened?" she asks, panic in her voice.

"I told them the truth," I say defiantly. "Why did this happen?"

"Some people do not want to hear it," says Qilla, the first words that come from her mouth. "You know this, Sister Emera."

"Is it true?" our green-haired friend asks, facing me, struggling with the next words: "Is Dragos...dead?"

Sister tells her: "If Flora saw it, she remembers perfectly. You see, you may not have seen it when you were healing her, but there is a slug in her head."

"Yeah," adds the Challenger. "This blue slug gives her perfect memory of everything she ever saw."

"Come inside, I cannot keep you cloaked much longer," says Qilla, walking to the wooden door at the top of three stone steps, bunches of leaves floating from her feet as she goes. I take a quick look around the courtyard, noting the soft shadows from the trees. There are two alleyways, the one we came from to the left and another to the right between two more buildings.

We enter. It is cool in here, on this first floor that has a ceiling four times our height. There is a wooden counter at the front covered in cobwebs and beyond are shelves of books shrouded in dust. It looks as if no one comes here and I ask Qilla if this is so.

"Myself and Hue," she says.

"Hue?" Fauna asks, glancing about the dusty room.

Qilla smiles and says: "Hue!"

"Did you call me, Sweet One?" a man's voice asks, seemingly from above us. I look up and freak out a bit. I see an old man's face, his head with only a few white hairs and a longish silver beard that is hanging; he is upside down! His body, his torso and shoulders are small and he is dressed in a plain grey cloth tunic.

"What are you, a bat?" the Challenger asks and Fauna giggles.

"I wish I were sometimes!" he says and smiles, the wrinkles on his face shifting as he lowers himself from the beams at the ceiling, one single long wooden leg reaching the floor. Now I see it, his legs, all four of them.

"Whoa!" my sister cries. To her side the Challenger and Emera's mouths hang open as the man lowers himself to the floor, hanging from one leg as his three other legs land, the last one letting go when the rest of him is set before us.

"Welcome from the two denizens of the Library of Dragosia," Qilla says. "More of the folks spend their time in the temple rather than the library. Here is empty of people but full of knowledge."

We all gaze at the old man named Hue. He has his two upper thighs and pelvis, but instead of normal legs he has four long slightly curved things made of dark wood, two in front, two in back, the bottom of each of them curving sharply, likely so he can grasp things. He stands nimbly upon these large legs, twice as tall as the Challenger upon them.

"You are using these instead of wheels?" Emera asks him.

He nods. "Wheels cannot climb. I lost my legs some time ago," he says and smiles, showing half his teeth are missing. "Ah well, this is who I am."

"Is there a way out of the Vale?" asks Fauna. "We didn't mean to cause problems here, honest!"

Hue shakes his head. "There is no way out. I have tried with my mechanical legs. At night I have climbed the mountain walls, tried to get to the top of this bowl, too steep!"

"Is there way to climb back in from the other side?" the Challenger asks and I wonder why he asks this.

Hue shrugs. "There may be, it is said that the other side is not so steep. One may come over from the other side, and travelers have done so before but then they could never leave!"

"We are Aboves," Qilla explains. "We wish to find ways to the outside world and we have long suspected that Dragos is not returning."

"Oh," I say at this news. "Are there others?"

"More than you know," says Qilla and Hue nods, resting forward a little on his front two legs, his two aft legs lowering a little.

Emera shrugs. "I know there are those that didn't believe Dragos would return, but I always thought He would." And then she looks afraid and says: "I need to get back to my daughter!"

"Is she with her father?" the Challenger asks her, looking concerned in his one eye.

"She is with her uncles," Emera says solemnly. "But I need to warn them that commotion is coming! I don't know what, but the townsfolk seem upset and Gemok—when he gets angry…"

The Challenger immediately offers to escort Emera, and I am a bit taken aback at his concern for her. I think it's sweet of him.

"I cannot make you unseen if I am not there, and not for long," says Qilla lamentably.

Hue laughs and I see his belly shake a bit. "Oh, we have some stuff in the Dramatic Arts Department. Come! We've got some fake beards and old robes, have you two looking like wayward sages in no time!" He walks like a tall spider, leading the Challenger and Emera down the way between bookshelves.

It is just Qilla, Fauna, and I now in this dusty chamber, when I ask about the slug. She tells me that she had one specimen in the library long ago, but knows not where it came from and has found no reference in any book, only that when it escaped its cage it crawled in her head and gave her the ability to retain all learned knowledge. She liked it at first, she explains, and as she aged it became stronger and gave her telepathy and the ability to make her and others temporarily unseen. Qilla tells me that it had made her far weaker and exhausted whenever she uses it now. I ask her how to remove it and she tells me she doesn't know, but advises me to do so if I ever can and soon.

Fauna asks her a few questions, and I tune out, thinking about this thing in my head. After a short time I hear the footfalls of Hue's wooden legs and he appears from a door at the back of the room. He greets us, telling us that the ranger and the healer have left in full disguise.

"Good," says Fauna. "Now, we need to figure something out. The mines, can we travel underneath?"

Qilla gasps. "Oh, there are ways, or so we are told, through the mountain; the Under the Dark we call it, but it is said

145

that there are things down there more frightening than anything in the above world."

Fauna says to me: "This might be our way out."

I begin to ponder, but am interrupted by a loud smash. There is, or was, a glass window behind us near the front. Evening light beams in and a single stone the size of my head lands near my sister.

Fauna sprints to the window, looking out.

"We know you're in there!" we hear the voice of Gemok shout. "Come out or we burn the library!"

Outside on the floor of the cobbled courtyard stands a row of figures and I know the two tall ones with thin necks and long faces are the Dragon Guards, whatever they are. In their fists I see pole-arms, the light of their gem axes glow in the shadow of the tower we are in.

"Come out!" calls a man.

"That's the Constable we ran into," Fauna laments. "He must have seen us when we were made visible again."

Through the small smashed window I see the man with a black round cap atop a head too big for his thin body. To his side a slightly taller man in green steps forward, a dragon-head scepter in hand, Gemok. His face is twisted in an enraged snarl and his cheeks flex as if he is fighting a battle with us with his stare. The little man with the trumpet is at his side, peering out from behind the priest's robes. There are more, miners, the burly man who'd gotten poked by the Challenger earlier. He looks angry as he stands with two other miners bearing their spades. More come from the alley to the right, shadows at first, then I see some bearing pitchforks while we hear shouts of *"Blasphemers!"*

"They're farmers," we hear Qilla say. We notice she and Hue have come over to the space right behind us and are peering out the broken window.

"I knew that," says Sister and turns back to the scene.

146

"I count eighteen," I say.

"Me too," says Qilla.

"I third that," says Hue and takes a wooden step back and then raises three of his legs up in front of him to show us. Qilla beckons us all away from the window. Once we move Fauna gets her sword out and I am rummaging through my pack-sack (or whatever you call it) for my magnet and Delipha's Rod, putting my bag back on my back as I hold both items in my hands, my dagger at my belt. I don't want to use it. There must be a way out of this that's peaceful!

"Alright," says Qilla. "You girls hide. I'll deal with them. And Hue, try not to show your four-legged self to the villagers this time?"

"I am only a village legend, keeps people in after dark lest they be spotted by the Four-Legged Wanderer!" he half-laughs and then begins to step on his wooden legs backward into the shadows of the inner library.

Fauna moves to intercept Qilla. "I got an idea," my sister tells her.

As far as Gemok and the gathered folk can see, only the old librarian emerges from the front door and steps into the light of the moon and the crowd's burning torches. She speaks: "Good-night to you, Gemok. There is no one here save for myself!"

Some of the miners behind him snarl. The two sentinels wheel forward a little.

"Lies!" Gemok declares and wags his dragon-headed scepter at her and pouts his lips, his bushy eyebrows flinging into his tall winged cap.

"No one save me!" returns Qilla, though in truth my sister and I and Hue are present.

The High Priest 's face turns red and his head looks like a tomato with a long double winged stem. He moves toward the older woman and, scepter in both hands, he charges hard, checking Qilla across the shoulders, the rod of his staff slamming against her frail frame. She falls back, making a small noise as she hits the street beneath. I hear two more cries, angry ones, my sister and Hue. All three of us are beside Qilla, having been made unseen by her, but now her concentration breaks and we all appear at her side. Fauna, closest to Qilla, has already unleashed her sword and stands poised to cut as the blade arrives near Gemok's neck.

The priest freezes as he sees the glint on the weapon. Sister pauses her stroke. I see a wooden leg swing from one side above, smacking the side of Gemok's head. Hue hovers over him now, pouncing all four of his curved feet upon him, pinning him to the ground. Members of the mob shriek at the sight. I run to Qilla.

Coughing, she leans up and gives me an eager nod to tell me she is fine. "So long as my head is unhurt," she says as she stands. I tell her she should get inside, but she won't leave her husband. Hue picks Gemok up by the neck in a curved leg and throws him across the courtyard. The little trumpet retainer screams like a frightened rooster and runs after him into the shadows. The Constable runs as well. Fauna still has her sword drawn.

"Sorry!" she shouts to Qilla. Two of the miners step toward Sis, the biggest one swinging his spade. Fauna ducks as it comes exceptionally close, and then she cuts her blade twice in the air, causing the miners to jump back to the others in the crowd.

I hear Gemok shouting from afar: "Stop them! We need inquisitive questioning!"

Before me the green dragon guard slides toward Hue, swinging the turquoise pole-arm, prompting the old four-legged man to lean back, his two front legs raised before him defensively. He gingerly backs to the library as the sentinel move forward. Hue shoots a curved end of a leg at the middle of the pole-arm, grasping and pulling. Now they're tugging back and forth, clasped together at the staff's midpoint, Hue glaring up at the long face that peers down at him.

Qilla reaches an arm towards her husband and the dragon sentinel, and then Hue vanishes. The guard, though its face is in a permanent grimace appears stunned, and it falls back a bit, seemingly surprised that its adversary seems to be gone. Its big boxy fingers are still rolled about its gem tipped pole-arm, yet something else grips it, Hue's unseen wood feet/hands, and I see it fling from the guard's grasp and then hover above its tall head. The sharp green-blue blade comes slicing down into the dragon-face of the green automaton and bright gem-coloured light splits from the impact; I see Hue's form, looming over the fallen thing, and he raises the pole-arm once again, slicing hard against the green face.

I tear my own face from the sight as bright light emerges from the impact, looking to my left to Fauna, who shields the side of her vision with her free hand. The blue sentinel now wheels towards her, slowly at first, but it seems to use the distraction of its fallen comrade to sneak up on her. When Fauna realizes it's moved in the dragon guard is standing right over her, and she looks up and raises her blade.

"Qilla!" I call, and leap to Fauna's side, raising the Mighty Magnet in my right hand and Delipha's Rod in the other.

The magnet does nothing, and as I get a close look at the big form I see that there is no metal, only painted wood.

Delipha's Rod! It shoots forth seawater! The stream hits the fake maw of the dragon face, filling its fake mouth, pushing the fake head upwards, jolting it for only a second. I keep spraying, moving the stream downward to its chest (which is also fake). Salt water is splashing in my face. Through my burning eyes I see the mighty sentinel move back. Fauna jumps to her left, and the pole-arm comes crashing down where she stood. I am still shooting the water. The long blue face glances about, ignoring the water that is still ricocheting off of it and hitting me.

"Duck!" Fauna shouts to me. She usually calls me an Owl.

I dive and start scrambling away and, hunching over like an ape, I run. Leaving puddles behind me, I hear the wheels of the sentinel give chase. Instinctively in panic, I roll to my side, the gem ax missing me…barely, and I see, for one split moment, that Hue is now surrounded by villagers, the green sentinel crumpled beneath him. They wave their torches at him and he backs off in the shadowed alleyway behind him. My attention snaps back to myself as I next see the gem ax come for me again, this time from my other side, and I roll back the way I came. It misses once more, but then it turns about as quickly as I dash around the sentinel's form.

I hear the trumpet blare from the far end of the courtyard, from the shadows where Hue had earlier tossed Gemok. I raise the Mighty Magnet again and I wave it as I activate it. My feet move while I quickly point the two thick ends of the item at the crowd and the courtyard. *"Pull!"* I cry, suddenly stopping as I stand with the looming sentinel between myself and the crowd.

The trumpet, at least six pitchforks, four shovels, the dragon-head scepter, and a few other metallic tools all fly from the crowd, slamming against the dragon sentinel at various places. The flying objects that smash against it's turned side only serve as a distraction. This is enough for me to run to my sister, who is now beside Hue, swinging her blade at the space between the four-legger and the crowd now bare of any weaponry save torches.

"Freak!" I hear a man shout to Hue.

"Get some wheels, blasphemer!" someone else yells.

Hue is backing towards the library, Fauna and I at his side. Qilla is with us too, and she makes us unseen once more. I am still dripping seawater. The mob edges forward slightly, all taunting us even if they only see water pooling in our place. The sentinel that still stands, the one I just ran from, rolls to us, ready to swing at the space we occupy.

"*This is my fault,*" I think.

The blue sentinel raises the gem pole-arm again. I gaze up in horror.

Two ropes appear from behind it, two ropes with loops tied at the ends. One goes about its long neck, another on the end of the pole-arm. A third rope, a bigger one, shoots up and goes about its body, about its arms. Next I see a figure, two figures, up on the dragon sentinel's massive shoulders.

I hear Qilla's voice in my head: "*Is that not your friend?*"

The Challenger!

The other's face is covered in green and black cloth!

Our ranger friend begins slashing the side of the long face of the automaton with his blade. The other person, attired in black clothing, lowers onto one of the thing's bulky arms, and then leaps to the ground. I see two other folks come forward from the crowd, and at first I think they are part of the mob, but I notice they too have their faces covered save their eyes. In their hands are large brass vials, which they promptly spew at the automaton. I then see another person, a woman, I think, with green cloth over her mouth and nose. She grabs a torch from someone's hands and throws it.

The dragon sentinel is aflame! It backs away fast, the fires growing, and then it wheels away down the alleyway, lighting up the shadows as it flees.

My sister and I begin laughing in massive relief as members of the crowd seem confused. I look over and see around a dozen folks now, faces covered, their backs to us, fronts to the mob, some pushing them away. I hear Gemok yell something: "This isn't over!"

Soon the courtyard is cleared of the torch wielding mob. Only our small party, Qilla and Hue, and the masked folks, about a dozen or so, remain.

The woman with the green cloth on her face removes it.

"Emera!" I cry in amazement.

The healer smiles, but promptly puts a finger to her lips. Qilla has made us visible again.

"And my brothers," she says, introducing us to two other masked men who nod to us. We thank them and everyone else who came out to protect us.

Fauna pats the Challenger on the shoulder and both smile. "You think I would miss a fight?" asks the ranger cockily.

Emera looks to the downed dragon sentinel, the one that Hue had destroyed. "I have a feeling we have a long fight before us," she says.

"I'm so sorry," I say. "This is our fault."

Emera shakes her head. Qilla does the same. They insist this was an eventuality, someone would have revealed the truth.

"Because of what happened we found new allies," says Qilla, looking to Emera and the others before looking at us three visitors. "Now friends, do you wish to leave?"

Fauna and I exchange looks. Both of us can tell the other thinks that it's for the best. The Challenger tells Hue he wants to return one day, coming over the other side of the mountain, as Hue had told him earlier was possible. The ranger looks to Emera and quickly tells her that he will return. Qilla then tells us that Hue and her will escort us into the mines and take us deep where the Under the Dark begins.

"The priests warn that the land beneath is full of dangerous things," says Emera.

"Same priests that say that Dragos is returning?" I ask and she shrugs.

"Thank you for everything," Fauna tells her.

"Thank you, Dragosia Antifa Chapter!" the Challenger says to those wearing masks as Qilla makes us unseen once more.

Qilla and Hue travel with us through the Vale. I wish I had proper time to see Dragosia but we soon come to an immense cave, the entrance to the mines. We follow tracks, of which there are many, and we follow one a long way, slowly moving downward as the floor of the mine descends. We reach an open chamber that's lightened only by a few sparse torches on the walls. There is a portal, an entrance-way only a bit bigger than ourselves. Beside it is a wooden sign that reads: **To the Under the Dark, Forbidden by Holy Decree.**

Qilla makes us seen once more. Hue stands over us, smiling with his kindly face. I will miss this cute couple. They bid us farewell and assure us that they will watch over Emera and her family and that more villagers are willing to join them in the fight against Gemok.

We three stare into the dark tunnel before us.

Fauna turns to the Challenger. "Do you wish to stay and help them?"

"Part me does, but I won't let you two venture alone into a dangerous place," he says and smiles. "I am with you until we reach daylight."

Qilla hands us a bag full of breads. Hue waves with three of his four legs.

We depart into the Under the Dark…

The journey continues…

THE END

The Challenger in the Under the Dark

We departed the Vale of Dragos and thus entered this sub-terranean domain, getting access through the old mines. I'm gracious most to Emera, that green-haired friend who hosted and healed us, and also to Qilla and her multi-mechanical limbed husband, Hue, for they had protected us. The three of us now make our way through an enormous tunnel.

Our ranger friend, The Challenger, lights up a torch with the fast burning wood we were gifted, and he says to us "Stay close together. There are older and fouler things than kobolds in the deep places of the world."

To my side my sister, her glowing face glowing, clasps the leather straps about her shoulders. We sisters both carry our party's supplies in these backpacks. She and the Challenger both seem apprehensive now, but I think that I am the only one who is truly afraid. At Fauna's belt dangles her sword, while her bow is secured about her. The Challenger too has both a sword and a bow, though between them only have a few arrows left in each of

155

their quivers. I look at the Challenger, the ranger a step behind us, catching the shimmering light in his uncovered eye. Before proceeding further in the dark we take a quick pause. Not wanting to hear the silence of this dark place, I ask Sis how many supplies we have. Fauna swings off her small knapsack, checking as we slow and then stop our steps. She announces that we have enough bread for two days. The Challenger, peering over her shoulder, adds that the pieces of wood can last likely less than a day.

"At least it will be dark when we sleep," our ranger friend adds dryly. Our clustered trio continues moving.

Here I am barely able to see the walls, though sometimes when the torchlight flickers I see the faint rock-face through the shadows. At our feet we follow a decrepit track. This used to be part of the mine, and I wonder if it's an expanding tunnel that was abandoned long ago. Further we come across a little wooden cart on its side, its dark brown frame half rotted into the cave's floor, a clump of dry black substance spilling from its edges. The Challenger kneels here, raising his torch over his head (in case the stuff is flammable) and runs a hand through the black mass, retrieving a small green thing, a near perfectly spherical gem. He shows us the dozens of tiny lights glinting within its surface from the torchlight.

"This could be some foreshadowing, this gem," he says, pocketing it, and I don't get what he means and Fauna looks like she doesn't either.

"It's the gem or precious stone that the vale's denizens mine," I say, recalling what Emera and the others told us.

"Yeah," adds Sister. "Wasn't that what powered all their thingies? No use to us here."

"We shall see then," the ranger says and we continue on our way.

156

We soon come to a huge wall, the end of this great open area, and to our lefts and rights the walls run far and both ways disappear into shadow.

"Which?" asks Sis, both her hands clasping her belt, looking to me. "Does your brain slug tell you anything?"

My ability to recall my memory perfectly isn't helping here. "I never read or was told anything about this place," I say, shaking my head. I look at the Challenger, who is sniffing the air.

"I don't know, girls, honestly," says he with a defeated shrug. "Either way is as good as the other."

"Okay!" shouts Fauna and her voice echoes far and wide. She begins to twirl herself like a top, sticking one of her legs out and speeding up, jumping in one movement away from the wall. When she slows down and finally stops spinning her booted foot is pointed to the left.

"She took classes back home," I tell the Challenger and he shrugs again, starting to walk down the wall to the left. Now that we've turned, the rock wall runs to our right and to our left is the big dark space we had just came through. I begin to wonder if anything can see us from afar. The glow from the Challenger's torch only emits a few paces around us. The wall, shale-coloured, has some patterns, swirls here and there, dark lines elsewhere, and as we get further along we see what appear to be embedded shells and numerous patterns of bones. I immediately know that these are the remains of long deceased animals, and I postulate that this place may have once been underwater.

I look down to Delipha's Rod. It is tied onto my belt, nestled in beside my dagger. The rod is a magical item I have had since before we were in the Vale of Dragos. It shoots seawater on command. At my left hip I have fastened the Mighty Magnet, another item I attained on that past adventure. The Challenger raises his torch-bearing arm a little, revealing more of the wall. We see the bones of a small fish, and as we walk we see another fish, much bigger, embedded behind the small one, its skeletal jaws open, frozen in poise, seemingly once ready to eat. We keep moving and soon see upon the rock wall another big fish's skeleton, this one turned around, seemingly fleeing, and then we see a whole school of smaller fish chasing the big one.

"Fish unionization is important," mutters the Challenger.

"Huh?" Fauna asks. She points ahead and says: "Hey, look!"

I see some scratches on the wall up ahead and as we reach them our ranger friend raises his arm the highest he can, illuminating the rock surface. We can clearly see that these are letters, words, but it's not in the common speech, but rather glyphs of some kind. "What is this, Flora?" Sister asks me.

I take a moment, but then I see patterns and I know what it says. "This is an ancient tongue," I say.

"I thought it was writing on a cave wall," says Fauna.

"It's pre-Common, the words," I say, laughing a little.

Fauna looks it over, a perplexed expression on her round face. "Tell me it says something encouraging?"

"Yeah," agrees the ranger. "An abandoned brewery nearby or something."

"Preserved drinks, you think?" Sister asks him excitedly.

"Fermented for thousands of years, distilled in magma and cool caverns for your present enjoyment," the ranger mutters, raising his torch yet further.

I gaze upward to where the stretching words begin and I begin reading them (somewhat) aloud: **"I have just departed a great empty vale. My winged steed fell in a thunderstorm."**

"This must be the Vale of Dragos," reasons Fauna.

I agree and continue reading. **"I am Xelia, First Knight of Glacia."**

"Glacia?" Fauna asks.

"They were very ancient peoples," I say after pausing to recollect all I know about the Glacian Empire.

"Thousands of years old. I have seen their ruins before in my ranging. They once ruled nearly all the lands on this continent," the Challenger says, lowering the torch so I can read the next verses.

"My beloved Firebird did not survive. I must return to the Citadel to serve my Empress. I could not scale the mountainous walls, so I seek a way out underneath the mountains. I have explored some of the tunnels nearby. All the ones this way lead to dead-ends. Ah," I say next. "Here is an arrow pointing to our right, so good thing we didn't go that way earlier. Nice choice, Fauna. Let's see, uh, it says: **I am to proceed. I was once told by the Empress's sages that there are monstrous things in the Under the Dark."**

"Under the Dark, eh? That'll get Salvatore off your scent," says the Challenger, pointing to those last words.

"Flora, does it say more?" asks Fauna.

I push up my spectacles on my nose, pressing the frames against my brow. "No," I answer.

"Maybe she wrote further on?" suggests Fauna, walking into the darkness before her, to the opposite direction where the carved arrow points, the direction we had already been traveling in.

"Yes," agrees the Challenger, catching up to her and lighting the way. He calls back to me: "And if we see more writing then we know we're going the right way."

Suddenly I find it romantic, the idea of following an ancient explorer, a knight on a flying steed in the employ of the Glacian Empress herself. I just hope that this underworld did not become Xelia's tomb. I'm keeping up with the two others now, eager to enter the next tunnel we come across.

At one point the Challenger pauses in his steps, telling us that he suspects that we may be being followed. I ask him how he knows this. He says it is only a feeling, no evidence yet.

We soon come upon a portal in the wall, tall and oblong in shape, as if it were purposely etched to resemble a door. This stands taller than the Challenger, and is as wide as two of him. He lets us go first, staying close to us, holding the torch above our heads, his sword drawn ready in his other hand, telling us he can smell something faint, something rotten from further within. This passage runs deep, and so we keep moving, waiting for some change in the scenery, something beyond the sterile brown walls that we can barely see.

Soon we take a short break in the tunnel. The Challenger has to light another piece of wood as a torch, and we eat some of the bread to keep our energy. I know I've pushed myself before, but I'm feeling urgency; I want to see something to show us we're on the right track.

We continue onward.

"Look!" says my sister after we move a few dozen feet, tapping me, pointing upward. I see small bluish glowing things far above us. Here the ceiling is so high. The glowing things are like stars, spread out far, only little dots on the dark ceiling. Further on the light things are closer together, whole bunches of them, and the more we walk the more the roof is overtaken by them.

"Mushrooms," says the Challenger, grinning. He takes a big breath and blows out the torch. We have more than enough light to see the place. Very soon the shimmering mushrooms stretch down along the sides of the walls from the cave ceiling, so thickly that there is not a single space between them, and the glow is so bright that it feels like we're in a fully lit room!

I gaze up at them, fascinated by the sight of layers upon layers of sprouting flat, wide, and bulgy blue radiant caps that grow so thickly like fur upon a beast. Their brightness is brightest on the biggest mushrooms, the smaller ones more faded, but they are all consistently blue.

"Wow, wow," stammers Fauna when we come to a section of the tunnel where the ceiling has become lower. She stands on her toes, swings her sword, and collects some of the bigger mushrooms that fall. She holds a handful and we both look closely at them. They are thick in the stalks, their caps even thicker, and all of their body glows steadily at the same luminous level.

I search my mind, unable to find any information on them. We encountered glowing mushrooms underground before, in truth, at the start of our journey, but I knew nothing of them then either. I know which mushrooms are poisonous on the surface of the world, and which ones are scrumptious, and which ones are exuberant, but there seems to be no literature, at least nothing I've read, on fungus beneath the world.

The Challenger, as if he understands what I am thinking, simply says that they may kill or give energy or heal or just be food.

"If we run out of bread and can't find anything else to eat then we got nothing to lose and we might as well die weirdly at that point," says my sister, packing many handfuls into her bag. "Hopefully we can find some underground stream, catch some juicy fish without eyes if we're lucky? I think we can!"

"Yum," says the ranger, his scruffy face fully visible from the glow of fungus that grows around us.

When we press on further the mushrooms begin to spread out, their numbers dwindling and the tunnel darkening. Before long we emerge in what is either a cavern or a subterranean chamber, I don't know which. Here there are only a few mushrooms, mostly on the walls behind us, this great new room stretching forward, only dimly lit. It is wide enough for us to walk side by side, with space for a few more of us if we had companions. Fauna tries to point out something. I already see it. Before us stands a single big jagged rock. As we come right up to its surface I see glyphs, but it's not bright enough here to read. Fauna retrieves some mushrooms from her backpack, still glowing, and holds them between us and the rock.

"Okay! Xelia made it! Yay! Let's see—**Here, beyond this archway before you is an underground valley. Beware the beasts of this realm. In these colossal caverns I have sensed something unexplained, but I do know that to survive in the depths you need not only use your mind and your body, but also your heart.**"

"Your heart?" asks the Challenger, chuckling dryly. "Sounds like she maybe had some mushrooms herself?"

"Well, that's what it says," I say, perplexed as to what she meant. I begin to wonder if this was an expression in her time, but I can't find anything in my memories about this being a Glacian thing. The Challenger reaches into my sister's backpack gently, bringing out a new piece of dry-wood for him to make into a torch, and their two efforts double our light. I look up, able to see the cave roof way above us. It's full of pointy stalactites that re-mind me of a decadent chandelier in a mansion that spans an en-tire ceiling.

I walk now in the middle between the two bearers of light.

"Look!" the ranger shouts, pointing his flaming stick.

In the illuminated space before us I see something some twenty paces away, a small ball-like thing, greenish-yellow or yellowish-green in colour. It moves, rolls along slowly, leaving an oozy trail behind it.

"A blob?" Fauna asks/gasps, laughing a little.

"Slime," answers the Challenger. "Nothing to worry about though! Observe, *get lost, slimeball!*" he barks and throws his torch at it. The fiery stick lands on the piece of slime and a hissing shriek shoots through the chamber while the slime oozily dashes away.

The Challenger laughs, running up and retrieving the burning torch. He then chases the slime as it scurries towards the far wall, and there it zips into a tiny round hole, not unlike a mouse hole in a house, and vanishes.

"Slime!" the ranger cries after it. "Anyway, believe me, even a bard could slay those things!"

"We could really *use* some music now," quips Fauna. We only hear distant dripping noises, each drop echoing five times.

"Xelia said there is an archway ahead, and that leads to an underground valley," I say, eager to reach it as I am wondering what else lives in this area, glad we've only encountered slime thus far.

Fauna charges ahead of us, and I see in the blackness ahead a single bright bit bouncing along, the mushrooms in her grasp. "Guys!" she calls as we begin to catch up to her. We see her standing, looking down before her. As I come around to her side I see that she is gazing into a pit. Even with the torchlight and mushrooms we cannot see beyond a few feet down into the shadows.

"Toss a shroom," I tell her.

"Now?" she says.

"I mean throw it down," I say.

She tilts her hand, letting one fall. Eventually, even though its light is faded and it looks tiny from where we stand, it lands. This pit is deep, at least two stories of a building down.

The Challenger steps around the hole, which is about as wide and as round as a big carriage's wheel. "I wonder what's down there?" he asks me. He closes his eye. Sister peers down, a look of apprehension coming over her.

"Deep," she says.

"I smell something rotten, like before," the ranger utters. "And I hear something scurrying. I too hear something coming together, coalescing, forming, bubbling…"

Fauna asks: "From down there?"

The Challenger's eye swings open. Sword raised, he turns and yells: "Here! Watch out!"

Something is coming for us from the darkness, something from back the way we came. It's big and green, thick and wide, a slimy bulging thing in the shape of a puffed hand that sweeps, palm open, toward us.

I hear my sister shriek as she reaches to get her bow off of her, and one of her hands snatches an arrow from the quiver at her side. The Challenger steps forward in a fighting stance, and he swipes. The big hand is too fast and his blade barely scratches it. It hits him, knocking his torch and sword from his grasping hands in one motion. Fauna gets one arrow off, too little too late. Coming at us is a great strength, a heavy mass. It sends me falling backward. If it weren't for the pit I think it would clobber me, crushing me into a pulp, but I fall from its reach, my sister beside me, and the Challenger on top of both of us.

My back takes in the immense pain of the rock hard floor of the pit as we land, and I feel my legs are flung up near the Challenger's head, and Fauna is now underneath my elbows and back.

We all breathe hard and heavy as we struggle to regain our composure, but it takes some time to squeeze our way onto our feet and stand side by side. There is so little space here, we can only move slightly on both sides without crashing into one another. Fauna has a deep gash along her forehead. I see her face in the dim light of the few mushrooms still in her hands.

"What was that?" she asks weakly.

"It was slime!" I cry.

"Not slime! That was strong!" shouts the Challenger. He looks up, and we sisters follow his gaze. The pit's top looks like a small circle from where we are. We see only the light of the Challenger's torch up there, still burning, but we all know it won't last much longer.

I mutter softly, realizing that we are stuck two stories down. The wall of the pit is slippery. I can feel nothing to grab onto, no bricks with creases, or vines, or protrusions—nothing!

"No!" Fauna yells. "After all our adventures we end up in a deep pit we can't climb out of?"

Everything had spun as we plunged together to the bottom of the pit, this cylindrical hole-thing! It had happened so fast! It's so common to not feel anything in the moment, but then have it all throbbing once you've settled. I had landed sideways-like, my feet at the Challenger's shoulders, my bottom hitting the hard ground while other parts of me collided with my sister. We now stand and gaze upward with our five eyes to the distant circle of light, the surface of the hole.

Fauna, with a big fresh gash on her forehead, holds her bow in the limited space between us. It is broken, both the string and the curvy wood snapped. She tosses it at our feet, cursing.

"Ow," the Challenger groans, lifting his arms. He carefully reaches his palms to the back of his head, his jutting elbows nearly hitting both of our faces.

"Bleeding?" I ask.

He shakes his head, now looking at his hands. He grabs his bow from off his back. "Do either of you have rope or strong thread?" he asks us.

"At the bottom of my bag, under the bread!" says Fauna.

"Where is your bag?" I ask her.

"Up there! It flung off me!"

I only have a tiny bit of our bread supply in my own bag. As I back up against the wall behind me I can feel my little carrier still clasped to my back.

"Well," says the Challenger, holding now his three remaining arrows from his quiver, all of them bent at the middle, so we couldn't use them anyway. "What does this leave us?"

"Our swords!" declares my sister. Hers is still at her belt and we're lucky that neither of their blades stabbed anybody when we fell. Fauna then waves one of her hands full of glowing blue mushrooms. "And these?"

The Challenger looks to me and I see that rare look of fear in his eye that is not covered by a patch. Maybe it's not fear, he's always hard to read. He is at my left, while my sister is wedged to my right now and the Challenger to her right in turn.

"I have the Mighty Magnet," I say. With my arms barely able to move, I grab my other item and feel its smooth body in my clasping palm. "And this, the Rod of Delipha!"

"What good are they now? We can't use magnetic force or seawater to get out of here, can we?" says the Ranger.

"You have the slug in your brain," says Fauna. "You can think of something, Flora! I know you can!"

I simultaneously shake my head and my eyes, letting images form underneath my eyelids. I see myself on the play-scape back home at Silver Coast and I also see another girl, a littler girl with pink hair—I remember stepping to her side. She looks down at an anthill. With a tiny shovel she built miniature canals. It had rained that day and now the canals stream with water into the base of the anthill, into underground tunnels she also constructed.

"Ah! Do you remember that little pink-haired girl who flooded ants?" I ask, my eyes flicking open. My sister furrows both her red eyebrows. She begins asking me why I'd bring that up now. I raise the rod in my hands. The Challenger chuckles and he appears to know what I am thinking.

"How long can you two tread?" the ranger asks us as I place the Mighty Magnet back at my belt.

Fauna mutters, rolling her eyes, seemingly understanding now. She looks up and says: "Can't we just stand on one another?"

"Won't be enough," I say, calculating our combined heights, and I point Delipha's Rod at our feet. "Prepare your socks to be soggy! This looks like the only way."

Fauna groans as I call on the Sea Goddess. I feel rumbling in my palms. Seawater shoots from the item's bulbous tip and we smell strong salt at our feet, and then our shins submerge and I feel strong arms around my shoulders. The Challenger, giving me an assuring look, hoists me up and around onto his own shoulders.

"Sorry for not asking first!" he cries and I tell him it was a good idea to put me up here. I am now pouring water down his side, the rising watery firmament now at his waist. "Climb on me!" he shouts to my sister.

"You'll drown!" she protests.

"Just go! My mass will displace the water, will send you both up faster! Trust me!" he replies quickly, and Fauna steps onto him, climbing him like an ettercap ascends her web.

Soon my sister and I face one another, both of us standing upon his broad shoulders, keeping balance by leaning against the walls of the narrow pit. I worry if I am hurting him as the water level rises to his chest. I call down to him, holding down Delipha's Rod in one hand as my sister lets me lean on her, the water coming faster now, thicker, more splashy. I see a starfish fly out, smacking against the ranger's face. He shakes his head, flinging it off just as the water surface reaches his bristly chin.

"Don't worry--*bbbllllllppppp!*" is the last thing he calls as his head goes under.

We two sisters are treading. I only move my legs. My arms point downward. I look up, calling to Delipha to assist us more. I feel strong waves emitting from the blessed item in my hands. My sister moves all four of her limbs and she suddenly drops as she notices my head is bobbing in the water, I'm almost going under! Beneath me she goes, pushing me up with her body. I take a big breath and then I let myself fall as she gets back into her treading position.

Again, I am submerged, still shooting water, and I look down and see the Challenger's dark form rise. He gently but firmly thrusts me back to the surface where I take another great breath!

We are nearly at the top of the pit. My legs are weak, too heavy to move. I feel my sister push me up, and then the cycle repeats, both of them taking turns propelling me to keep the water flowing.

Fauna grabs the lip of the pit, our ranger friend having pushed her upward, and she pulls herself up onto the cave floor, panting loudly. I feel the Challenger shove me again. Soon I am at the curb where I reach with one hand and place it atop cold rock. My sister's hand grips my wrist, pulling me, and I soon stare up at the cave ceiling. With my remaining strength I look over and see a single shot of seawater shoot forth from the tip of the rod, and I bid Delipha to cease, thanking her once more for saving us as the rod goes flaccid in my hand.

I hear heavy breathing, followed by a thud, and I know our ranger friend is up. I know why he managed to do what he just did, remembering that he was given the capability of superhuman feats.

"Th—thank—thank you!" my sister stammers to him, coughing.

He only laughs, coughing up seawater himself and they pat one another on the back for a bit.

168

As we rest, the Challenger leans up, gets more dry-wood from Fauna's knapsack (which was up here, so most of the bread isn't soggy and none of the firewood is spoiled) and he lights another makeshift torch. He appears over me, dripping, his ranger tunic and cloak and breeches all soaked. He helps me to my feet. I feel dizzy as I find my bearings.

"Slime?" Fauna says, glancing around at my side.

"Don't see it," answers the Challenger. "It must have fled."

"Was that slime, that green hand thingy?" I ask him. "Was it mad that you threw a torch at it earlier?"

He shrugs.

"We might have a subterranean enemy," says Fauna, and she asks me if she needs to carry me. I tell her I am fine, just that we should move slowly as we proceed. I take one last look at the hole that is now filled to the brim with seawater. We are exhausted and drenched, but we only have a bit of food that we know we can eat (and we have the glowing mushrooms, but we don't know what they do).

"A big archway should be ahead of us," I tell the others after our short rest, remembering what I read on the rock back there before the slime hand appeared. Xelia had passed through here. We are following her pathway through the mountain tunnels, or so I hope.

The Challenger, munching on a piece of bread and walking a little ahead of us, suddenly points forward. When my sister and I catch up to him I can see by the light of his torch a dark oozy trail on the ground before us.

"Slime," says the Challenger as we cautiously follow it through wide open space. I sigh in relief as I soon see an immense stone archway emerge from the blackness. Our drenched feet reach it and my friend raises the torch. I can just barely see the high point of the arch.

There are many things piled up where the giant portal stands – enormous slabs of rock, rounded and square-like boulders, rectangular massive brick-looking objects, some pieces of shining surface wedged between cracks, thousands of individual piled up stones – everything and anything that can be found and shoved and filled to the brim from one wall to the other. Someone or something has made it so no one can pass. We cannot go through. The way is shut.

The Challenger moves his torch to reveal dark green streaks that run up onto the grey and brown wall of rock and brick, seemingly vanishing into a sliver between two crusted mortar bits. The ranger steps forward and peeps through this tiny space with his eye. He tells us he can see a very distant bit of light through immense darkness.

"Outside?" Fauna asks eagerly.

Shaking his head, he says: "Doubt it, we've been underground less than a day."

I calculate the distance we've moved, realizing he is probably right that we haven't moved very far underground, but the thought of light *is* encouraging.

"Night and day be hard to determine down here!" Fauna says, pressing her small hands against the makeshift wall. "I don't see any cracks we can get through."

She then puts some of the glowing mushrooms onto the sword at her belt. The Challenger, after handing me the torch, does the same with the bright fungus. Both blades are turned into luminous skewers and placed at their respective belts.

"We might find a way!" Sister says, placing a foot between two rocks, beginning to climb again like an ettercap. The Challenger follows, taking the left side of the massive clogged archway as she takes the right, and I, with the torch, watch my companions and their dangling, shimmering swords.

170

"I am experienced at breaking fourth walls!" the ranger proclaims.

"We'll find a space!" says my sister.

"Hey guys!" I call up, wiping salt from one of my eyes beneath my spectacles. "Remember what I read on the rock back there, from Xelia?"

"Yeah!" Fauna giggles, side-climbing to the edge. "Something about using our hearts?"

"It wasn't our hearts that got us out of that pit!" sneers the ranger.

I am about to say that my brain saved us, but I remember that I couldn't have escaped without them keeping me afloat. Randomly, I ask: "What would you do if you were to use your hearts *right now*?"

"Let it beat again and again, keeping me going, that's what it does, doesn't it?" calls Sister.

The Challenger, high up, suddenly lets go and lets himself fall, reaching the cavern floor a few paces to my side, landing smoothly on his feet. "No holes," he says, leaning up from his stance.

"I wonder how Xelia got through," I say, recalling the two inscriptions from her.

"It might not have been clogged back then," the ranger says and reaches into his damp cloak, retrieving the tiny green gem he had earlier picked up.

"Ah, that gem reminds me of Emera," I tell him, thinking of our green-haired friend back in the Vale of Dragos.

He says: "I semi-wish she were with us."

"I wonder if we should've stayed in the Vale?"

He looks at me, a thoughtful expression in his uncovered eye. "They had magic and gadgets. If we'd stayed we would've eventually figured out a way to escape together, I think."

Fauna climbs down halfway and then drops, landing gingerly beside us. She states that she also found nothing that any of us can fit through, even us sisters. "We left because of the High Priest. As long as we were there he would've hunted us," she adds to our conversation.

"A small fanatical group can ruin everything," I say lamentably.

The Challenger nods eagerly, and then he looks back at the wall. With the combined forces of the torch in my hand and the two glowing fungus encrusted swords we can see the wall better. It is in this triple illumination where I see something shiny, something rectangular and tall and right before us near the exact mid-point of the archway's width.

After handing my torch to the Challenger, I hastily grab the Mighty Magnet from my belt as I notice that this big block looks to be made of something metallic, copper or bronze. I utter the esoteric words to activate the Mighty Magnet in my hands, holding its two ends in front of the big glittering slab. I see that the rock piece right above it is rectangular as well, running horizontally across the metal bit as well as the other rocks beside it. Using the magnetic force, I pull the metal piece out, stepping back as I drag it with me a few paces backwards. Fauna and the ranger part to let the tall oblong piece through.

"It's perfect!" stammers Sister as the block scrapes against the cave floor.

I release the force, and then walk around the tall metal block before me, seeing a stable portal into the dark beyond the wall. It is tall enough for us to get through, with the Challenger ducking a little as we pass one by one.

"I wonder what it is, who made it?" says the ranger, stepping back to examine the rectangular thing.

Fauna shrugs. "No idea," she says. "This metallic block was probably here long after Xelia came through, no?" We three go through the newly made portal.

"Mind two, heart zero, I guess," I say once we are on the other side. Fauna half laughs, raising her beaming blade. We have entered a new place.

To our sides, about twenty paces of either side of us, we see rock walls again. Here is even bigger than the last chamber! And I see the tiny spec of light in the far distance. Placing the Mighty Magnet at my belt, I stand in the middle of my companions and their glowing swords. The ranger still carries the torch in his other hand.

"To the light," Fauna whispers and her whisper echoes.

We walk and walk, the light only seeming to get a little bit bigger, closer. At times the walls at our sides seem to vanish and I know not how far they expand. This place must be huge, this valley that Xelia's carvings warned about. After a long time trekking in silence over unobstructed ground we come to a protruding rock that stands in the middle of the immense cavern. It is as tall as a medium-sized person and I can see from the lights we hold that there are words on it, ancient words:

"I, Xelia of the Glacian Empire, have made is thus far. Beware the beasts of this underground valley! Here I met a thunderous beast as well as its underlings! They fell at my blade, for they knew not my power. There is light in the distance and I go now to it."

As I read it to my companions I see looks of hope form on their faces. We continue toward the light, parting shadows. I see something in the blackness a short way away. It is immense and, as we near it, I can see it is bone white before realizing that I am looking upon actual bones.

"Thunderous Beast!" growls the Challenger.

It is something long dead, a great colossal skeleton – this rising mass of bones! It leans against the enormous cave wall to our left, having likely fallen over as it died, and we see the many vertebrae of its back and long tail, and its big crumpled limb bones underneath a thick rib-cage. As we pass we eventually come to its skull. I look into its deep eye sockets that are as big as I am, admiring the long teeth in its protruding jaws.

"Gods!" the Challenger says, his face aglow in the light of his torch. "I've never seen such a thing in the flesh!"

"And look!" says Fauna, lowering her mushroom-covered sword toward her feet. Beside the big bones, sits a smaller skeleton, a two legged thing with a rodent-like skull that is covered in cobwebs. A pair of big teeth juts from its upper jaw. It must have stood just under my height in life.

"Kobolds, little 1D4 feckers!" the Challenger says, and we all soon notice more of these smaller skeletons sprawled about the dark area.

"Xelia was tough!" declares Fauna as we continue, coming across more and more long-gone kobolds.

"Talk about a random encounter!" says the ranger and then adds: "I guess there's nothing to fear unless there's some necromancy here!"

There must be such a thing as a cursed mouth because within seconds I can hear what sounds like clattering of bones. One of the kobold skeletons stands up slowly, wobbly at first, but then turns its snouted skull towards us and then raises a rusted spear in its hands. Two more stand, sprouting from their places.

"What are these?" asks the Challenger in clear disgust. "Stal-bolds?!"

I see underneath them tiny bits of green moving about – slime! It must be animating them!

174

And then I hear thunderous clattering. The skeleton of the big monster is rising like a surfacing whale. One big skull and dozens of tiny ones gaze at us.

I calculate our odds, not good.

"Run?" I ask the others.

They both nod at once.

Putting exhaustion on hold, I glimpse over my shoulder. Against the backdrop of darkness I see giant moving bones, the littler skeletons clinking against the rocky floor. The giant four-legged bestial skeleton towers behind them, the great thing slamming each of its thick bony feet, steadily booming, looking as if it might crush the smaller skeletons charging in front.

"It's the slime!" the Challenger shouts. "It invigorates the bones!"

We desperately make for the distant light. I see now faraway earth-and-rock walls to our sides. They rise steeply and culminate in thick stalactite encrusted roof more than two hundred paces above.

Slime, I abruptly remember, is vulnerable to fire. "The wood!" I huff while I remember the fast burning sticks in Fauna's flapping knapsack. I charge to her side, exerting extra energy. "Fire!" I say, quickly untying the strings over the cover of her knapsack as it bounces.

Something slams the ground behind me, where I would still be if I hadn't sped my feet just now! The kobold skeletons are throwing their spears! My feet flash with fury as I retrieve a piece of wood. Fauna reaches over her shoulder to snatch it from me and I grab another from her bag and we strike them together once.

FRPPPPP!!

Both of our sticks burn!

The faraway light is closer now! We must be almost half-way—

My sister shrieks. My arms flapping like hummingbird wings, my feet pummeling the ground like rain, I twist and see the long rock that she's tripping on. She falls. The nearest of the kobold skeletons reaches her. The Challenger and I, still at full speed, share a glance, a sigh, and unable to stop, we sharply curve apart, turning steeply, charging back to her.

She immediately springs to action—good old Fauna!—waving her flaming torch at the first two short skeletons before her, prompting them to bounce back. She swings her blade, slamming the snout of the next nearest! I reach her side and swing my burning stick at two more of the skeletal kobolds that charge in at our right. I see the dark sockets of their rat-like skull-faces, and I see tiny pieces of green slime wedged between their bones, connecting them, making them move.

I wave my torch at the closer of the two, pushing the fire where its arm and shoulder meet, prompting this thing to loosen its bony grip on its spear, yet making no whelping sound since it has no vocals. The Challenger swings in at my left, slicing down his sword and his torch, removing both arms from the other undead kobold, causing it to run away, disarmed. Another leaps at him, spear jutting, but the Challenger, too fast for it, kicks upward at the wooden shaft, breaking it, and then, with his hand clasped about the hilt of his sword, punches the skull, smashing it into white powder. The gaunt body fights on, trying to slap him, but the ranger simply knees its chest, cracking the ribs, causing little globs of slime to flee the crumpling mass.

Another kobold skeleton comes at me now. This one is slightly taller than the others, maybe their once leader. It holds a double-bladed ax in it's spindly hands. The sneering undead foe raises the weapon and I bring the fire to its face, a shrill hiss emitting from the meeting of bone and flame. Still, the ax comes down at me!

A piece of wood, its midpoint burning, flings in from aside of me, and I see that Fauna, having already dispatched others, has struck her shrinking torch in the path of the plunging ax. Her wood crumbles, but I manage to move, her futile block saving me time to cartwheel out of there, sweeping to the side, hitting a smaller skeleton, likely a runt, shattering it immediately.

As I get back to my feet I see that my sister has leapt backwards. She is unhurt, having managed to dodge the ax. The Challenger calls out, pivoting over to her, his sword aimed at the gaping jaws of the tall undead kobold. It tries to move quick, tries to lift the heavy ax again, but before it can do so the ranger's sword shoots out from between where the back of its skull meets its uppermost spine. The Challenger pulls up, and then Fauna moves in and they both keep chopping until it falls over and the slime flees the splintering bones.

"Oh no," I groan when the shadow of the impending Thunder Beast skeleton completely envelops us.

"Dino-Lich," the Challenger mutters.

I move to stand with my sister. There is no time to run, the great beast is already upon us. A massive skull rises overhead of our party. The giant thing parts it jaws and I see teeth like white javelins.

I take a step back. So does Fauna. Between us the Challenger places his sword at his belt, and from his back he draws his bow, and he places his burning torch onto the string, fire-tip first, and pulls back as the bone maw opens wider.

"You two, run!" the ranger says, drawing the bowstring as far as he can.

"You've taken us far," says Sister. "We won't leave you."

The head comes down at us. The ranger releases the torch. It whizzes into the mouth, into the non-existent throat. The flames cause it to close its jaws, bits of tiny slime falling from within.

Fauna dashes rightward, I to my left, and we charge around the huge bones. In the moment I reach the side of the towering rib-cage I see the Challenger's form jump onto the monster's shut snout. The wilderness wanderer hops along the top of the skull to the protruding spine.

I swerve, charging over to the nearest of its ribs, for it suddenly lowers its midpoint. The nearest curving bone is easy for me to grasp. With the torch in one hand, I manage to bring myself up onto it, squeezing my frame between the next big rib. I balance my feet on the crescent-shaped curving part, my free hand grasping onto the upper part. I wave the torch, frantically finding the small spaces where slime is wedged between the bones above me. I hear sizzling, followed by groans as tiny bits of slime fall from the heaving spine. Across the way I see Fauna flitting about the ground, looking as if she were behind a wall of shifting white pines. Her tiny form moves fast, still waving her torch, narrowly avoiding a sideways kick from one of the giant feet! Above me the Challenger's eager footfalls against the spinal column send each pair of ribs shaking from the front to the back of the beast.

Everything is trembling! My fingers lose grasp of the torch. It falls onto the ground and gets stomped upon by a toe, so I press against the rib I'm riding, squeezing both of my arms about it.

"What is the plan?" I ask myself, seeing Sister chuck her torch at the base of the tail and then duck as its long spindly tip swings at her. The Challenger busies himself above, still stamping, sending bits of bone and slime down through the rib-cage.

I cry out. The ranger begins to slide down the tailbone, I can see him as I look up. In seconds everything quakes even stronger, and the dark ground, rushing past me one moment, is now rushing up to me. I shut my eyes, tightening my grip further, as tight as I can, pressing my chest and shoulders, feeling a sharp smack against my side as my sight spins.

I manage to look in time to roll out of the way as the rest of the big bones fall towards me. I keep rolling.

Strewn about a slightly more illuminated area now (for it seems the skeleton beast has carried us far) I see first two long and wide leg bones, and then a few ribs and spinal chunks.

"Fauna! Challenger!" I shout, feeling dizzy, my body miraculously only a little sore. My sister emerges from across the many bones, curving as she runs towards me, and I soon see the Challenger popping up from a nearby pile. Up ahead I see the great skull. It writhes among the vertebrae of neck bones, but it soon falls over and I can hear slithering, the creeping of fleeing slime.

The three of us assemble quickly before the dead bones, asking each other if we are hurt, thankfully no one is badly, save some bruises and bumps.

"Okay," the Challenger tells us, panting more than a little. "I think...that we are...okay for now."

Fauna reaches behind her and retrieves two pieces of wood, and she lamentably tells us it's the last of it. Thankfully, we are nearer the lightened space, and I see that it is less than a hundred paces from us now. I also see vague things, structures and shadows, but we are still too far for me to discern anything fully.

"Xelia must have come here," I say to her, finally fully catching my own breath before glancing around, looking for more rock carvings to find more of the ancient adventurer's scribbling.

"After all that just happened, what was that she said about using our hearts rather than minds?" asks the Challenger, scoffing, looking over at the lopsided big white reptile-like skull, seating himself on a sideways leg bone across from it. "Ah, it was all the slime, eh?"

Fauna groans when we hear more clinking, more rustling, more movement...

I see from where the big open space we had just fled there is more slime now, trails of it on the ground around and behind us. My sister lights the two last sticks in her hands instantly, giving one to the Challenger and the other to me. My dagger, Delipha's Rod, and the Mighty Magnet are all tied at my belt, all useless in this context as far as I can tell.

"Stop the slime!" declares the Challenger, and he begins walking towards the nearest bulge of green matter moving towards us.

"Enough!" Fauna shouts, and then she pulls from her bag a handful of the glowing blue mushrooms. "I don't know what this will do, but the last time we ate something unknown it made us super!"

"Oh yeah, that," I say, remembering those many days ago, when we dealt with Lobster-Man and his minions.

"I don't care what it does!" she shrieks, looking desperate. "I am eating these glowing fungus thingies—consequences be damned!" and she plops them all into her mouth.

The Challenger by now has already started circling the collapsed skeletal body of the Thunder Beast, hitting the fast slinking green slime as he moves, seemingly frantic to stop the impending slime from reaching the bones again. All the ooze suddenly stops creeping forward, and all at once coalesces into a blob-like mass of green, and I worry that it's going to shape-shift into something dangerous!

Instead it rushes to Fauna, far quicker than before. The Challenger dashes towards us sisters as this happens, but for once he is too late.

It has already grabbed her! It is a greenish hand once more, like the one that had pushed us into the pit earlier. My sister cries out, chewing wildly what she'd just shoved in her mouth as thick fingers wrap around her. The oozy form stretches, becoming taller and thinner, flinging my sister upside down right in front of us. I reach to grab her dangling hands. A small tendril shoots from the slime, pushing me, causing me to fall hard on the cave floor. Another tendril emerges and strikes the Challenger, slapping the sword from his hands. I get to my knees, pull my dagger from my belt, but the tendril turns and slaps both my dagger and the torch from my hands in one quick move.

"Ow!" I yell. "Let her go!"

"Why?" a shrill voice (if it could be called that, for it sounds more like the hissing of steaming water) demands. *"You are on our lands, passing our blessed paths, eating our sanctified crops!"*

"Oh!" Fauna yelps, still upside down, her red cap falling off and her red hair fluttering over the cavern's hard floor. "My belly hurts! Whatever those mushrooms do, it's doing it!"

"It is poison for solid folk!" says the slime.

"We're solid folk!" the Challenger retorts in protest.

I frantically search for something to say, surprised that now the slime has decided to communicate with us. The mass takes on a slightly pinkish tinge for a split moment, and then two more tendrils shoot out from its side, and it slaps Fauna's back, prompting some bits of blue mushroom to shoot from her mouth. She makes a 'yuck' noise, and then spits out the rest of the glowing substance, reminding me a bit of the first time she drank wine. The slime releases her, letting her down unexpectedly gently. Fauna gets up immediately, rubbing her belly, smiling a little while she looks at the still glowing tiny chunks beside her on the ground.

She looks up at the slime next, saying: "Okay, it's out now and I'm feeling better!"

The blue-green-pinkish slime has now coalesced into a roundish blob, like a big translucent ball about twice the size Fauna's size. I am beginning to feel there was some miscommunication somewhere. The Challenger is tip-toeing behind the slime blob, having grabbed his blade again, looking ready to strike it.

"But *you* attacked us!" I say in protest, trying to get our older friend's attention with my hands, seeing if I can get him to pause for a moment. The ranger does so, raising his brow above his eye-patch, looking to me.

"We saw you trespass our realms!" the hissing voice speaks. *"You came from the old mines! Do you know why the miners from the Dragon's Vale abandoned those mines long ago?"*

I shake my head and then say "no", hoping that I can reason with the slime, feeling too fatigued to fight or run any further.

"We didn't know," says my sister, who is now at my side, placing her cap back on her head. "You saw me eat poison things, so you've got to believe me — we're not from around here!"

The slime ball, having drawn back its tendrils inside itself, projects now what looks like a skinny green arm with a small hand on its end, which it uses to scratch its top, clearly mimicking head-scratching.

"We are passing through," I say, trying to sound calm, though I feel my heart thumping like a drumbeat in front of a crew of oarsmen.

"We were lost in the Vale of Dragos and we are trying to leave the mountains," says Fauna.

We are standing side by side now, and the Challenger waits five paces behind the slime, looking impatient. "You tried to hurt us…twice!" the ranger snaps.

The slime spins around to 'face' him and says: *"Trespassing! We were merely trying to scare you! The bones cannot hurt you!"*

"Well," says the Challenger, looking thoughtful. "Maybe, I mean, even kobolds with muscles and flesh are weaklings, let alone kobolds made of bone!"

"Yes!" replies the slime, and I think I hear something resembling cheerfulness in the unreal voice.

"Yes!" I then agree. Without thinking further, I blurt out: "We were following Xelia's footsteps!"

The slime seems to gasp in many voices. I am about to speak further, but I hear something, other sets of footsteps. The Challenger, who had just lowered his sword, quickly raises it again.

"Is this a slime trick?" he shouts as he turns his head and body sideways, towards where the new noises come from.

"Now what?" Fauna asks, and then she yells and grabs her sword.

Within seconds two figures emerge, shadows in front of the light down the way through the cavern. They are tall. I cannot see their faces, only what they carry stretched out between them. They are only a few paces away when I realize they are trapping us!

My sister shrieks though her voice is muffled. I feel the two others smushed against me. My face, I think, is on my sister's hair because I feel rough bunches and smell old lemons. I also feel what I think is a muddy boot against my cheek. We are hitting hard ground together in this constricting net.

Fauna yelps: "I see nothing! Can you?"

"No!" I say to her ear.

"I *can* with my eye!" the Challenger cries from near my feet. "We're coming upon the light!"

"Do you see up?" I ask.

"Yes!" replies the ranger narrativingly. "Far above, taller than any city I've seen, spans the roof of the inside of this mountain! Like immense cracks, this whole open section above, as if a god sliced it! Whatever has us, this must be their home!"

"What *has* us?" I inquire frantically.

"Two-leggers, men maybe!" he answers, and he calls to our captors. "Hey! Who pulled you out of the turnip patch early?"

We hear a loud grunt, and then I feel the tight net flip over. I try to move my legs, but barely can. I feel something soft against the back of me, and I hear something soothing as I realize that the slime we are bagged with oozes itself out around us, softening each tumble of the net.

Through my sisters red hair I see what the ranger just described, for we sisters face upward now and the ranger is on the ground. Brightness overwhelms my sight. Having traveled underground, having left the Vale of Dragos during night, I now see daytime sky for the first time in a while. When my eyes adjust I see puffy clouds too! The faraway walls of the interior of the mountain near the top look purple from here, so distant. Fauna gasps. The slime oozes over the rest of us, covering the sight. We can breathe, but we're enclosed by slime. We are dragged longer, but eventually our captors halt.

I hear a soft whooshing and the slime in the net suddenly falls from us, sinking weakly to the base of our huddled forms, no longer cushioning us. There's massive sunlight upon us, brighter than before, for we're directly below the great hollow.

There are two forms above us. The rope netting around us loosens quickly.

We're freed!

"Thought you slime!" says one of our captors.

"Not us!" says Sister.

"We were *fighting* the slime!" declares the Challenger as he gets up.

I roll off of my sister, onto the floor of the cavern, gazing up at faraway sky. After fighting off slime-animated bones and being dragged in a net, I'm exhausted. Standing slowly, I'm feeling bruises on my legs and arms. My blue coat and hat are dusty. I pat myself down quickly.

"Slime change shape sometimes!" says another voice, slightly higher and more grating than the other.

"But always weaken in sun!" adds the deeper first voice.

"Sunlight best disinfectant!" agrees the second.

Beyond our former captors are some peculiar sights. Around us stand trees, all tall and perfectly straight, the loftiest of them reaching a tenth of the distance to the cavern's roof. Some are heavily leafed, others of pine, all of them evenly spaced apart. Closer to us grow long shafts of golden and green grasses and soaring veggie stalks. They too all seemingly reach upward. Growing things (I remember thanks to the instant recollection slug in my head) are shaped like this when there's a singular source of sunlight directly above. The Challenger stands aside my astonished sister. He's seen more things than us, yet he too looks amazed. Further from us there stand two wide structures made of dark logs. They are side by side, square-shaped and two-storied. Upon their flat roofs sit big and wide objects, curved bowl-shaped things, and I can see (in this short distance) long tubes emerging from under them. These things must collect rainwater, I deduce.

"Wow," says Sister.

"An underground niche farmstead!" I stammer.

"Nice groves," compliments the Challenger, looking to the trees.

The two strangers are odd, which was not unexpected. They're tall and thin, as much shaped like long beans as people could be, though their arms are quite muscled. Atop the pair's lanky frames and long faces sprout mops of hair that literally look like encrusted old stretchy mops where each bristly fiber sweeps upward and then sideways, one yellowish, the other reddish. Their complexions are pale yet tan at the top and forehead, likely the re-sult of a lifetime under the one light. Their necks are red and their eyes seem small for their faces, as do their noses. Their mouths are large and wide, mostly frowning.

185

"Twins?" I ask awkwardly, trying to remove tension.

The yellowish-haired one nods. I gaze at their simple garments, thin partly sleeved set of tunics and plain white sarongs over their lower halves.

"We're twins too!" says Fauna. Both she and the ranger looked angry a moment ago, but they both now appear relieved. Between us and them lay the unraveled net and the now coiling slime. Its pinkish-greenish mass shrinks into a puddle formation, drying, looking more like dough. The sun, I realize, causes slime to weaken massively.

"They not slime!" says the deep voiced, reddish-haired twin to the other.

I tell our names, explaining that we're passing underground, and about the fight with the slime. Sister shows a glowing mushroom to them, still having some in her knapsack and on her sword. They both laugh, and then the reddish-haired brother wraps the slime with the net again and hoists it onto his gangling but large shoulders.

"Capturing the slime?" Fauna then asks them. The twins already are headed to the nearer of the two log buildings. I shrug, feeling a bit bad, especially since the slime had told us that we'd trespassed on its blessed lands, that it had only meant to scare us, and because it had just cushioned us while we were being dragged. I wonder if the three of us would've been able to work things out peacefully back there if we hadn't all gotten swept up?

"We're safe?" whispers the Challenger to us.

"Yeah," says Fauna, putting the glowing fungi piece in her pocket, pulling the straps of her knapsack at her front. "Ugh, can't believe I ate one of those back there!"

"And the slime saved you," I remind her as she shrugs back to me.

"Well," the Challenger mutters. "Before *that* it pushed us into a pit to die, and *we* saved ourselves!"

186

"Come!" calls the yellowish-haired brother.

We follow them between the tall crops, to what I assume is their stead. Some little fowl, blue in feather, hop around lightly, and I see a small pond near the edge of the yields. Along the walls of both of the structures there are more of the hose-like things that stretch down from the big rain-catchers, some that run into the crops. There are lots of wooden buckets strewn about as well.

"Beautiful," Fauna compliments, and I can tell she's open to being friendly.

The yellow-haired twin opens the door to the stead. Slight smoke and steam escape. Our apparent hosts enter, and we follow, Sister first, Challenger second, me last, standard for our trio. The place is big and wide, yet cluttered and stuffy. On our right is a pile of worn boots aside crates with tools in them, as well as stacked stools and pots, and further inward along the wall runs a row of thick wooden barrels to the midpoint of the chamber. To our left runs a long line of curtains that hang from the ceiling, a bright blue one nearest to the front, while the proceeding curtains are of white and brown along the wall. Before us runs a tattered muddy carpet over wooden planks. Where the long carpeting ends the floor raises a single tall step, and upon this elevated region stands a crude lengthy table near the right-hand wall, while nearer the middle of it sits some furnishings. From between these a column of smoke rises.

We companions gaze at the ceiling far above. Among a maze of beams and the tops of six wooden pillars I see numerous bunched baskets that are tied to the beams with pulley ropes. I spot two particularly long straw-weaved pods that dangle side by side over the entrance-way, and I gasp as I notice two faces, each peering over the side of their respective pods. They look shriveled, one bald of hair, and the other with a woolly knot of whites.

This latter one, an elderly woman I believe, speaks in a weak yet piercing voice: "You bring in slime folk, Lumpen?"

"Slime?" says the bald one in a gravelly yet deeper voice, shaking over the edge of his pod. "Over Bub's shoulders, is it?"

"Shush you!" screeches the crone beside him. Her pod lowers a bit. "It's sun-dried slime! What of those girls and patch-eyed man?"

"They not slime! They were lighted!" growls Bub to them, the reddish-haired twin, passing from this cramped entry space.

I nod to the two above, quickly calling our names to them. Bub turns and waves a hand: "No need to meet rotting fruit!" grunts he, stepping along the carpet toward the elevated space near the middle of the chamber.

The white-haired crone curses at him.

"Shush you, Gram, or I'll poke you with my stick!" yells Bub in reply, calling over his shoulder. Her face contorts, but her pod slinks back up to the jumbled roof. I give Fauna and the Challenger a weird look. We all shrug.

"Lumpen! Bub! What you boys brought?"

The booming voice, like an uglier rendition of Bub's voice, startles me as I see a rotund head rise from behind a long piece of furniture up ahead. Fauna follows the carpet, coming up behind the tall brothers. The Challenger trails her. They both call reserved greetings, introducing themselves.

"Fauna? Challenger?" rumbles the thick figure near the hearth. "What sorta names are those?"

"Your name, friend?" Sister asks as I speedily join her, arriving at her side. I sense hostility. These are strange folk, indeed people. Living underground may have made them peculiar. I see the owner of the intimidating voice. Standing at the end of a crude brown couch now stands a man, late middle-aged. It's obvious he's the father of two. He's wider than them, both his body and his face. Over his broad torso sits a furry black shroud parted at the middle, the collar of a tunic poking where the furs meet. On thick legs he wears muddy pants. His beady brown eyes overlook each of us. I feel nervy as they come to me.

"You were fighting slime?" he asks us from across the short distance.

"Yes," says Sister. "It chased us from the beginning of the valley here, animating walking bones, if you can believe it!"

"Yeah, they do that trick," sneers the older man. He turns and sits on the couch, his back to us again as he says: "Put them in the barn for tonight, Bub."

"Lumpen can do that," says Bub, flinging the net across from the fire-pit on the raised area.

"Fire dying, magic reeling!" says a shrill voice from an unseen source.

"May we come up?" Fauna asks. The Challenger looks to us sisters one by one, and I can tell he too has a strange feeling.

"Don't care!" answers the father.

Sister steps up. We follow. A low table covers most of the right side of the platform, while the left half directly before us consists of two long wooden couches that face one another and a single big comfy-looking green chair. In the exact middle of the furnishings is the fire-pit, the home's hearth. I can see embers and small flickering flames at the bottom of this deep hole.

"What they pay?" asks the shrill voice. I see her now. She is in the green chair on the far left of the slightly elevated living room. In the declining glow sits a thin figure shrouded in a sprawling multi-coloured blanket. I see a frail looking face, gaunt, with a tiny mouth only partly open in a disapproving frown.

"Pay?" asks the Challenger.

"Maybe we can do some farm work?" asks Fauna, smil-ing.

"Bah!" says the big man.

"Here," says the Challenger. In his unarmed hand he holds a green shiny stone, the little gem that he had picked up back when we first entered the Under the Dark. He says to me: "I told you this would foreshadow something."

Bub, the red-haired brother, coming over from the edge of the fire, grabs the round gem, revealing a grin with five white teeth and two golden ones.

"We came from the Vale of Dragos," the ranger says then.

"Yes, we've been reading the words of Xelia, do you know of her?" I ask, figuring they must know since they live here.

The father shakes his big head. "No," says he.

"Where are you folks from?" I ask politely.

"The Dropped," says Bub, putting the payment in his pocket before he turns and shouts: "Lumpen, show them their lodgings!"

The yellowish-haired twin walks on past the living room, and as we follow I get a good look at the woman in the chair. I see that her expression hasn't moved, nor do her eyes as we pass, and I notice too that her skin is grey and stone-like.

"Peculiar folks," I say in my head, but I try to remember how Mother taught me not to be judgmental. Lumpen leads us down into the back space of the long home where I see many red flags, or red towels or something, hanging above on the beams. This part of the homestead is roomier. Lumpen pushes through a short door, bending over as he passes through. We sisters do not need to duck. Outside this backdoor the wall of the barn stands right before us, only a watery ditch between the two structures. The barn doors, where Lumpen takes us, are bigger. Inside the floor is covered in pink straw, while the walls and ceiling are shrouded in thick clusters of glowing blue mushrooms that light the immense spanning interior. In the blue light I see some forms move in the distance, what I guess, or hope, are some kind of cattle.

"Wow!" gasps Fauna. "You grow them here?"

190

The yellow-haired brother heads to the nearest wall, grabs some mushrooms, scooping them with his long arm into a sack. He ties the bag once it's full and heaves it over his shoulder.

"You don't eat it, do you?" my sister asks. "Because that's not a good idea!"

"Fuel to fire," Lumpen says sneering. "Fuels our magic!"

"Magic?" I ask, not finding it likely that these folk are spell-casters.

Lumpen chuckles and I notice his two big front teeth. He waves a hand back toward the closed barn doors behind us. The heavy doors creak and then swing right open!

"Come," he says and brings us all back to the home where we return to the elevated middle space, and the two brothers unload at once their contributions onto the fire. The yellowish-haired brother pours the fungus into the hearth and the fire blooms, while Bub flings the dried out mass of slime in next and we hear the high voice shrieking in the flames.

Fauna's face goes wild.

The wide father and thin brothers begin moving their arms, all of them standing around the fire-pit, and I see something forming in the smoke. The fire crackles before us. Dark smoke envelopes the middle of the musty room. I hear, over the sizzling, the shrieks of the slime that Bub had only just poured into the sunken hearth.

Earlier that same mass of slime chased us. Now it burns at the mercy of this strange clan of under-dwellers. Who are they? *"The Dropped,"* Bub mentioned earlier.

I look at the tall twins, Bub the reddish-haired and Lumpen the yellowish-haired. They sit now across from us, their spindly legs arching forward. A bulgier version of them with grey thinner hair, the father, sits to the left of his offspring. On the chair to *my* left I see the mother, the wiry grey woman under the blanket. She looks intently at us. Beside me is Fauna. She franti-

191

cally tells our story, mentioning that we sisters are from Silver Coast. The father waves his long hand quickly, and I see shifting in the smoke, an image brilliant and sparkling, the shining walls of our home city, lofty spires rising from behind.

"Yes!" I exclaim, pointing.

"That your city?" the Challenger asks and I nod. He sits further on the right side of me and Fauna.

"We may live down here, but we know of the outside!" snorts the mother, once more her mouth unmoving.

"Yes, the cursed outside!" grumbles the father.

When the representation of Silver Coast fades in the smoke I decide to ask them about the magic to conjure such images, but instead my sister continues our story, telling of when we parted the city for the chance at a quest, and how we met the Challenger. She quickly tells of Hare-Neck Valley and Lobster-Man, the Old Campus, and then mentions our crash into the Vale of Dragos.

"From there we entered the mines," she says finally, huffing before she hastily explains our encounters with the slime. She mentions the two brothers scooping us in a net. Bub chuckles. Fauna looks to me, and then she adds that we've been following the trail of Xelia, the ancient warrior who came this subterranean way and wrote her journey on rocks.

"We hope her carvings will lead us out!" I add when Sister is finished.

"Twins?" the mother stammers from the green chair at our side, her mouth still agape.

"Yes!" says Fauna, smiling weakly to her. Beads of sweat trickle down her raggedy red bangs. I think she wants to ask about the slime in the fire.

"We're grateful for your hospitality! Really, we are!" I say next, looking them over through the billowing smoke. I hear the

Challenger's belly grumble. I would feel hungry myself if the slime were not burning there.

"What kind of a name *is* The Challenger? asks Bub then, blinking his beady eyes at the ranger, pouting his lower lip. "I would've called him The One-Eyed!"

Lumpen and the father chortle.

"Why are *you* called Dropped?" the ranger asks, looking at the reddish-haired brother.

The scene is tense. The fire sizzles and the smoke rises to the roof, some of it seeping into the holes and nooks in the wood and straw.

"Dropped by Dragos?" I inquire. I remember the villagers in the Vale told us they were brought by Dragos long ago. Did the mighty dragon drop these ones here by mistake, or maybe *not* by mistake?

The father looks at me oddly, cocking a grey brow.

"The dragon?" my sister asks. "The Vale is named for Him!"

"You say weird names!" declares Bub, looking into the flames between us. "Dragos! Xelia! Challenger!"

"Xelia was an ancient winged-steed rider!" I say enthusiastically.

The father shakes his big head, waving his hand faster now, leaning his arm from his furred mantle, and shouting: "We here forever, our clan, Dropped!"

We hear the slime beneath us making pained gurgles. I can tell that Fauna is becoming further riled. I speak, hoping to come across as more diplomatic than she would.

"So, friends, why do you burn the slime?" I ask. Fauna nods eagerly at my side.

The woman whom I think is actually made of stone, snorts piercingly. "She asks why we burn slime!"

I hear cackling laughter from behind us, from the dangling members of the clan that hover over the entrance in their swaying pods. Both brothers look at me. I cannot read their long faces. Am I overstepping the boundaries of our stay? I think back to Silver Coast, at Academy when the Professors taught us about ethics.

"It's sentient!" I follow-up.

"The capacity to speak does not make one brainy!" says the Challenger.

"Thanks," I mouth. The 30-something ranger shrugs.

"This is their territory, isn't it?" my sister asks with grit in her voice. Fresh flames flicker and smoke surges from the hearth.

"Slime *hates* sunlight!" calls a voice towards the front of the home.

"Be silent, Gram!" Bub shouts.

The father cries: "I'm hungry!"

"Fire dying, magic reeling!" calls the stoned woman. "Bub, get more!"

"Lumpen, get more," says Bub in turn. He stands and holds a small twirling ball of reddish fire that floats between his palms. The other brother grunts, stands, and goes to the home's back part. The father waves further. I see things floating from the unseen pantry at the back, blue eggs nearly the size of my sister's head, hunks of red meat, and a buzzing cloud of chopped spices that move like a swarm of bugs.

"Tasty slime," the big man says, bringing the hovering items toward the hearth. I shudder.

Fauna taps my knee and calls: "Group huddle!"

My sister leads us over to the front. Here more walls of curtain hang. Fauna leans on the wooden door a little, and nods to the ranger, letting him speak first.

"Listen," he says. "We won't feast on the slime, no doubt I don't want to, but we can eat the other food they're offering, no?

And they can tell us about this underground realm, what we can expect next as we try to find a way out of here?"

"Hee hee!" a crackled voice rings out above us.

The Challenger frowns. I follow his gaze and see the two elder denizens peering over their roped baskets, both gaping of maws and wide of eyes.

"We already know a way out," Sister whispers, sliding her small form to the big door we first came in, reaching both arms at the edges, opening it.

"The slime," I say as I follow her out.

"Bee are bee!" the ranger calls to our hosts, passing briskly, letting the door fall into place behind him. Outside is not bright as it was before. The trees and crops and stalagmites around the farmstead cast lengthening shadows. Far up at the ceiling of the cavern I can see the twilight sky and part of the rising moon through the great parting in the cavern's roof.

"Hello—ellooo—looo--oooo!" Fauna shouts, her screechy voice echoing throughout the colossal chamber. "Wow, this is something! Do you think Dragos dropped them while flying over the mountains long ago?"

I find myself remembering the dragon's skeleton that we saw those days ago on the side of the mountain, back when we had a flying ship—we've really have had quite a quest so far!

"Look," says the Challenger to the discussion at hand. "We got hosts here, yeah? We can eat, lodge, and by morning be on our way."

"Our way is up," says Fauna, pointing to the faraway sky.

"And do we have enough rope? No," says the Challenger. "We've nothing, unless Flora here wants to flood the entire place with Delipha's rod!"

Unsure if he's sarcastic, I reach for the magical item at my belt. I do quick calculations in my head. "No," I say. "Too many tunnels and crevices, water will flow out."

"Well, we can't leave the slime," Fauna says, and she glances about the nearby groves. "It cushioned us as we were dragged in the net, remember? It was trying to help, and it spoke, reasoned with us!"

The Challenger guffaws. "After it tried to slay us twice! Let's just make friends with these weirdies."

"Could we talk them into freeing the slime?" asks Sister.

"I agree," I concede, shuddering as I think of the poor slime burning in that hearth. "If slime can reason with *us*, then we *can* reason with *them*."

The Challenger grins gawkily.

"What?" I cry. "We can!"

The ranger sighs, one of his eyebrows cocking. "Well, just remember what happened the last time we interfered."

"The Vale of Dragos?" asks Fauna. "When *she* revealed to them that the dragon they worshiped lay dead on the face of the mountain?"

"Oh yeah," I concede further.

"And the hosts we had, they treated us well," says the Challenger. "Emera especially."

"Emera didn't cook sentient creatures," I say.

"None that we know of," adds Fauna. "But she didn't seem the type."

"She *wasn't!*" insists the ranger. "The point is we're being hosted and fed and if we're lucky we'll be shown a way out."

"If not, we still have bread left…" my sister trails off. She looks around, twirling a red hair that streaks down from the base of her cap. She points to the nearest of the tall perfectly upward reaching trees.

"Chop?" I ask.

"A task!" sneers the Challenger. "A bit of a side-quest to make such a ladder!"

"Oh! You come as guests and you talk of such things!" calls a snortful voice from an unseen source (namely behind us). I feel dread as I glance over my shoulder. The brother Lumpen stands there, clutching two pails overflowing with blue mushrooms. From the short distance I can see how pale the front of his protracted face is, and how sunken his eyes are.

"We gift you food and that's how you speak!" he snarls as he steps toward the front door to the massive home.

"I won't eat *those* mushrooms again," laughs Fauna. "And it was the slime that saved me when I did!"

"You speak of making a gigantic ladder? No one leaves through up where the sun streaks across the gaps in the rock!" cries Lumpen, looking above at the darkening sky.

"Where do we leave through?" I ask, trying to sound calm. "Any tunnels leading out of the mountains to outside, the above world?"

The tall man spits at his own feet. "Slime blocks all the underpasses that lead through dark!"

"Really?" I ask him, trying to recall if I've read anything about slime being so prevalent underground. Did Xelia mention anything of this in the carvings I read down here? I suddenly remember what we'd earlier read on the rocks, back before the slime had attacked us that first time. She wrote:

In the colossal caverns I have sensed something unexplained, but I do know that to survive in the depths you need not only use your mind and your body, but also your heart.

What did this mean?

Lumpen frowns, saying: "Our magic makes it so sunlight keeps them back even at night! We catch rain, but sun too!" He then huffs and opens the front door with his foot before stamping inside.

Us three exchange looks as the door shuts behind him. At the roof of the home I see the massive bowl that I'd thought was only for collecting water. It shimmers, intense light now emanating from its basin like a torch. The surrounding land begins to lighten once more. Above us the black of night has already unfolded, yet the groves and the crops of this farmstead remain bright as day. I fan my eyes and peer far, noting that the light goes to the end of their trees and crops. We stand in a single bright space in an expanse of black shadow.

"Keeps the slime away," I say.

Sister nods. "Let's go," she says. "We've waited too long."

"Yes," agrees the ranger. "And this is cliche, but to speak of getting higher, reaching the top? Well, as I always say, I'm chaotic. With chaos," he adds, pointing up. "You can climb?"

Fauna tilts her head at him, her expression seemingly puzzled yet thoughtful. Our trio enters the home again. The hearth broils as Lumpen pours fresh glowing mushrooms in. Overhead the two elder clan members snicker as we pass under their swaying baskets.

"It was *you* turned yourself into stone!" cries the father to the mother near the hearth. Bub stares at us from the distance in the middle of the great room, now with two floating balls of fire in his hands. We three walk in a wide row, quickly nearing the raised hearth spot.

"There's One-Eye! Bub, look!" shouts the bald hovering elder from the front.

The reddish-haired brother goes wide-eyed, and he lobs a fireball towards the pod of the bald old one, seemingly annoyed. The small flaming ball whizzes over our heads, nearly singing my cap. In pure reflex, I reach for Delipha's rod, snatch it from my belt, and then spin myself quickly calling upon the goddess, sending a stream of seawater upwards towards the fireball. The waters reach just in time to douse it before it hits the old hanging one. Oddly, I expect the clan to be relieved I stopped a potential fire in their home. Instead none of them save Bub even looks at us, oh and how he gazes…

If he was annoyed before he is enraged now. He readies his arm to shoot the other fireball, this time at us! No longer holding back, Fauna runs first, dashing up the small steps to the raised space, towards the fiery hearth, towards the slime.

The Challenger shouts "Now!" too late, but he charges along her side, his sword unsheathed and ready to cover her.

Chaos is happening. I move too keep up with them. This won't be easy, whatever is about to happen. Sister ascends steps to the raised platform where the two brothers stand. The Challenger strides aside her, sword in hand. Another fireball bursts from the red-haired brother's fists, passing over my companions, zooming at me!

I raise the magical rod. Seawater shoots forth, ending the threat.

Frantically, I shout: "I was just trying to prevent a fire, there I've done it twice!"

"Ah!" the big father snaps, waving dismissively, belching as he stands by the two brothers. "I've the power of cold don't you know? Was under control!"

"Hospitality privileges revoked! Insulted us!" the clan-mother cries from the big chair across from the others of the clan. The Challenger leaps across the hearth, challenging (hence his name) the two brothers at once. He waves his sword from one side to the other, bidding them 'move back!'

"Can we yet de-escalate?" I wonder.

No. Fauna is dashing into the sunken hearth to rescue the slime. I leap up the little steps next, raising Delipha's Rod in one hand, pulling out the Mighty Magnet from my belt in my other. I call upon the Sea Goddess again, splashing beneath my feet to the blazing hearth. I see Fauna's red cap moving and I drench the spaces beside and behind her in a circular frenzy as she moves her arms around the quivering mass, the burning slime.

A great weight is suddenly pulling on my arm. I gasp, realizing the stream of water has become solid ice! I nearly topple, but the long frozen stream breaks off, and I yank myself backwards, falling off the raised platform, back onto the lower ground toward the entrance. I land on carpeting, cushioning my fall.

"We're taking the slime!" I call as I realize I am unhurt. Barely aching, I lean up and look upon the scene: directly across from me on the elevated flooring the stout father stands, his frosty thick arms protruding at the sides of his furry mantle, his bead-like eyes fixated on me. The Challenger, his back to the squelched hearth, flicks his sword about, and Bub (red of hair) steps back from him, face contorted as he chants deeply. At his side the brother Lumpen (of blonde hair) has backed even further from the ranger, now twirling his hands about.

"Fauna!" I cry to my sister. Unaided, I see her hand reach the lip of the hearth. Her clothes are damp, yet she remains unscathed by the fire. The bulging mass of the slime, crisped, she pushes above her onto the floor to the base of the chair across the way, the chair where the lady of stone sits. Fauna pulls herself up onto the raised floor. At her right is the Challenger, keeping the others at bay, the father too having stepped back from his swordplay.

"Insulters!" shouts the father, his fists covered in ice.

"Farmer Ice!" cries the Challenger assertively, slashing a wide X as he shouts: "Allow us leave!"

"The slime comes with us!" calls Fauna. I get up and run to her side, calling upon Delipha once more to pour over the slime. I hear what sounds like soothing moans emanate from its broad mass.

Something creaks. The stone mother on the chair stands before us and we sisters both gasp.

"Oh girls, did you really think I was immobile this whole time?" she asks, her mouth still gaping. She pulls back an arm and swiftly punches Fauna, sending her back into the hearth. I duck as another rocky fist swings at me, lowering my face close to the slime's surface.

"Thank you," a limp voice speaks.

I glance up and see a stone foot rushing at my face, yet I manage to tumble away sideways along the side of the hearth, back towards the couch we'd earlier been sitting on. I get to my feet and glance frantically to the father across the way.

Our ranger friend does one of his high jumps just as the thick icy man is about to ram him, letting the portly farmer bash into Bub instead, interrupting his incantations. As the Challenger lands, Lumpen sends a whirlwind from his hands, flinging the Challenger, sending him shooting over my head toward the front of the big room.

"No fire! Fire squelched!" shouts the mother to the others then. "No fire, magic reels!"

Fauna jumps from the doused hearth, landing at my side, her blade drawn. The stone mother runs at us, while the father and two brothers scramble along behind her. The three men behind her abruptly trip on something unseen. From my vantage, over the shoulder of the stone attacker I see for a split moment the slime is at their feet, wrapping their ankles in newly sprouted tendrils!

Fauna waves her blade at the oncoming stone woman, slowly backing from her. *"Sword won't hinder her,"* I hastily think. My magnet and water rod are of no use either, I realize. I turn toward the front entrance, charging towards the Challenger.

The ranger is on his feet again, having slammed against the wall. Now he is being assailed from above. Pots and pans and other little things are being chucked by the two hanging elders, the one of white hair, the other of none. Beneath their dangling pods, the Challenger dodges their thrown items, hopping from one foot to another, all the while retrieving his bow from his back, dropping his sword for a moment as he fits his only arrow (not sure where he got it from) onto the bowstring, and he then pivots to dodge a plunging glass bottle, and shoots upward.

This arrow flies diagonally toward the ropes that bear the two swaying baskets, piercing one of each in its flight, lop-siding both pods, sending both elders to the floorboards. They feebly lay slug-like at the Challenger's feet, but as he retrieves his sword they promptly scurry away together, vanishing behind the curtains to the side.

"Fauna!" I yell.

"Slime!" she cries back, lowering her blade, still slashing the area between her and the stony mother. Our slippery ally, having already tripped the three men, now oozes towards us at the front. The stone woman turns about and steps heavily with both feet upon the slime, stopping it in its slime tracks. Fauna charges her, slicing her sword, smacking the back of the rocky mother's head until sparks appear.

"Magic reeling!" shouts the stone woman again to the others of the clan, ignoring Fauna. "More glow mushrooms! Hearth dies! So too will our powers fade if not re-lit!"

"Stop telling them!" the father bellows.

I take the Mighty Magnet and I say the words to activate, flinging some of the pots and pans that had earlier been hurled at the Challenger, flinging his too sword in the process. The items barely deter the mother and Fauna is still making sparks on her side as the father and his sons rise again behind the mother. The Challenger, catching his sword after I use the magnetic force to swing it back at him, steps over to the large curtains on the wall at his side and he gingerly lifts the flap of one with his sword's end, revealing a small room with a thick cauldron.

"Chuck it!" he says, smiling over to me as he too notices it.

"Fauna!" I cry. "Move!"

My sister moves swiftly, ducking, and then rolling toward the Challenger at the side wall.

Magnet in hand, I pull the mighty iron pot towards me. It moves slowly, scraping the floor as it heaves. I sidestep toward the Challenger and I switch opposite magnetic force, pushing hard, sending the cauldron at the raised wooden platform that is the living room. The cauldron, after smashing the stoned mother, then the father and Bub and Lumpen, crashes into the wood of the platform, sending splinters everywhere as four voices cry out.

My sister had moved in time, ducking, then rolling toward the Challenger at the side wall. The slime slides along towards us, and the Challenger aggressively swings open the front door. Thinking it might come in handy, I grab the fallen curtain off the floor, the one that was just hanging before the cauldron. I then dash out behind my sister and the slithering slime. The last thing I see inside, as I slam the front door, is the cauldron rolling away from the middle of the room, the clan all out of sight among the splintered wood.

We run as one column into the cold underground night. The curtain in my arms is huge. I nearly trip on it as I run after Fauna. I toss the curtain over the slime at my side, hoping it might protect it from the sunlight that comes from the strange lighted-up bowl that sits atop the home's roof! Fauna, seeming to understand, kneels over hastily to scoop the blanketed slime into her arms. A soft voice speaks from underneath her: *"Their magic is fading, but the light still beams. Hastily, to the barn!"*

"I guess after all that we're friends with the slime now!" speaks hastily the Challenger as we three curve our running trajectory to our left, turning along the corner towards the back, towards the barn with the magic fungus. The Challenger, longest of leg, leads, my sister and I behind him, the curtain flapping in her arms. Tiny blue fowl birds jump out of our way, clucking in annoyance as we run alongside the wall of the big home.

Fauna tears open the barn's big door when we reach the space between the two buildings, rushing in with the slime in tow. The Challenger and I stand at the entrance, catching our breaths, readying ourselves for more action. With his blade drawn and my magic items both at the ready, we stare at the back door of the home just past the narrow ditch.

Over my shoulder I see everything inside the barn glows. The blue mushrooms on the walls pulsate wildly and in near unison they detach from the wall and begin to float.

"They look like jellyfish!" the Challenger grunts in amazement, taking a glance.

The blue mushrooms, brighter now than ever, all hover above the slime, encircling it, then they dissipate in a flash, their forms fading into shining mist that cascades onto the slime as Fauna gazes on. The slime's whole being glows.

"Ah, Sacred crop, Ancestral lifeblood!" says the slime. It's form begins to make random patterns, bulging, stretching, bubbling. *"Xelia, yes. Xelia, my friend, on rocks of our homeland She carved ages ago. She used her Heart, the first of the surface world to treat us kindly. I see Xelia lives in your Hearts!"*

Fauna smiles as the slime turns into a big pinkish-green heart-shape for a moment. "Thank you. Hey Sis! Did you hear that? That's what the riddle meant!"

"Ah!" says the Challenger, nodding over to her, then me. "You didn't catch that with your brain slug, eh?"

I shrug. The back door of the home across the short distance shakes, then it flings open. The Challenger raises his sword higher. I raise my rod.

Lumpen stands there in the archway, anger evident on his long face. He hollers: "Squelch my brother's fire, but can you withstand my flurries?"

Behind him the great light bowl fades slightly. Lumpen shoots strong winds from his fingertips, sending both of us hard against the wooden barn's front. I maintain the grips on my magnet and rod, but my hands are flung at my sides, I cannot move!

"Guess they still have some magic!" barks the Challenger at my side against the wall.

Something shoots through the barn door then, something green, flat, blue, and wide. It hugs the ground, zooming underneath the gusts. This mass spins around Lumpen's feet, tripping him, stopping his winds, allowing the Challenger and me to drop. Fauna runs out beside us, immediately taking off alongside the home again. The Challenger and I shake ourselves a bit, and then follow, passing by the slime as it morphs into a bigger form, turning into that hand form that it had used to slap us earlier! I see it chuck Lumpen into the barn just as I round the home's corner.

Far above us, through the crack in the mountain, is a black starry sky. I see it only for a moment, stealing a glance. Now the slime follows us and we all tear along the side of the wall, dodging patches of crops and the weird blue hens. I hear commotion as the slime, now a big turquoise ball that is twice as tall the Challenger, rolls rapidly alongside us.

"What's the plan?" asks the Challenger.

"Where can we leave the underground?" Fauna asks the slime quickly.

"Xelia found a way, but the pass She took has been blocked for centuries!" replies the slime hastily, its voice sounding strong once more, like a powerful torrent of hissing steam.

"There they are!" shouts a deep voice. I see the father emerge at the front corner of the home. Bub and the stone mother arrive behind him. The red-haired brother bears the great net which he had originally caught us in.

We all halt in our tracks. The Challenger cries out, standing aside my sister, both of them raising their swords before themselves.

"No more!" shouts Fauna at them.

"We leave here! No more battle!" declares the Challenger.

I feel the air is suddenly cold. I see the father, standing a ways from us, holding out his arms, sending forth from them an immense arctic blast.

Delipha's Rod! I raise it again, stepping in front of my party, splashing out a great wave of water. My liquid stream streaks hard into the oncoming freezing air, the waters arching upward, becoming an immense wall of hard ice!

I keep splashing forth, standing firm as I watch the whole region in front of me become a single white-blue mass. The frozen water protrudes like a singular tear-shaped bulge, the heaviest part falling first and it falls towards our attackers.

The three farmer folk scuttle from under the shadow of the plunging formation, and then shards of ice upon ice shatter before me!

The slime projects forth its wide bulk before us, shielding us from the debris before it envelopes us completely. I see nothing, only feel softness around me. In front of my nose and mouth is open space, somehow I breathe comfortably, though my heart is thumping.

"Be calm, friends," I hear the slime speak as I feel movement all around me. I know the slime is stirring quickly. It won't hurt us, not after all this, and it quickly asks: *"Doth I have permission to grab hold of you all and flee from here?"*

"Yes!" I say, echoed by the Challenger and my sister.

Things crash, the voices of the clan cry out. It seems that the body of the slime begins bouncing and bouncing, and then it springs what I assume is upward. I feel force pushing me and soon I can see again. My sister calls beside me, but I can only look forward, for just my face is uncovered.

"Do you have your cap?" I call to her, nearly laughing, though I am terrified as I gaze into night sky, the stars all spinning. I soon see the white curtain above me. It shoots out and the zooming pace begins to slow. We are floating now, floating, gliding downward. The great curtain is stretched, its ends held firm in grasping arms of the slime.

"Gods!" cries our unseen ranger friend. "We are above the mountains!"

I see it, the range far beneath, some of the peaks covered in snow that gleams in the moonlight. The slime coasts for a short while upon the high airs toward a long plateaued niche region beside the massive crack in the mountain. I realize the slime must have bounced so hard it cleared the whole subterranean valley!

Soon the slime lands, rolling, covering us once more in itself. Though a bit dizzy, I'm relieved when everything ceases and the slime finally softly pushes us from it's expansive body, depositing us upon smooth ground. Our clothes are surprisingly dry.

The Challenger stands, declaring: "I was wrong about you, slime! For that, I am sorry!"

The slime mouthlessly mutters: *"Truly, ranger, You are a goodly being!"*

"Well," the Challenger laughs, getting to his feet, rubbing his chin with the back of his hand. "Chaotic, maybe a little good."

He grins at us sisters as we too stand, Fauna beginning to do some stretches. "That was quite a ride!" she says to the slime.

"The clan folk are surrounded by a fresh moat," the slime beams and its big mass deflates into a long snake-like form that begins slithering around us gracefully. *"The fire son, he melted it when we were fleeing up here."*

Behind where we stand expands the great crack, and we hastily gather side by side to peer over the immense distance. As the slime says, the homestead far below (visible because the bowl of light is shining again) is encircled by waters that appear thick and deep. I can see specks moving into the home, the clan, and I can see tiny blue fowl floating calmly on the surface of the new waters.

"You're lucky I'm out of arrows, Bub!" the Challenger roars down the immense fissure.

"I know of ways back inside," says the slime, and it becomes a green ball the size of a bull. *"They have not access to more of our crop, at least for now. I shall return to my slime-folk and organize in the time we have to protect against the clan!"*

"We would love to help, but I'm thinking that we're finished with the underworld," my sister says and I nod eagerly in agreement.

"You have helped more than enough. I shall remind the others that there are some from the surface that are Good-Hearted, some like Xelia. Your names?" the slime asks, its surface rippling a little.

We three tell our names.

"Flora and Fauna, two sisters," says the slime, bubbling in amusement. *"And their friend, the Challenger! Slime-folk will know your names!"*

With no further words the slime bids us farewell by turning into a hand and giving a curt wave before it dissipates into a puddle and begins scuttling down the steadily curving mountainside.

We stand now on one of many mountains that surround the Valley of Dragos. The sight before us is breathtaking, a great steep expanse of rocky ground that eventually becomes lush halfway to the base of the slope. There are forests and beyond that we can just barely see meadows. I know that this is west and south and that this is where we want to go; it is to the north and east where the hundreds of craggy mountain peaks stand. We are here at the end, nearer than ever to where we began this quest.

"South and west," says Sister, she too understanding the remaining journey ahead of us.

"To home?" I ask Fauna, immediately remembering that Silver Coast is only a few days from this point. We were so blessed to have had such a detour underground! She removes her red cap, hitting some of the dust off her sleeve and shoulders with it. As she places it back on, she nods once. I can see how weary she is, despite her big relieving smile. I feel a grin of my own forming.

"So, is that a *yes*?" I ask, laughing.

"To home, yes! Our luck might run out if we stay questing too long!" she says, pulling on the string to her little backpack.

"You two are not low-level anymore," says the Challenger, placing his sword back in place in the old scabbard at his side near his two belts. He looks off from us, turning partly towards the great crack in the mountain. "I think that the Vale of Dragos is that way, if I can remember rightly."

We can see that there is a level ground that spans around the crack, eventually leading eastward.

"You're the ranger!" says Fauna jestingly. "You would know better than we!"

"My slug tells me that's the right way," I say. "And from when we were flying in the ship I saw pathways between the peaks. There *is* a way down there, down that big bowl into the vale."

He looks back to us. "Will you two be alright on the road home?"

"Well, yes, and we can pay you the rest of what we owe?" I tell him, remembering how we first met him in the tavern.

"It's been a great quest, friends," he says, placing both hands on his belts after waving his hands to refuse payment.

"What?" I ask, not liking where this is going.

Fauna's mouth is hanging open as she looks to the ranger. In a moment, as the Challenger once more looks away, she appears to compose herself, and to him she says: "Emera?"

The Challenger nods. "We left the Vale of Dragos in a not great place, didn't we? I felt kind of bad for leaving her and the others like that."

"She did a lot for us," I say, thinking back to the lovely green-haired woman who hosted us.

"What made you decide this?" Fauna asks.

"Something Xelia said long ago," he says.

"Do your thing," Sister says after a moment. She's now looking to me. "I think she's single?"

"Either way, she may need help, as well her daughter, her brothers, and *everyone* of sound mind in the Vale of Dragos!" says the ranger. He then looks to us, adding: "I'll someday come to collect the rest of the coin, and maybe another quest? But, will you two be safe?"

"Challenger!" I laugh, motioning to my rod, my magnet, my dagger, and my sister.

After eating what's left of the bread we hug three ways, a long friendly and warm embrace, and then the ranger parts to go ranging over the range. I hope we meet again.

We sisters turn now westward, and we trek down, reaching the mountain's base by morning. Here stands a tiny village called Xelia. Its denizens are strong and proud and we're told that they're the descendants of the great warrior herself. Once on the surface she had come here to this calm valley and settled. We have followed *such* a legacy!

Completing our quest is all!

THE END

The Scouring of Silver Coast

We earned such a rest after all our adventures, having just come from the underground world. My sister and I stayed at an inn within the simple mountainside village for three days. Parting on the third morning we find ourselves on an earth pathway that sprouts westward. This mostly flat land stretches onward, south of the realms we had initially come through.

Just north of here is where we'd first met the Challenger, our ranger friend who accompanied us through our quest. On that northerly trail we had become trapped in Hare-Neck Valley where we partook involuntarily in a gigantic game between three strange players. After that we'd met the surviving player, Lobster-Man, and we faced his augmented kobold army. From there we had gone eastward to the ruins of an abandoned campus where we fought the dreaded Straw Man, an old adversary of the Challenger. From there we ventured in a flying ship over immense mountain ranges, crashing into the Vale of Dragos, and then, as you likely remember, reader, we traveled under the mountains to end up in the village, Xelia.

We no longer can count on the Challenger, for he parted us once we'd emerged from the underground. I can say that we sisters did enough questing for a lifetime (or at least a while). By late afternoon the pathway becomes stone road. The grasses we pass on either side of us are greenish-yellow, waiting for some rain so the blades can transition to a deeper green. There aren't many clouds, so it looks like they'll have to wait.

"I can't believe how we lucked out," says Fauna as we walk side by side, keeping a medium pace. She has her sword at her belt, a fresh bow across her form, and a quiver of new arrows at her back.

"You wanted a quest, did you?" I ask her.

"Yes," she laughs back. "But you came too!'

"Truth," I say, looking at the thirsty grasses swaying in the breeze.

"And we wouldn't have gotten far without the Challenger," she says. "Although we pulled our own too, didn't we?"

"We did," I agree, taking a glance at my belt, seeing my dagger alongside my magical items that I've gained, Delipha's Rod and the Mighty Magnet. Such luck! In my mind I calculate the chances of our survival in each of the adventures – the three of us likely should have perished, really.

"Never been here before," says Fauna, looking about. We had explored the outskirts of Silver Coast when we were smaller, but never here this far south of the city. A green river splashes on just north of us, its muddy banks a small ways from the road.

"I know *of* the area," I say, having seen the maps of this region. "The Silver River here, I think, pretty sure. We'll be at the southern gates before twilight."

My sister smiles as the sun lights up her already bright face. "The brain slug?"

I nod, feeling my own smile fade. She's referring to the creature in my head.

"Mother may know of a way to remove it," Fauna says, looking back to the grass.

"Maybe," I say. It's now that I remember that many of the items that Mother gave us when we first set out had been lost during the quest. We have none left of those tiny alchemy bombs!

Something happens as we move onto higher ground – I hear a greeting voice. I glance about, seeing no one save Sister. The voice is feminine, less youthful, and I begin to recognize it from our adventures.

"Flora, can you hear me?" it calls.

I pause when Fauna and I reach the rising ground's summit. Beyond a wide valley before us I see the tallest rising spires of Silver Coast, and I breathe in relief at the distant sight. My right hand goes to Fauna's left arm. She pauses, and I tell her what I hear.

"I hear you," I respond, amazed that I find myself speaking in my head. I remember now. It is Qilla, the older woman we met in the Vale of Dragos at the library. She told me that she too has a brain slug and had spoken to me this way before.

"It is I, Qilla," she responds with a faint laugh. *"I reach you all the way from my home in the Vale of Dragos! It seems your slug too has evolved, become telepathic it has!"*

I reply, just thinking: *"My sister and I are near our home, safe and well!"*

"Flora, what are you doing?"

"I'm talking in my head, talking to Qilla," I say. Sister looks apprehensive.

"Your ranger friend has made it down here, two days ago, a sturdy and intrepid adventurer he truly is! He says 'hello'!"

"The Challenger!" I tell Fauna and feel my mouth turning into a grin. "He's made it safely to the Vale!"

Fauna silently cheers and then sits herself on the round summit, grabbing a wayward apple that had fallen from the single nearby tree and biting into it (the apple, not the tree). "Greet him for me!" she beams as bits of juice run down her lips.

"*We are delighted he has made it! Please tell him!*"

"*I will,*" replies Qilla. "*The Challenger and Emera are going for a walk now. He seems to have a sweet side to him.*"

"*Yep!*" I think back, giggling loudly.

"*Flora,*" says Qilla. I can hear a seriousness in her telepathic tone. I gaze onto some distant wispy clouds floating over my still distant city as she continues: "*I must warn you. Something stirs, something on the coast of this great continent, not far from where I sense you stand now. A mind, possibly too with a slug, one that is far older and more embedded than yours, even mine...I sense it, something powerful!*"

"Another slug?" I say aloud, and Fauna looks concerned as I say this. I repeat it in my mind to Qilla.

"*Possibly, though something odd about it,*" says she. "*Ahh, sorry friend, Hue chipped his foot, got to help him!*"

She bids me farewell, telling me that she may contact me again if she gets more information. I hastily relay this all to Fauna who in turn simply shrugs her shoulders and says: "Well, we have so many scholars here in the city, so many libraries beyond just Mother's. There could be another in the city lodged in someone's head?"

"Yes," I semi-agree, uneasy.

We move down the big hill. Here there are small houses, wooden and stone ones, and a beige brick roadway that winds about them. The great white walls ascend beyond. I still see the spires and towers, and between them the famous blocky wide turreted fortress. This fortress was built in the feudal era, that's Mother's generation.

"Home," I say in astonishment. From here I cannot see Mother's library, for it's all the way in the Northwest Quadrant of the city. "Ah, we approach from the South and the East! Through this valley and we're at the walls!"

Fauna has a smile paved on her face, a look of contentment I've not seen for a long time. There are ups and downs as we move along the twisty road, little vales at the bottom of the hills. Each time we ascend to a summit we see more of the oncoming city. Every now and again we see a home or two, some side by side, most nearer the high points of the rising and falling land. There are folks about, some, and we sisters keep greeting people joyfully, both of us just so happy to have completed our quest.

"There," says Fauna after we finally make our way out of these hilly outskirts and cross a long stone bridge over the Silver River. The mighty city walls rise about twenty paces from us now. Before the wall we can see a short procession of folks, about twenty deep, all lined up, some with wagons. This is one of the two entrances—there is one here at the southeast and one further at the northeast. A pair of familiar tall bronze-ish gates are flung open as is usual for the daytime, though I am a little perplexed at the slow moving lineup. Usually folks are able to just wander inside. As we get closer along this last street in front of the wall we see that there are guards posted at the doorway, questioning the first in line.

"Strange," I say.

"Things have changed since we left?" Sister says, leading me over the beige cobbles to the back of the lineup. I glance upward, noticing more guards on the top of the wall, each of them clad in greyish-blue.

"Names? Work? District?" one of the two guards in the shadowy archway says to the family before us once we are closer to the entrance-way. A woman with lightening-white hair answers quickly as her partner grabs the wrists of one of three children, bidding the little one to keep still while the other two hop in place.

"What district are we?" Fauna asks from my side.

"Northwest," I answer, unsure if she really forgot that.

"Oh yeah," she says, smacking the side of her head playfully. "I need a slug of my own!"

The small clan before us begins moving through the open gates, and the nearer of the two guards moves his hand to motion us to approach. Sister tilts her cap in greeting as we step over to the guard. He looks to be around the Challenger's age, mid-30s, though his face is fair more clean-cut and he has both eyes, two greens.

"Names? Work? District?" he asks in an unsmiling disposition. Both guards lean against their pikes on opposite walls, the further one, a woman with silvery hair with a thin dyed blue line running through along her ponytail, looks us up and down.

Sometimes I'd race to answer before my sister, but not this time. She tells our names and that we are returning from an adventure, and then she adds: "We're from the Northwest."

"Campus District," I add plainly. Beyond the arch I can barely make the stones of the entrance square, nearly able to hear the distant splash of fountains. The first guard looks to the second, the second shaking her head underneath her cone-shaped helmet.

"Campus District is sealed over, as you must already know since you live here?" says the nearer guard.

"It's been a month to two and a half, a near season," Sister tells him. "What do you mean, *sealed*?"

The other guard brings both hands to her pike, no longer leaning. "You're not with one of those shell houses, are you?" she asks gruffly.

"And where have you two been exactly to not know this? Underground?" asks the green-eyed guard warily.

Fauna eagerly nods while she brings her backpack off of her, unfastening the strings and reaching in to bring out a handful of glowing blue mushrooms. "Don't eat them, poison-ish, but see, yes, we've been underground!" she laughs.

"What do you mean by sealed? What are shell houses?" I repeat her question, adding my own, as the second guard steps over and peers at the glowing fungi. I'm suddenly worried about Mother and everyone else we know in the city. *"Sealed?"* I ask myself, fully unsure of what that means.

The female guard approaches and plucks one of the mushrooms, inspecting it. "You could sell these at the markets," she says to Fauna.

"As long as no one tries to resell them as food," Sister replies.

"I believe it now," says the first guard then. "You girls have not been around for a while. The canals are on fire, magic fire."

"The bridges are all burned," says the second.

"And the fires won't stop," finishes the first.

"Magic—magic fire?" I stammer, immediately thinking they are kidding with us, playing mind games with us because we're younger and they are tripping with their power.

"Wait, does this mean we can't reach home?" Sister says, seemingly more to me.

I nod, already knowing this, and I hastily make a wide circle with my finger in front of her, explaining: "Remember the city is round like a wheel, so Southeast, Southwest," I say and dab my pointing finger at the bottom and top of one side, hoping it makes sense on her end. "The wall runs here along the East."

She nods quickly and points to the imagined left side (my left) of the imagined map. "This is the Silver Sea," she says, moving her whole hand downward. "All along the open water runs the western half, I remember."

"Yes," says I, and then I put a perfect criss-cross with my finger from one end to the other and from the top to the bottom. "The canals here, so they are on fire. That's what you mean when you say *sealed* isn't it?" I ask the guards. They both nod curtly.

"We can head to the Southwest Quadrant and get a ferry to the Northwest?" Fauna asks me.

"You cannot get to the Southwest in the first place because there is fire between you and it!" barks the second guard, and she peers over our heads to the growing line-up behind us.

"You mean to say we're stuck in the Southeast?" Fauna suddenly gripes, the usually rosiness on her face vanishing.

The two guards nod, and then I nod and say: "It would seem so," and then I sigh and ask: "What caused this magic fire?"

"No more time to be answering!" says the male guard, gripping his pole-arm, stamping it's base against the cobbled stones beneath. "Move on now if you're entering the city!"

"Are we entering?" I ask Fauna, but she is already moving, shaking her head at the guards for their pushiness. I call behind me as I jog to catch up to her. "What caused the fires?"

"Ask someone inside!" calls the woman guard before she turns to attend the next party.

We are beyond the archways, stepping onto the familiar brilliance of the first square of Silver Coast. Somehow we are close to home, yet so far at the same time. We're going to have to get informed fast on what's going on if we're going to find our way back. I've got a feeling this might be bad.

"Welcome home," we sisters say to one another as we step out of the archway.

I immediately recognize the scape, the slug in my brain, the one that grants me instant recollection of everything I ever learned, reminds me. We are inside the walls of Silver Coast. The splashing of fountains is the first thing I hear and the second thing I see after the immense cobbled square, the entrance of the city, as it was when we left though maybe only a third of it's usual crowd. It must be because the city is cut off from itself; the four canals, as we learned before entering, are seemingly on *fire*, magic fire. The whole city is cordoned off into it's four major quadrants; we are in the Southeast, our home is in the Northwest.

As we walk from the walls things become busier. A few throngs of pedestrians pass through markets, and I've counted at least a dozen carriages drawn by burdensome beasts, many belonging to merchants either heading to or leaving from these busy markets. We consider buying some food as we look upon sultry flat-breads, fruity pastes, and honeyed syrups, along with steaming pies and buttery biscuits, but we opt to instead eat the leftovers the villagers gave us back at the mountainside hamlet. As I bite into the stale-ish bread I think of the contrast between that place and here, even if the crowds are not as large as usual. As we munch Sister leads, taking a turn down a narrower way. On our left side stretches a row of two-story buildings, and at our right side there are numerous houses, many stacked together, some four or five stories.

I can see a few of the tallest spires in the distance to the North and West-ish, beyond this quadrant. Ever since I was really little those sky-piercing towers gave me a sense of lofty majesty, especially on a clear day or at night when the lights from within make them appear as star-filled themselves. Mother's library is among some of those towers, further to the Northwest, the campus district. I feel annoyed that I cannot now waltz in, step on through the great sunny atrium and find a desk to get lost in a tome or two, or at the very least take a long nap in my old room. Sadly, we might not even be able to see Mother for some time still. We have left the corridors between structures and are in another square. Here there are two fountains, one at either end of the wide space, each with a bronze fish-shaped spout.

"The most crowded place I've seen in weeks, yet I've never seen this place so uncrowded!" Fauna says as we move along between more market stalls. These are largely small wooden desks or portable carts that folks have set up. I see some with jewelry, others with tools, and more than a few with glass bottles, some with waters, milks, and a few of bright colours, potions, all beautiful and some obviously magical.

I remember this place, recalling having come here more than once with Sister or friends, usually after classes were done. We were younger and interested in buying shiny stuff with whatever coinage we had, and then we'd go northward to a place called The Slope for some entertainment. The Slope is at the edge of this Southeast Quadrant, right where the four canals meet. There is an X shaped series of bridges that connect them all.

"Where are we going to stay for the night if we can't get home?" I ask Fauna once we've reached the middle of the square. Looming over us is a silver statue of a tall javelin that rises thirty feet in the air. I recall the history, but am too preoccupied. By now the light of the sun has faded and the lights of the city are taking over.

"Have you ever slept on the street?" she asks playfully as we come to one of the many benches sprawled out around the spear statue. I place my backpack on it and Fauna does the same with hers.

"Before meeting the Challenger I wouldn't have considered it," I say of our ranger friend. "We've toughed it in the bush and mountains, but for the last few days and nights all I've thought about is sleeping somewhere cushy!"

"Me too! Maybe an inn?" says Sister, unfastening the strings on her pack and rummaging through coins and mushrooms. A crowd passes by, some stragglers at the back decked out fully in dark red robes. Small children play in the pools, some of their nearby mothers calling them out as it is getting darker.

"Shell house?" I ask her, suddenly recalling the strange term.

"Huh?" asks Fauna, raising an eyebrow into her cap.

"Remember? The guard at the front? 'You're not with one of those shell houses, are you?' she asked us? What did that mean?"

"Oh," says Fauna, closing up her bag and placing it onto her back again. "Well, you have the slug in your head, what does it tell you?"

"Nothing," I answer, shrugging. "I never heard of 'shell houses' before. They must be new, something that happened since we left."

"Well, Qilla also told you there is another brain slug somewhere in the city, so lots of weird things going on?" Sister says. "We have some coins, maybe an eccentric innkeeper will take some glow mushrooms? Best brassy inns are in the Entertainment District, center of town near the Slope."

I catch the glint of emergent moonlight in the surface of the silvery javelin monument and I ask her: "Do you have any friends in the area?"

"We don't talk anymore, she knows why. An inn looks like our best wager," Fauna says, flicking a curl of red hair from her face. "Unless we can figure a way over the fire."

"If no one else has figured a way I doubt we can," I say.

She smiles. I can read her expression—she thinks after all we've lived through that we can find a way and I wonder if she may be right, but I'm still doubtful. I know already that magic fire that burns on a body of water cannot be doused by water, so my water rod is useless here. Maybe I can use the Mighty Magnet to bring down a massive building and squelch…no, I won't be doing that.

"Well," Sister says, glancing about the semi-crowded square. "To the Slope. From there we'll figure out what to do." With these words she mimics pulling out her sword from her belt, though not really because it's an unwise move in a crowded urban space. She points her arm instead to what she thinks is North.

I curtly nod, noticing a single horsed cart that is idle against a lamppost. It's conductor is slowly crawling up the side, lifting their small body shawled in black. There is a snug-looking bench positioned in the back. I look to my sister and she immediately knows what I'm thinking.

"We have coin and mushrooms, take your pick or both!" she calls as we make our way through the shifting crowd.

The cart-driver looks down, having just set down upon the front perch. This is an older one, one I cannot tell is man or woman, not that it matters. The cart-driver's eyes are piercing and has a withered long face that looks to be partly scowling.

"Where to?" they grumble, nodding toward the backseats.

Fauna places a handful of coins and glowing fungi aside the conductor, cautioning to eat neither as she reaches for the side rail and pulls herself into the back. I follow nearly as gingerly, ourselves and our belongings soon nestled nicely in the carriage.

"To the Slope please," says my sister.

"Why the red clothes?" the cart-driver asks her as the horse begins to trot.

"My favourite!" she answers.

The driver conducts the horse to start galloping once we're clear and I feel a breeze as the heads of the crowd float by like ice flows on a frozen river. We move from the square down a wide alleyway between squat buildings. There are fences in front of many of them, these open shops and lavish homes.

The cart turns into another aisle, this one more cobbled than the last, sending the cart into a frenzy of tittering movements, prompting me to reach for the rail. There are stone balconies a few feet overhead, whole rows of them zipping by, dangling flowery vines smacking against our faces. Next we are moving uphill on a more even street. Overhead at the summit is a stout chocolate brown-bricked structure. The cart-driver takes us along its side for a while before scurrying around another corner.

Sister gasps. Beyond her side of the cart stands a blackened structure. We can see that the bricks are bright red where they are not charred with soot. A single crumpled chimney sits atop a collapsed roof and one wall has fallen over, revealing a smashed interior as we whiz past it.

"Shell house," utters the cart-driver with a dry laugh.

"And what *was* a shell house?" asks Fauna, taking off her cap, placing it on her lap. I lower mine too.

"You two not from around here?" comes the response.

"Underground," my sister quickly quips.

"Not been around lately," I say. "The shell houses, there were none when we left?"

The cart driver tells us: "These shell houses have been popping up since as long as the canal fires burned. There was a bloke by the name of Sharkoo. He came when the fires burned, told the young ones not to be afraid. Some listened. Sharkoo told them the magic fire cannot hurt them, was only an illusion."

"Sharkoo?" I echo. "Such strange named beings we've met already!"

"Slug-Lord, Lobster-Man, Frog-Boy, the Straw Man, Gemok, Bub!" Sister lists some of our previous rogues gallery with a giggle.

"Yeah," I agree. "So Sharkoo started these shell houses?"

The cart driver nods. "They began popping up here and there, small at first. So many were confused, angry about the fires."

"The fires, what caused them?" Fauna asks the driver.

"Ah, you really have been gone a while!" the driver says while extending a hand to their front. We see the semi-distant wall of reddish fire in the distance. The cart turns onto a large wide road. There are some people walking along the sides here. The buildings here are larger, five to six stories mostly.

"It's said that they leaked from the Zoma warehouses," says the driver solemnly, a hint of anger in their voice.

"Zoma?" asks Sister.

"I remember them," I say, recalling with the help of the slug. "They were starting up when we left, delivering letters and goods throughout Silver Coast. Named after the Zoma Rainwood in the South."

The cart-driver nods and grunts. "They are destitute after this. Everyone knows it was their mistake caused this. We traded safety for convenience, aye? You girls wanted to be dropped at the Slope?"

Fauna gets out first, thanking them for the ride and information. Here we stand in a semi-crowded square as the cart drives off. A thickly set inn is near, just across the small way. My sister tells me that she will grab us a room and negotiate a good price. I give her my belongings, telling her to store them beneath a bed and to meet me at the Slope. I keep my magical rod and magnet on my belt, refusing to part with them. It's nearby, across the way.

The crowd becomes a little thicker near the canal. The Slope is built on an old hill, its surface covered in flat stone. It juts upward, this large semi-circle shape that seats around thirty, into the nearby canal, the X-shaped bridges just beyond it, accessible from the sides of the Slope. It is like a raised amphitheater, a stage. I can see the flames licking the air a fair twenty feet or so above the waters beyond. I move to stand at the edge of the canal where only a brass rail separates me from the burning waters. I've never seen anything like this. The flames burn high, as tall as five of me, everywhere the water flows. Beyond I can see spires and stouter structures. To my left the bridges start, and I can see the canal meeting another channel, not far from here the four of them criss-cross and that's where the bridges also cross over. The fires, I can see, have overwhelmed the stone bridges.

We cannot cross over there, no way.

"This must be some twisted magic experiment gone seriously wrong!" says someone nearby. I see there are two young boys looking to be near my age standing further along the rail. The one who just spoke has short dirty blondish hair, not unlike the Challenger. At his belt is a small bug catcher net, must be a collector. The other is a bit taller with darker hair that runs to his shoulders. Both are wearing plain brownish clothes, tunics and breeches.

"Well, I heard it was Zoma's excess fuel," says the other one, a lanky one, shaking his head. I look away when the first one who spoke glances over at me. I see now that there is a small crowd filling up the little stools on the wide end of the semi-circle that is the Slope.

"Come on," he says to the other. "Carma's show starts!"

"Flora!" my sister calls. She bears a great smile. "We got a giant-sized room! They took the rest of the mushrooms, except this one," she says, holding a big blue one in her hand. "Also, left the weapons, can't be out in the street with weapons they said. Fair! So, that's my sword, arrows, and your dagger. At least we get a nice cushy sleep tonight!"

I feel a bit of joy erupt inside me as I thank her.

"Whoa," she says, gazing upon the flames.

I nod in answer, and then I look over at the Slope to my right. I see there, standing with her back to the fiery river a young

226

woman who looks to be maybe a bit older than us. She is decked out in a short purple robe, and has bright red pants, her hair black with silver and pink strands. Like me she wears spectacles, only not as big as mine. She is speaking loudly into a broad horn that expands her voice. Fauna is looking curiously over at her as she hands me a small vial of water while holding one in her other hand, telling me that they are complimentary from the inn. We sisters walk over, finding a small set of stools in front of a little round wooden table that resembles a tree stump. The rest of the seats and tables are occupied with folks, many of them young, the two boys I saw earlier at the next table over.

"Welcome, welcome, welcome! I'm Carma!" calls the apparent host, the strangely decked out young woman, a great smile upon her roundish face. The fire burns directly behind her. None of the audience seems phased by it, likely adjusted to it by now.

Fauna takes a drink of the water. "Ah!" she says in refreshment. "I missed this city."

"Okay, so we've got some jokes, some stories, and a special guest tonight!" cries Carma, raising her free hand in a friendly wave.

"Who's the guest?" calls the dirty blonde-haired boy from the table over from us. Some snickers rise up among the assembled.

"Oh! You will find out! But first," Carma reads a tiny piece of paper in her hands. "Up on our open part of the show, we have Ridley and the Snail!"

"That's us!" declares the lankier of the two boys, though I do not know if he is the Snail or Ridley. Both of them go to the front of the small stage, the dirty-blonde haired boy speaking as the taller boy brings out some glass jars from a bag. I squint closely and see that there are things in the jars, little things, bugs! Some glow, others hover. There are nine jars in all.

"Ridley, the Snail, and their troupe of buzzers!" declares the dirty-blonde haired boy to some early applause.

Both of the two then pull out tiny flutes and begin playing a melody, beginning soft and forlorn, the bugs moving to the music, most of them hopping, others darting up and down slowly with their wings. As the two boys speed their tempo, merging into a joyful, and then a triumphant stretch of music, the tiny critters move accordingly. Their last few notes consist of all the bugs in unison moving the fastest yet, the glowing ones pulsating with radiant colours, one of the flying ones splitting into two separate bugs by the end of it!

"Wow!" stammers Sister before the immense applause from the other guests follows.

The ones called Ridley and the Snail take deep bows, some of the bugs doing the same in their jars, or something that looks like bowing, and then they are collected back into a small bag by the taller of the two.

"Bug trainers," I say to Fauna. "That's really amazing."

"We free them eventually," the dirty-blonde haired boy says to me with a friendly smile as the pair of them pass us and sit back down at the nearby table.

"Wow, wasn't that something?" cries Carma, bubblingly as she returns to the stage. "Now, are you ready for our special guest?"

"Yes please!" calls Fauna, looking excited.

"And here's what you came here to find out! Our guest tonight, even though he's been called 'the enemy of the people of Silver Coast', and is said to be very dangerous, I thought it would be good to extend a peace token and bring him over here! Please welcome Sharkoo!"

We sisters both gasp, others in the assembled crowd following.

"Wait? What?!" someone shouts from a few tables over, and then a silence overwhelms the space as I take notice of a group of red cloaked figures approaching from behind the seats – a small throng of these along with a taller figure: this being is easily the height of three of me, he too decked in a long red cloak, towering over his underlings. He throws back his hood and I see a big crimson head, the head of a shark, it's jaws set open in a frozen shriek. Between rows of knife-like teeth I see two red eyes and I realize this is only a costume.

"You know he is dangerous yet you bring him here?" my sister suddenly shouts to the one called Carma at the front of the little stage.

"Well!" she laughs in reply, speaking into the horn. "My plan is to mock him while he's here! Hey Sharkoo! Made anyone leap into fire lately? Ha ha!"

The one called Sharkoo seems to peer beyond the fake jaws at us sisters for a moment before patting one of the shorter robed figures on the back. I just know something bad is on the verge of happening.

My sister and I are seated as the tall shark-dressed being called Sharkoo waddles his way awkwardly to the semi-circle stage. Carma, the host, has stated that she considers him a nemesis and a public danger, and yet she has invited that same dangerous nemesis here to her show.

"Why is he here?" someone calls, and I look over and see it's the boy with dirty-blondish hair.

"Calm down, Ridley," says his friend, the Snail, on the seat next to him, the taller dark-haired boy. "Let's hear what he has to say."

"Like your friend says!" calls Carma, giggling on the slightly raised platform that is the stage. "We all know that Shakoo is wrong, so what harm can be done in hearing him out?"

229

Sister stands and she says: "If we *know* he is wrong then there is nothing worth hearing!"

"Truth!" agrees Ridley loudly.

Carma just smiles as the one called Sharkoo arrives aside her, towering over her, his minions scampering at his side. These shorter beings are decked completely in crimson robes, and at first I think they are kobolds like the ones we encountered on our adventure, but then, as they all fling back their crimson hoods I can see they are merely folks, though strange to look at—one of them has patches of hair on his face, another has tiny eyes but a big nose and mouth, and one particularly thin bespectacled one has a single tuft of dark hair on the crown of his head – all odd looking fellows, I count six in all.

Sharkoo stands in place for a moment, seeming to relish the disagreements that his presence has caused. He is so strange to look at, this costumed man, or whatever he is – I see the two red orbs between fake serrated teeth and false open jaws. For a moment those eyes gaze upon Fauna and I, as if we've given him pause. There are jeers from the crowd, while others clap, a split audience.

Unsure, I say to Sis: "Should we leave? I don't like the looks of this, but…" and I look at the small crowd of about twenty spectators. There are others lingering beyond the seats as well, many who look curious, likely recognizing the shark figure. And then I hear voices that seem distant at first, all flowing from beyond the burning fire on the far side the theater.

"Shame on you!" one voice calls from the other side.

"Oh, come now!" retorts Carma, turning her head to the canal, and she hands Sharkoo her speaking horn and steps aside.

Sharkoo then turns about, facing the fires, his tail-fin bouncing as he turns. From where I stand I notice that the flames seem to be lower than they were before.

"Detractors on both sides of the fire!" cries Sharkoo, his voice far more plain than expected, yet powerful. He turns and faces the audience.

"Begone Sharkoo!" calls a woman's voice from beyond the flaming canal.

"Oh! Oh!" declares the being dressed in a shark-skin suit, both of his apparent flippers for arms grasping the speaking horn. "You see, my present assemblage, how hard it is for me to even speak in the public realm! Oh, forlorn it is for me when once our city was free!"

"What is this?" Sister says, seemingly to me, Carma, and the crowd.

"Now, let us be calm. The craziness of my critics must fade," says Sharkoo. There is something about his voice, something familiar. I hear the sounds of stool-legs scraping against the cobbled floor. People are sitting now, Fauna included. We share a look. I see apprehension on her face, yet she seems to have become settled. The boy named Ridley too is silent. I see the same sense of serenity on the faces of others, and I feel strangely tranquil.

"Don't listen to him!" a lone voice calls over the flames.

"Fire dying," I whisper to myself, thinking of our time underneath the mountains, remembering the hearth in that subterranean home. The fire here is indeed dying, it's flames falling further into the waters, so much so that I can now see beyond the canal to the other side. A small crowd is gathered there, though too far for me to make out faces. I'm wondering if it's too early to be optimistic that I will soon be able to cross into the Northwest.

"Fear stops so many of you!" exclaims Sharkoo. "Fear of future, fear of flame! It takes great bravery, a tremendous sacrifice of courage to overcome such! Who among my supporters has this eternal spirit? Who has the will?"

Confused, I watch as the six of his robed followers rush up to Sharkoo's sides, each of them begging to be chosen. The lanky orator swipes both of his arms, bidding them back, pausing for a moment, and then he pats one on the shoulder with his free flipper.

"Something's wrong," I say to Sister. She doesn't even flinch at my words, too absorbed in the situation before us.

"I'm Hudaji!" declares the small chosen underling in a nasally voice. "Sharkoo has chosen me!"

"I have, don't make me regret it," says the being into the horn. "You've toughened up. I've taken you from chaotic nothingness. Of all the followers, *you* may be the bravest. Show us!"

"Yes, Father Sharkoo!" declares the one called Hudaji. He smiles widely at the small audience, the fuzz on his chin betraying his youth.

"Fire, even magic fire, cannot hurt those who are truly courageous!" Sharkoo tells him.

"Carma, stop this!" shouts come from the other side of the canal.

"It's an expression!" she snaps back, unmoving from her place.

I feel dread as the follower, Hudaji, quickly scuttles over to the edge of the canal. Even my sister just watches, as do the two boys nearby, and everyone else. Hudaji climbs onto the stone rail at the lip of the canal, and with one swift move he plunges down into the fire, eliciting horrified gasps from both sides of the burning waters. From where he fell a blazing plume of fire erupts, rising tall into the night, and then the surrounding flames grow in size and intensity.

With or without the brain slug, I piece together what is happening.

"Awful," Fauna mutters, seemingly still dazed.

"Well!" Sharkoo strongly declares, shaking his tall costumed head. "I have immense confidence that the *next* one who leaps will be in truth the chosen brave one, the true succeeder of vital principle!" and then he turns to us, the gathered audience. "And *who* among you others wish to demonstrate your constituted quality?"

"This is madness," I say, trying to shout, but something holds me back. There is something that affects everyone, though I seem to be able to resist it the most. Hypnosis, I realize. I must be able to resist slightly more because of the brain slug in my head. One of the audience members stands. It's the friend of Ridley, the taller boy, the Snail.

"Your name?" asks Sharkoo.

The dark-haired boy, foggy as the rest of us, smiles slightly as he responds: "You may call me the Snail."

"No, no!" cries the now angered being, thrashing his costumed flippers as he shouts into the horn: "I don't have to call you by your made up name! Now, show the city you are braver than the ill-fated Hudaji! Leap boldly into the flames!"

The Snail steps over while his friend, Ridley, passively calls out for him to stop. Using whatever will-power I have, I reach for the Rod of Delipha at my belt, aim it's pearly head at my face, and then chant to the goddess. Seawater sprays my nose and mouth and eyes, and I feel completely free of the spell. I spray my sister next. She sputters and shakes her head.

"Fauna!" I yell. "It's Lobster-Man!"

"What? What!?" she cries, wiping the last drop of salt water from her cheeks. She leaps to her feet and shrieks: "Lobster-Man!"

"Ah! Crazy! I can't control them!" calls the one we know is not really called Sharkoo.

"You refuse to call people by their preferred names!" I say. "You're keeping the fires burning! The fuel is people!"

"I would've gotten away with it too!" Sharkoo drops the horn, suddenly reaching his fins into his robes, retrieving something.

"Spray them all with the dolphin rod!" Fauna asks of me and I oblige, ignoring her error. I run around the little amphitheater then, letting loose the waters of the sea goddess into each face. Everyone snaps out of their fugue, all parting from their chairs, outraged at what they just witnessed. I spray Carma last, standing from a distance from Lobster-Man and his minions, but it doesn't seem to make a difference on her.

"Stop that!" she snaps, sputtering.

"I *am* Lobster-Man! This is my home city and I must be in charge, in power!" declares the upright lobster. "And you villains have slain my friends, to which I avenge once and for all!" With that the lobster-being dressed as a shark-being raises in both fins a small vial with blue liquid within. Immediately I know what it is, the antidote. Lobster-Man pours the whole thing into his gaping fake jaw.

"Delipha, give me watery strength!" I shout as the surviving underlings in red charge towards me. The seawater shoots forth from the rod, and I strafe it from left to right, dousing all of the lackeys, creating an impromptu stream that sweeps them from their awkward feet and washes them away down a long alleyway, the lot of them thrashing and feebly whining as they flow away.

"No! That was my remaining fan-base!" calls the red being.

"What are you doing?" cries Carma. "You guys are ruining my show!"

Lobster-man grunts, then chuckles menacingly. He is changing, growing. The bogus shark head rips apart, revealing beady eyes and dangling antennae, as the fins tear and two immense claws emerge. Fires flicker at his back as he grows three times in height and breadth, an over-sized lobster-beast with a hulking upper part that stands on two legs, the shark costume gone, only parts of his robes remaining covering his mid-section. I rush back through the seats as the crowd disperses, all save the boys called Ridley and the Snail, while Carma leaps behind a stool to the side of the stage.

Fauna, unarmed, stands upon a tree-trunk-looking table and utters: "Final boss," a line that would be more expected from the Challenger.

"Take this!" I tell her, swinging to her the Mighty Magnet, quickly naming the magic words for her.

"I wish we were nearer that giant javelin, then I'd skewer this crustacean!" she spits, then shouts: "Look out!"

The enlarged Lobster-man charges his immense self towards us, slashing both of his giant claws. Fauna runs right, I veer left, the gigantic red body smashing the table we had just been at.

I'm moving rapidly towards the canal rails now, towards the stage. Lobster-man has turned, his red eyes upon me. With the fires at my back, I can see him stamp his feet, readying another charge. I begin to move, feeling a dream-like hesitancy in my feet. I know instantly I cannot move in time. Feebly, I raise Delipha's rod, running, veering to my left as Lobster-Man comes nearer and nearer. I'm in his shadow when he pauses abruptly. Something is hitting him from his side, hard enough to slow him.

I move, dashing, taking no time to look.

Rock and marble crash behind me. Over my shoulder I see Lobster-Man is tearing apart the amphitheater, savagely smashing the rails where I just was, sending bits of rock into the flaming canal. I keep my feet moving, encircling Lobster-Man when I see Ridley and the Snail both standing on the one remaining table. The Snail is loading Ridley's bug net with a large pebble, which Ridley then casts towards the Lobster-beast, using the net alike a catapult. The pebble smacks against the side of Lobster-Man's head, prompting him to turn quickly with one long step, facing the two boys.

"Now Delipha!" I shout over the ensuing crashing foot-falls. The seawater stream merely splashes against the thick cara-pace that covers Lobster-Man's rear-side, not at all hindering him as he rushes at our new allies. Ridley and the Snail dash away to either side, each of them getting slammed by the gigantic swiping claws. The Snail flies towards where my sister stands, while Rid-ley smashes against the stone rails. I quickly lower my rod, letting forth some water at the back of Lobster-Man's feet, causing him to stumble a little, just enough to give Ridley time to scramble away.

Sister emerges to his right, now picking up with the Mighty Magnet every piece of cutlery that was spilled, shooting little knives and forks to our foe, most of them bouncing off against his hard shell, angering the Lobster, making him redder.

"Is that all you've got, girly?" roars Lobster-Man.

The boy called the Snail leaps at him then, carrying before him one of the overturned tables, pushing against the monster's torso like a shield. I shoot water from where I stand, splashing it at his feet, hoping it trips him up, but he manages to maintain his place. He shoots me a quick glare, grunting, reaching for the Snail, gripping from him his makeshift wooden shield, clawing it instantly into two pieces that plunk to the ground at his sides. Lobster-Man lunges at the Snail, grabbing him by his mid-section in one of his pincer claws.

"Stop forcing people to call you fake names!" booms the Lobster, swinging the Snail around like a rag-doll. Some of the glass jars with bugs in them fly out, the dancing bugs in turn flee-ing as their vessels are broken against the hard floor.

"Okay Sharkoo!" shouts my Sister mockingly. She is run-ning towards the feet of the bipedal lobster. Angered, he swings his free claw at her. She ducks from his grasp, hastily side-stepping his swipe. Lobster-Man grunts, dropping the Snail from his other claw, now striking both towards Sister. He sends one claw towards her head, another towards her legs, but she manages to jump and duck in time. Out of fear, I suddenly want to splash her away from the swiping claws, yet Sister seems to be keeping her pace, twirling herself now around Lobster-Man, causing the massive red beast to slowly turn about.

One of his claws manages to lunge as Fauna dashes about him, taking hold of part of her tunic, lifting her. I raise my rod, readying to try something, even if it doesn't work!

"Why do you stand in the way of me? I only aim to bring order!" bellows Lobster-Man in frustration.

Fauna is laughing as she hangs in his pincer. "Order?" she stammers between rapid giggles as her feet dangle above the cobblestone floor. "You see, Lobster, I know what really motivates you and it's not order!"

"Ah, and what is that, pray tell!" says Lobster-Man, hunching over, leaning his bulgy face towards his new captive.

Fauna raises one hand, pointing the two ends of the Mighty Magnet at him. She speaks and the foe yelps as the magnetic force pulls him downward. At first it appears as if Lobster-Man has fallen unto her, his body fully smashing against the floor of the amphitheater area, creating a massive split-second quake that sends up stools, utensils, and little bits of stone.

Maintaining my footing in my place, I think she is crushed, but the great crustacean suddenly flings upward and I see her, Fauna holding the magnet, standing defiantly upon the cracked cobble, unhurt.

"How? How?" I stammer in wonder, stepping over to her.

"*Pull!*" she cries.

Lobster-Man, having landed on his back, is jerked upward once more, the unseen force pulling him. Some coins shoot out

237

from unseen pockets, slapping and sticking against the ends of the Mighty Magnet.

"Push!" Fauna roars just as the big carapace is nearly upon her once more. Lobster-Man, on his feet again, managing to raise his claws to shield himself uselessly as Fauna pushes him towards the stone banisters and the fires beyond them, silver and gold coinage streaming out from both of his sides.

"Ah, the coins!" I realize, and then I cry for Delipha and, standing moving over to my sister's side, shoot forth a current of water, prompting a flailing Lobster-Man back further. His back against the rail, he begins to rapidly shrink, and I remember that his version of antidote is temporary, as it had been when we sisters once drank some.

As the great lobster looks about to fall backward into the flames, something small and blue suddenly squeezes from the hole that is his left ear. As our foe returns to normal size, the two of us cease our attacks, watching in awe as a blue brain slug crawls among the fallen coins on the floor, moving fast for a slug.

"That's it!" I say. "What Qilla was telling me about, the other brain slug in the city!"

As Lobster-Man collapses we see Ridley dash out from the side of the rail, his little net swinging as he catches the fleeing blue slug. The Snail soon arrives at his side with a glass bottle in hand. I look to Fauna and laugh in shock and relief.

We can study it and maybe I can find a way to remove my own brain slug. Maybe, I'm not sure.

Fauna and I are more concerned with Lobster-Man for now. We step to look over his soggy body. He is small and thin once more, his claws twitching, and he moans pitiably.

"Oh!" says Carma, suddenly appearing from seemingly nowhere. "Lobster-Man, is that what you are called?" she asks the sprawled-out being.

"Meh," answers the defeated demagogue.

"Well, I can help you! Come, you can be my new father!" says Carma and she looks at us and adds: "I have seventeen siblings!"

"Don't feed him this," says my sister, tossing her the blue mushroom. Carma catches it, nervously smiles, and then drags a semi-sentient, semi-protesting lobster away.

THE END

<u>Epilogue</u>

The sleep that night—so satisfying! It's never the same as one's own bed, but the inn's offered a nice reprieve from the wilds of the lands. We came so far in our journey, having left Silver Coast and explored the surroundings lands. Once we had met the Challenger we had gone on to explore lands that I had only heard of or read about. Seeing these new places with my own eyes is so much more rewarding, and still there is so much more of the world I yearn to one day see.

Now I'm standing in the courtyard, not far from the cracked amphitheater where last night's dramatic events unfolded. My favoured items are at my belt, the rod of the sea goddess and the Mighty Magnet which my sister had used to save the day, and everything else is in my backpack strapped tightly against my form.

It's after midday, poking into very early evening, for Sister and I slept heavily, allowing the inn to charge us for two nights instead of one, which we were more than happy to pay. The place out here is busy, full of people, some moving in and out of the area in mercantile haste, others wandering slowly through, while a few folks are resting at the various terraces, clusters of benches, and numerous balconies. Birds chatter above me, some of them fluttering about and swooping to street level to grasp bits of things people have dropped.

This is home.

Most importantly, and I sigh long and relievingly when I see it, the canals are no longer on fire.

"Magic reeling," I mutter to myself and smile as I see that the flames are completely gone, likely dissipating in the night. The bridges are open and horses, buggies, hooves, wheels, and feet once more are crossing from this district to another or from another district to this one. I think I hear too some celebratory fanfare in the distant, though I know not which quadrant it emanates. The city is opened up after all this time, all these delays. I can't help but imagine that the celebration is singularly for us returning, though I know it's not. Still, it's fitting timing and matches my mood.

"All ready?" my sister, Fauna, asks as she comes over at my side, her blade at her belt, sheathed in a brand new red sheath she'd just bought. Her bag is firmly on her back as well. She has some scratches on her face, earned from last night, but they look like they will heal soon enough. We're both lucky to have come out of all of this with no permanent damages, unless you count the slug in my head as one, which I don't.

"Ready," I reply to my sister.

Last night, before we retired to our rented beds, we spoke with the two boys, Ridley and the Snail, explaining almost everything about our long adventure and how I too had a blue slug within me just as Lobster-Man had. They were understanding, and so they agreed to hand over the bottled blue slug that had come from our now defeated foe. Lobster-Man's ex-slug is now in the glass bottle in my bag, having stopped writhing in the night. It was resting when I last looked upon it before we left the inn. We'll find it a more humane domain, maybe a terrarium in Mother's library, give it lots of space, see if we can communicate with it as we study it. Figuring out more about this specimen will teach me what to do about my own. Who knows? Maybe if I get mine out they can be friends?

Fauna is smiling, and I'm sure I am, as we walk through sun-soaked streets, making our way to the nearest bridge behind the amphitheater. As we pass onto it's stone surface we see a crude wooden sign has been put up, **Hudaji's Bridge** it reads.

Throughout our quest we saw so many things, so many instances of recklessness, and examples of why one must always be careful about whom one follows in life. I am so glad that I have learned such things, to follow my own instincts and knowledge, learning from others, yes, but also realizing that there are some that can lead one astray if not questioned properly. Most importantly though, despite the foes we made, we also made a lot of friends on our journey.

"Ridley and the Snail gave me their, um, how do you say —their locations?" says Fauna cheerfully and I sense something from her. We're behind a slowly moving crowd, but we're soon reaching the middle of the wide bridge.

"Oh, yes, I told them too we could collaborate in the future," I tell her, remembering the night before after we defeated the baddie. "Between the two of them they have a huge bug collection, so I'd love to see if there's anything I don't know of. But who knows? Maybe they know stuff about brain slugs?"

"Maybe," she laughs.

Now we're coming upon the end of the bridge, into the Northwest sector of the city of Silver Coast. The first few acres contain bricked walkways of grey and white, while further on from us there are numerous square-shaped ponds, each with a plot of green where a great tree grows; these are samples of every known tree on the continent, this famed collection on campus. Lofty flagpoles expand upward between the watered trees, each with the colours of their respective colleges. Mother's library can be seen yet beyond that, among a cluster of behemothal buildings at the end of a long stretch of neatly trimmed grass. I see to my far left a row of red and brown bricked squat structures, all of them thriving with vines of green leaf and ivy.

"Finally," I say as I see them.

Here we begin towards the walkway that leads home. I sense something then, like I had when we first entered the city yesterday, a message that streams into my mind, the voice of Qilla! She speaks to me now, and I cannot wait to tell her the latest. I extend my arm towards Fauna, pointing to the nearest bench. A pair of white and blue robed pupils pass by as we reach it. It's quite crowded here near the treed ponds.

I tell her what is happening.

"Speaking to you now?" she asks, scratching her forehead a little.

I nod, and I wonder if the brain slug in my backpack has sensed this, though I feel no commotion. Our conversation is fast, as she says she cannot speak long. She reports that the High Priests are still causing trouble in the Vale of Dragos, and so the Challenger had left yesterday, saying he wanted to return underground for help, coming back over the mountain at night with the flying bones of Dragos at his back.

The slime! I realize that it had animated the skeleton of the dragon just as it had when it was trying to frighten us. I quickly tell Sister this, to which her eyes go wide and she looks like she doesn't know to laugh or shriek, but she does neither.

Qilla tells me then that she must go to a town meeting, promising to speak with me soon-ish, and I tell her something, a promise to relay a quick message to the Challenger for us – 'The Lobster is defeated' though Qilla doesn't understand it.

We know the ranger will get the reference. He gets all the references.

And so the two of us continue on our way, eager to reach home. Still, even in our hurry, each step I relish, coming back to acquainted grounds, letting the memories (of which I have now perfect recollection) come flowing back into my mind. We are not far from where much of our childhoods took place, much of our most treasured memories.

"Home," says Sister, beaming at me warmly. "After all our quests, Flora, we are home!"

When we're finally near, passing by a pair of familiar weeping willows that Mother had named long before us. I remember that when we first departed the campus Fauna had promised me that I could write about our adventures. That can wait, but I will be writing the story.

We're treading up the old pathway to the doorstep of our home. I smell even from here the baking scones and I can hear the whistling of Mother's great kettle.

As much as I look forward to returning to my room with my comfy blue bed, I know us sisters and Mother will be talking about our adventures with the Challenger deep into the night.

THE END END

Manufactured by Amazon.ca
Bolton, ON

26442984R00148